Danielle Steel

'Danielle's books always make me feel **strong, inspired and happy** – truly a page-turning experience' *Liz*

'She has a remarkable ability to write different stories at an **amazing pace**. Every time I pick up a book I know that I'm going to be taken through **highs and lows**' *Gillian*

'I feel like I've **travelled the world** through her descriptions of the places in her books' *Ann*

'Every book **gets you hooked** from page one' *Julie*

'Danielle Steel takes me to another place with her masterful story-telling . . . **Absolute reading pleasure** from the first page to the very last' *Holly*

'I have **drawn immense strength** from the characters in many of her books' *Sarika*

Moral Compass

Danielle Steel has been hailed as one of the world's most popular authors, with nearly a billion copies of her novels sold. Her recent international bestsellers include *Royal*, *Expect a Miracle* and *All That Glitters*. She is also the author of *His Bright Light*, the story of her son Nick Traina's life and death; *A Gift of Hope*, a memoir of her work with the homeless; and the children's books *Pretty Minnie in Paris* and *Pretty Minnie in Hollywood*. Danielle divides her time between Paris and her home in northern California.

By Danielle Steel

All That Glitters • Royal • Daddy's Girls • The Wedding Dress
The Numbers Game • Moral Compass • Spy • Child's Play • The Dark Side
Lost and Found • Blessing in Disguise • Silent Night • Turning Point
Beauchamp Hall • In His Father's Footsteps • The Good Fight • The Cast
Accidental Heroes • Fall From Grace • Past Perfect • Fairytale
The Right Time • The Duchess • Against All Odds • Dangerous Games
The Mistress • The Award • Rushing Waters • Magic • The Apartment
Property Of A Noblewoman • Blue • Precious Gifts • Undercover • Country
Prodigal Son • Pegasus • A Perfect Life • Power Play • Winners • First Sight
Until The End Of Time • The Sins Of The Mother • Friends Forever
Betrayal • Hotel Vendôme • Happy Birthday • 44 Charles Street • Legacy
Family Ties • Big Girl • Southern Lights • Matters Of The Heart
One Day At A Time • A Good Woman • Rogue • Honor Thyself
Amazing Grace • Bungalow 2 • Sisters • H.R.H. • Coming Out • The House
Toxic Bachelors • Miracle • Impossible • Echoes • Second Chance • Ransom
Safe Harbour • Johnny Angel • Dating Game • Answered Prayers
Sunset In St. Tropez • The Cottage • The Kiss • Leap Of Faith • Lone Eagle
Journey • The House On Hope Street • The Wedding • Irresistible Forces
Granny Dan • Bittersweet • Mirror Image • The Klone And I
The Long Road Home • The Ghost • Special Delivery • The Ranch
Silent Honor • Malice • Five Days In Paris • Lightning • Wings • The Gift
Accident • Vanished • Mixed Blessings • Jewels • No Greater Love
Heartbeat • Message From Nam • Daddy • Star • Zoya • Kaleidoscope
Fine Things • Wanderlust • Secrets • Family Album • Full Circle • Changes
Thurston House • Crossings • Once In A Lifetime • A Perfect Stranger
Remembrance • Palomino • The Ring • Loving • To Love Again
Summer's End • Season Of Passion • The Promise
Now And Forever • Passion's Promise • Going Home

Nonfiction

Expect a Miracle
Pure Joy: *The Dogs We Love*
A Gift of Hope: *Helping the Homeless*
His Bright Light: *The Story of Nick Traina*
Love: Poems

For Children

Pretty Minnie in Hollywood
Pretty Minnie in Paris

Danielle Steel

MORAL COMPASS

PAN BOOKS

First published 2020 by Delacorte Press
an imprint of Random House
a division of Penguin Random House LLC, New York

First published in the UK 2020 by Macmillan

This paperback edition published 2020 by Pan Books
an imprint of Pan Macmillan
The Smithson, 6 Briset Street, London EC1M 5NR
Associated companies throughout the world
www.panmacmillan.com

ISBN 978-1-5098-7814-7

1 3 5 7 9 8 6 4 2

A CIP catalogue record for this book is available from the British Library.

Typeset in Charter ITC by Palimpsest Book Production Ltd, Falkirk, Stirlingshire
Printed and bound by CPI Group (UK) Ltd, Croydon, CR0 4YY

Visit www.panmacmillan.com to read more about all our books
and to buy them. You will also find features, author interviews and
news of any author events, and you can sign up for e-newsletters
so that you're always first to hear about our new releases.

To Beatie, Trevor, Todd, Nick,
Samantha, Victoria, Vanessa,
Maxx, and Zara,

To my darling children,
Be lucky, be wise, be brave,
be honest, be kind,
be loving to each other,
stand up for what you believe in,
and do what you know is right.

I love you so very much
and am so proud of you!

Mom/d.s.

The only thing necessary for the triumph of evil is for good men to do nothing.
—ATTRIBUTED TO EDMUND BURKE

MORAL COMPASS

Chapter One

It was the day after Labor Day, one of those perfect, golden September mornings in Massachusetts, as the students of Saint Ambrose Preparatory School began to arrive. The school was over a hundred and twenty years old, and its imposing stone buildings looked as distinguished as the colleges where most of the students would be accepted once they graduated. Many illustrious men had attended Saint Ambrose and gone on to make their marks on the world.

It was a historic day for Saint Ambrose. After ten years of heated debate, and two years of preparation, a hundred and forty female students were about to arrive and join the eight hundred male students. It was part of a three-year program that would ultimately add four hundred young women to the student body, bringing it to a total of twelve hundred students. This first year, they had accepted sixty female freshmen, forty sophomores, thirty-two juniors, and eight seniors, who had either recently moved to the East Coast, or had some valid reason to want to change schools as a senior and not graduate with the class they'd gone through high school with until then. Each of the female applicants had been carefully vetted to make sure she was up to the standards, morally and academically, of Saint Ambrose.

Two dorms had been built to accommodate the new female students. A third would be finished within a year, with a fourth scheduled to be built the year after that. So far, all the new additions and changes had gone smoothly. There had been lengthy seminars for the past year to assist the existing faculty with the transition from teaching at an all-male school to co-ed classes. Its advo-cates had insisted that it would improve the academic standing of the school, as girls tended to be more dedi-cated to their studies at the same age, and settled down to academics earlier. Others said it would make the students better rounded, learning to live and work, collaborate, cooperate, and compete with members of the opposite sex, which was, after all, more representa-tive of the "real world" they would be entering in college and thereafter.

The school's enrollment had diminished slightly in recent years, with most of their competitors having already gone co-ed, which most students preferred. They couldn't stay current and compete if they didn't go co-ed. But the battle had been hard won, and the headmaster, Taylor Houghton IV, was one of the last to be convinced of its benefits. He could see endless complications as a result, including student romances, which they didn't have to deal with as an all-male school. Lawrence Gray, head of the English department, had asked if they would be renaming the school Saint Sodom and Gomorrah. After thirty-seven years at Saint Ambrose, he had been the most vehement voice against the change. Traditional, conservative, and privately a bitter person, his objections were eventually overruled by those who wanted the school to keep up with the times, no matter how challenging. Larry Gray's sour attitude stemmed from the fact that ten years into his tenure at Saint Ambrose, his wife had left him for the father of a tenth-grade boy. He had never fully recovered, and never remarried. He had stayed for another twenty-seven years since, but was an unhappy person though an excellent teacher. He wrung the best academic performance possible out of each of the boys, and sent them off to college well prepared to shine at the university of their choice.

Taylor Houghton was fond of Larry, affectionately calling him their resident curmudgeon, and was fully prepared for Larry's grousing throughout the coming year. Larry's resistant attitude toward modernizing the school had resulted in his being passed over as assistant headmaster for many years. He was two years away from retirement, and continued to be vocal about his objections to the incoming female students.

When the previous assistant headmaster retired, faced

with such a major change at the school, the board had conducted a two-year search, and was jubilant when they succeeded in wooing a brilliant young African-American woman, assistant headmaster of a rival prep school. Harvard-educated Nicole Smith was excited to come to Saint Ambrose at a time of transition. Her father was the dean of a respected, small university, and her mother was a poet laureate teaching at Princeton. Nicole had the academic life in her blood. At thirty-six, she was full of energy and enthusiasm. Taylor Houghton, the faculty, and the board were thrilled that she was joining them, and even Larry Gray had few objections to her, and liked her. He no longer aspired to be assistant headmaster himself. All he wanted was to retire, and said he could hardly wait.

Shepard Watts, as head of the board, had been one of the most ardent supporters of the plan to go co-ed. He readily admitted it was not without ulterior motive. His thirteen-year-old twin daughters would be coming in as freshmen in a year, followed by his eleven-year-old son in three years. He wanted his daughters to have the same opportunity for a first-rate education at Saint Ambrose as his sons. The twins had already filled out applications and been accepted, contingent on their performing well in eighth grade. No one had any doubt about that, given their academic records to date. Jamie Watts, Shepard's oldest son, was one of their star students, and would be a senior this year. His scholastic achievements were notable, as was his success as an athlete. He was an all-around great kid and everybody loved him.

Shepard was an investment banker in New York, and his wife, Ellen, was a full-time hands-on mother, and head of the parents' association. She had worked for Shepard as a summer intern twenty years before, and married him a year later. Taylor and his wife, Charity, were extremely fond of them, and considered them good friends.

Taylor and Charity had one daughter. She was married, a pediatrician, and lived in Chicago. Charity taught history and Latin at the school, and was excited that she'd be teaching girls this year. From a staunch New England family, she was perfectly suited to the life of being married to the headmaster of a venerable prep school. She was proud of Taylor and his position. He was ten years away from retirement and loved the school. Despite its size, there was a family feeling to it, and Charity made a point of knowing as many of the students and parents as she could. Like other members of the faculty, she served as counselor to a group of students, whom she followed for all four years. She would be working on college applications with her senior counselees almost as soon as they started school, writing recommendations for them, and advising them on their essays. Most of the students of Saint Ambrose applied to Ivy League colleges, and an impressive number of their applicants were accepted every year.

Taylor and Nicole Smith were standing on the steps of the administration building, watching students arrive, when Shepard Watts and his son Jamie drove in. Shep left Jamie to find his friends, and came up the steps to greet Taylor and Nicole. She looked bright-eyed and excited as she watched the procession of SUVs file in and go to designated parking areas for each class of students.

"How's it going?" Shepard smiled at the assistant head-master.

"It's looking good," she said, smiling broadly. "They started arriving at 9:01." The parking lots were almost full. Shepard glanced at Taylor.

"Where's Larry?" He was usually on hand to observe the arrival of the students.

"They're giving him oxygen in my office," Taylor said, and all three of them laughed. Taylor was tall and athletic-looking, with salt and pepper hair and lively brown eyes. He had gone to Princeton, like all his male relatives before him. Charity had gone to Wellesley. Shepard was a Yalie, a handsome man, with dark hair and piercing blue eyes, and was their most effective fundraiser. He simply would not take no for an answer, and brought in an astonishing amount of money from current parents and alumni, and he was a generous donor as well. Despite the demands of his business, he was a devoted father. For the past three years, he had amply demonstrated his dedication to the school.

The three stood on the steps, watching the SUVs arrive and go to the parking lots where they could unload bicycles, computers, and as many of the comforts of home as the students were allowed to bring. There were long tables manned by teachers, who were handing out dorm assignments. As always, there was a mild degree of confusion, as parents wrestled with duffel bags and trunks, boxes and computers, while returning students went to look for their friends and find out what dorm they would be in. All the information had been sent to them digitally a month before, but the dorm assignments and schedule for the day were being handed out again for those who hadn't brought the papers with them. Freshmen were assigned to suites with four to six students, seniors were in singles or doubles, and sophomores and juniors were in rooms set up for three or four students. The female dorms followed the same system. There would be a female teacher in each dorm to help anyone who was sick or had a problem, and to see that everyone behaved and followed the rules.

Gillian Marks, the new athletic director, had been assigned to one of the female dorms. Their old athletic director of twenty years had quit the moment it was confirmed that the school would be accepting female students. Gillian was an upbeat person and had been thrilled when they offered her the job. She was a star in her own right, and at eighteen had won a silver medal in the Olympics for the long jump. She had set a record that hadn't been beaten yet. She was six feet two, thirty-two years old, had been the assistant athletic director at a girls' boarding school, and was excited about the prospect of working with males too.

Simon Edwards, a returning math teacher, was going to help her coach the boys' soccer team. He had lived in France and Italy for two years after college, and loved the game. He had previously taught at a top private co-ed day school in New York and had come to Saint Ambrose the year before, wanting the experience of teaching at a boarding school. He had come back with enthusiasm now that they were going co-ed. He was the youngest member of the faculty at twenty-eight. He and Gillian had met in August to talk about his coaching the boys' soccer team. Tryouts for the teams were starting the next day. The school had an Olympic-size indoor pool, donated by a member of the alumni, and a strong swimming team. Gillian was going to be coaching girls' volleyball and basketball too.

Taylor and Nicole watched Gillian greeting the freshman girls in their parking area, and Simon Edwards was welcoming the freshman boys. Returning students and their parents knew the routine, and where to get their dorm assignments, as the students threaded their way between their friends, happy to see them after the summer. As they watched with Shepard, they saw Steve Babson arrive. He had the longest history of academic probation of any student in the school. He barely managed to squeak through every year. His father, Bert Babson, was a cardiac surgeon in New York, who rarely showed up at the school and was harsh about his son whenever the staff at Saint Ambrose communicated with him. His frightened, somewhat disoriented wife came to visit her son alone, and experience told Taylor, as well as Steve's advisor, that Jean Babson had a drinking problem, which she kept in control when she came to the school. There were hints that Steve didn't have an easy home life, with an aggressive father and unstable mother, but he had made it to senior year, and he was a sweet kid. He was a good-looking, slightly disheveled boy with brown curly hair and innocent brown eyes. There was a big, friendly, lovable puppy dog look to him that went straight to his teachers' hearts, and almost made up for his poor grades.

Gabe Harris had come up from New York with Rick Russo, and Shepard groaned when he saw Rick's mother. She was wearing a pink Chanel suit and stiletto heels in the middle of the country in Massachusetts. Her hair was freshly done, and as always she was wearing an inch of makeup. Shep knew that if he'd been any closer, he would have been overcome by her perfume. Rick's father, Joe, owned high-end luxury shopping malls in Florida and Texas, and was by far the biggest donor to the school. In the past three years, he had given them an annuity for a million dollars, so they put up with them. Rick was the opposite of his parents. He had light brown hair, a quiet demeanor, gray eyes, and could have blended into any crowd, which was what he wanted, so he didn't stand out like his parents. He was an excellent student. He was a quiet, unassuming boy who never showed off, unlike them. Shepard found Joe Russo unbearable, but as head of the board, he had to be pleasant to him, given the huge amount of money Russo donated to the school. Adele Russo was driving the new Bentley SUV that Shepard knew sold for just under three hundred thousand dollars. And the boy who'd ridden with them, Gabe Harris, was considered a good kid. He was a mediocre student, but he tried hard, and was one of their star athletes. He was hoping to get an athletic scholarship for college. He was one of the few scholarship students they had. He was the oldest of four children. Gabe's parents were investing heavily in him, to show his younger siblings that he could make it and so could they. His father, Mike Harris, was one of the most successful personal trainers in New York, and his mother, Rachel, managed a restaurant. They worked hard to keep their son at Saint Ambrose, and he did his best to live up to their expectations. He was going to play soccer as well as football as a senior this year, and was a powerful tennis player too. He had broad shoulders from working out with his father, and wore his hair in a buzz cut. He wasn't tall but looked manly and had intense blue eyes.

They saw Tommy Yee arrive with his father. Tommy was a gentle, kind, very sweet Chinese-American boy, an only child who had nearly perfect grades. His father, Jeff, was a dentist in New York, and his mother, Shirley, was the head of a prestigious accounting firm. Tommy spoke fluent Mandarin and Cantonese, was gifted in physics, strong in math, and a prodigy on the violin. He played in the school orchestra, and his parents expected nothing less than perfection from him. He was hoping for early admission at MIT, and from everything Taylor heard from his teachers, he would get it. Taylor knew that his parents pushed him hard and expected only the best from him. Their demands and expectations left him little time to hang out with friends.

Shepard left them then to find Jamie and get his room assignment. He knew he had a single this year, in the same dorm with several of his classmates. Shepard promised Taylor he'd stop by to say goodbye before he left. He had work to do until then, setting up Jamie's stereo and his computer, and a small refrigerator seniors were allowed to have in their rooms so they could eat or have snacks while they did homework, or studied for exams.

Boarding school was more like college these days, with

almost the same amount of freedom and independence for the older students, the privileges that came with age. The only difference was that cars were not allowed on the campus. Students could only go into the nearby town on weekends, with permission, on their bikes or on foot. But on campus, they were treated like adults, and were expected to treat the faculty and each other with decorum and respect. Drugs and alcohol were not allowed, and they had had only a few incidents, which were quickly handled. The students involved were expelled. There were no second chances where drugs were concerned, and the board fully agreed with the policy.

The therapist on campus, Maxine Bell, stayed in close contact with all of the advisors to make sure that they weren't missing any important signs of students with depression or suicidal tendencies. They had had a heart-breaking incident five years before, with a student who had taken his own life. He'd had top grades and strong family support, but had had a romance that went wrong. He reacted violently to it and hanged himself. There had been three suicides in the last twenty years, far fewer than their competitors. One of the top-rated boarding schools had had four suicides in the last two years. It was something all of the institutions worried about, but Maxine was everywhere, and knew an amazing number of the kids. She went to their games and some practices, hung out in the cafeteria, and knew many students by name. She kept her finger on the pulse of Saint Ambrose. Betty Trapp, the school nurse, was another source of information for Maxine, since all the students knew Betty, and went to the infirmary to have her fuss over them when they were sick. A local doctor came when called, and there was a hospital ten miles away, with helicopter service to Boston. The school functioned like a well oiled machine, and there was no reason for it to be any different now with girls.

Shepard left to find his son, and Larry emerged from the building to watch the arrival scene, which looked chaotic but wasn't. Having young girls in their midst was an unfamiliar sight, but not an unpleasant one. Several of the boys were noticing the girls around them, though none of the girls appeared to be speaking to each other yet. They had too much else to do as they unloaded the vehicles they'd come in, and argued with their parents about what to put where, and who would carry what.

The mothers of the freshman girls looked frazzled. Most of the fathers had come with them, and were struggling with their heavy trunks, with the occasional teacher lending a hand.

"The dorms will be drowning in hair dryers and curling irons by tonight," Larry said gloomily, and Nicole smiled at him. She was used to his complaints by now, after their initial meetings about the arrival of girls on campus.

"It won't kill us, Larry," she reassured him, as they all

noticed a particularly beautiful girl get out of her mother's car. There was no one else with them, and the girl with long straight blond hair down her back pulled out her trunk and two duffel bags without hesitation, while her mother managed some cartons. The girl seemed unusually poised for her age. She looked older than a senior and more like a college student, Nicole thought. She was strikingly pretty, like a model, and they all saw several heads turn to look at her, faculty and fathers as well as students. She was wearing cut-off jeans, a T-shirt and sneakers, and paid no attention to the admiring stares. She continued talking to her mother. Nicole recognized her from the files she had studied. She was Vivienne Walker, an incoming senior from L.A. Her mother was an attorney and had just moved to New York. Her father was a real estate developer in L.A., and they were getting a divorce. Vivienne had had top grades at her private day school in L.A. She and her mother had visited the school in May and she had been one of the last female students to be accepted, because they were short of senior girls. At best, it was difficult to lure seniors to a change of schools, except due to emergency or family circumstances, which was the case for Vivienne.

Larry watched Vivienne and her mother with a dour expression. She was exactly the kind of student he had been afraid of, a real beauty who would distract her fellow male students, and cause "drama," as he had put it. There was no question, every male in the vicinity had noticed her, the fathers even more than the sons. She looked like Alice in Wonderland all grown up. "That's exactly what I was talking about," he said, scowling, and walked back inside to his office as Nicole and Taylor exchanged a smile.

"He'll get over it," Taylor said optimistically, as he saw Adrian Stone arrive in a town car with a driver, also up from New York. Adrian was one of their most brilliant students, identified by his classmates as a "geek." He was very slight and had long brown hair that was always in his face and big, sad brown eyes. A returning junior, he suffered from social anxiety and asthma, and was something of a computer genius, who designed his own programs and applications. He had few friends, if any, and kept to himself, studying all the time or hiding out in the computer lab. His parents, Jack and Liz, were both psychiatrists, and were in the midst of a divorce that had turned Adrian's life into a living hell. They constantly dragged each other into court and filed court orders against one another, and the court-appointed psychiatrist assigned to the case for Adrian's benefit had finally recommended to the judge two years before that he be sent away to school to get him out of the middle of their war. In addition, the court had assigned a child advocacy lawyer, pro bono, to defend Adrian against his parents, who used him as a weapon against each other. He had flourished academically, and was a little less shy than he had been when he'd arrived. According to his counselor and teachers he was always afraid to do or say the wrong thing and get someone in trouble, or himself.

His parents almost never came to see him at school, and he always seemed reluctant to go home for vacation, where he lived with each of them on alternating days, an arrangement that he admitted he hated, but the only one both parents would agree to. He was better off at school. The driver of the town car helped him unload his suitcases, a duffel and some boxes, and helped him carry them into his dorm. As always, Adrian was the only student with neither parent there with him on opening day.

Taylor looked pensive as he thought about him, and then noticed a familiar black van appear and park in a remote corner of the parking lot designated for seniors. The windows were tinted too dark to see inside. There were two men in the front seat, a driver and a bodyguard, and Taylor could guess who was in it. As soon as the van stopped, a man with a perfect body jumped out. He was tall with well-developed broad shoulders and was wearing a black T-shirt and jeans, black cowboy boots, a baseball cap, and dark glasses. A tall, equally handsome boy got out after him, with the same build as his father and a mane of blond hair, although his father's was dark, and Taylor knew he had green eyes. A blond woman got out immediately after him, in jeans and a T-shirt, a baseball cap and dark glasses too, and they started unloading boxes immediately. The driver and second man helped them unload, but the boy and his parents headed across the parking lot alone, carrying all of his equipment to the table with the room assignments for senior boys. The two men stayed with the van, and no one paid any attention to the boy and his parents. Then suddenly you could see someone in the crowd give a start as they realized who they were. They were quiet and discreet, careful not to draw attention to themselves, as their son waved to friends in the distance.

Nicole Smith looked at Taylor then with a quizzical expression. "Is that . . . ?" She suddenly remembered that one of the senior boys, Chase Morgan, was the son of famous actor Matthew Morgan, and his wife, Merritt Jones, the most acclaimed actress of the last two decades, with two Oscars to her credit and countless nominations. This was his fourth year at Saint Ambrose, and Taylor always said that he had never met two better parents. They were totally focused on their son, kept a low profile and didn't embarrass him, and never showed off. They came to school for important functions, and visited him when they had a break in their busy schedules. They asked for no special privileges for them or their son, and met with his teachers, like anyone else. When Chase broke his leg on a sophomore ski trip to Vermont, his father was there in twelve hours, his mother in twenty-four. They both flew in from locations where they were filming, Matthew in London, and Merritt in Nairobi.

Even more remarkable, they had been separated for most of the past year, after Matthew supposedly had an affair with an actress he was working with, Kristin Harte. It was all over the tabloids. The paparazzi stalked Merritt for months. They were allegedly filing for divorce, but still came to school events together, and kept the whole mess away from their son. They appeared to be pleasant to each other when they were with him. Merritt carried one end of a trunk, and Matthew the other, and they chatted with Chase along the way.

Chase's best friend on campus was Jamie Watts, Shepard's son. Jamie found them quickly, and helped them with what they were carrying. The two boys could have been brothers; they were both tall, blond, and handsome, with broad shoulders and narrow waists, and an air of confidence about them. They looked like actors or models, and were accomplished athletes. They were beautiful to look at.

Taylor nodded in answer to Nicole's unspoken question about Chase's parents. "They're the easiest parents I've dealt with in nineteen years here. They're incredibly nice, discreet, responsible people, and Chase is a really great kid. He wants to go to UCLA and go back to the West Coast or Tisch Drama at NYU. His parents had wanted him to have an eastern school experience for high school, and they travel all the time. He's a terrific student and athlete and an all-around terrific kid. So is Jamie, Shepard's boy."

Nicole knew that Matthew produced and directed as well as acted. There had been some important parents at the school she came from, but she had to admit she was impressed watching the Morgans weave their way through the crowd, and observed how discreet they were. Seeing them there was so unexpected that no one paid any attention to them, and once in a while you could see someone recognize them and look shocked. They kept their professional lives as far away from Chase as they could. You would never guess that Matthew was currently living with another woman, and he and his wife were about to get divorced. They looked like any other family there that day. And Taylor had seen some bitter divorces in his time, but not theirs.

By ten-thirty, all the room assignments had been picked up. The students and their parents were in their dorm rooms setting things up, and where fathers were needed, they lent a hand for mothers who had come alone. Gillian Marks was helping the freshman girls as best she could, with two of her assistants. Most of the girls had brought their own hangers, towels, bed linens, and soaps, and there were stacks of empty cartons everywhere. Larry Gray hadn't been entirely wrong. Every girl in the freshman dorm had brought her own hair dryer and curling iron, and straightening irons too. It looked like a hair salon gone mad with special shampoos and conditioners, body gels, and face washes on every surface in the bathrooms.

At noon the entire student body had to be in the cafeteria, where tables had been set up for the faculty to greet them. As soon as everyone was in the room, as close as they could figure it, Taylor Houghton made a brief speech to welcome old and new students, and all the new female students. There was hooting and catcalls and whistles for that, while Larry Gray looked as though he had swallowed a quince. Taylor held up a hand and stopped it quickly, and introduced the new faculty members. Then he wished everyone a wonderful lunch. The noise in the cafeteria was deafening, but no more so than usual on the first day.

At one-thirty, what Maxine called the Vale of Tears began. It was time for the parents to leave. New parents always cried, and this time so did the freshman girls. But the school kept it short and sweet. At one forty-five, each class had to be at orientation, to get their list of classes and teachers, and the name of their counselor, and by two-thirty they had their first class. The school year was off and running.

Gillian Marks had reminded them before lunch in the cafeteria that team tryouts began the next morning at six A.M., and they each had a list of what tryouts were when. There was a list of clubs they could sign up for in the next few weeks, and special field trips throughout the year. She reminded them that the ski trips to New Hampshire and Vermont filled up quickly, and urged them to sign up soon.

An hour after their parents left, the students were so immersed in school that they had no time to miss them. And by dinnertime, which normally happened in three shifts, they were busy socializing, gossiping about teachers, talking about the classes they'd just been in, and were catching up with old friends, and making new ones.

Jamie Watts and Chase Morgan sat at the same table, as they always did. Steve Babson joined them a little while later, and Tommy Yee walked by them with his violin case, which never left his hands. His grandfather in Shanghai had given him a stunningly valuable violin made by Joseph Gagliano when he turned sixteen, and he took it everywhere with him. His classmates teased him about it at first, and now Tommy carrying his violin case everywhere, even to meals, was a familiar sight.

"Good summer, Tommy?" Jamie called out to him.

"I visited my grandparents in Shanghai. They made me practice my violin three hours a day." He rolled his eyes and grinned. He said he was going to the music tryouts after dinner. The drama club was meeting that weekend, which was going to be a lot more interesting now, since they could do productions with girls in them.

"How are you holding up?" Simon asked Gillian, as they picked up their meals on trays, and sat down at the same table for dinner.

"I feel like I'm running a hair salon in the freshman dorm, but don't tell Larry Gray." She grinned, eating a lamb chop and a double portion of string beans. He was eating lasagna. The school was feeding nearly a thousand people three times a day, and the food was surprisingly good. "All that gorgeous naturally disheveled hair that looks like they just climbed out of bed apparently takes a lot of work and hair products to get that way." She wore hers as short as she could. Being the athletic director left no time to worry about her hair. "I like the kids. You can tell they're good. How was your day?" she asked him.

"Busy, crazy. It will be for the next few weeks. I have twice as many counselees as I had last year, and half of them are girls."

"We start tryouts tomorrow morning, I'm going to be crazed with that. I have to be in my office at five A.M.," Gillian said.

"I'm doing soccer tryouts in two days." He looked at her seriously for a moment then. "Working in a boarding school, do you ever miss having a real life?" She thought about it for a minute and shook her head.

"Not really. My whole life has kind of been like this. I trained for years for the Olympics. Then I went back a second time. I went to boarding school myself as a kid, because my parents moved around all the time. My father worked for oil companies based in the Middle East and my mother went with him. I was always training for some team in college, so I went for what I knew. I've been teaching athletics in boarding schools for ten years. It's kind of nice living in a community. You never get lonely," she said, smiling at him. She was a happy person, it showed, and she loved what she did. "What about you?"

"Up until a year ago, I was working in a fancy day school for rich kids in New York. I lived in France and Italy for two years after college, then I worked for two years as a teacher in New York. I lived in SoHo, and thought I was cool. I had a bad breakup with my girlfriend and gave up my apartment, so I decided to try teaching here last year. I liked it, and it was exciting being part of the transition, so I re-enlisted for another year. Sometimes I miss living like an adult in New York though, going home at night, and doing whatever I want on weekends."

"You'll get over it. I don't think I'd know how to do that anymore. This works for me. In some ways, it's like never having to grow up. You just stay a kid forever."

"Yeah, but they graduate and we don't. I'm thinking I'll do this for another two years, and then see what I think."

"By then, you won't want to go back to New York. This life is addictive," she predicted with a knowing look.

"What do you do in the summer?" He was curious about her.

"I work at a boot camp for women in Baja California." She grinned at him. "They're tough, already in great shape, and expect to be pushed hard. It challenges me too. It's fun working with adults for a change. A lot of them are actresses from L.A."

"You are a glutton for punishment." They had finished their dinner then, and she wanted to get back to the freshman dorm and see how her charges were settling in. So far neither of them had noticed any particular mixing between boys and girls. Each sex seemed to be staying among their own. The returning boys stuck with their friends.

Gillian had noticed Vivienne Walker come in. Chase and Jamie had invited her to join them, but she had declined politely and gone to sit with a group of senior girls. They were all at one table in the back, getting to know each other. The dynamics were fascinating, and, contrary to what Larry Gray had predicted, it hadn't yet become Sodom and Gomorrah. There was no sign of it. The boys and girls were paying almost no attention to each other, except for an occasional glance.

Simon went to his male freshman dorm then, and Gillian went back to her brand-new dorm, where several of the girls complained that there was no hot water. Gillian reported it to maintenance. Lights out was at ten P.M., and they had to be in the dorm by nine. They were going to be introduced to the wonders of their state-of-the-art library the next day. By ten-thirty, Gillian was fast asleep, and the next thing she knew, her alarm went off at four A.M. She took an icy cold shower, since there was still no hot water, and she left a message for maintenance again. Then she headed across campus to get to her office at five and start her day. She made herself a cup of coffee, heated up oatmeal in her office microwave, and went over the list of students who had signed up for tryouts. When they started to wander in at six o'clock she was ready for them. She had freshmen swim tryouts first. She could hardly wait to start working with them. And the one thing she was sure of was that she had the best job in the world.

Chapter Two

Vivienne Walker stayed up until midnight on her first night, texting and FaceTiming her friends in L.A. She had broken up with her boyfriend that summer when she left L.A., because neither of them felt they could handle the responsibility and burden of a long distance relationship, with college looming in a year. It seemed too complicated to both of them, and they hadn't contacted each other since she'd left. But she missed her girlfriends. Her two best friends, Lana and Zoe, had gone to school with her since second grade and it seemed strange to be without them now. They called themselves the Three Musketeers. Lana's parents were TV producers and had gotten divorced when she was ten. She had been supportive of Vivienne when her parents split up and assured her she'd be fine. Zoe's parents were still together. Her father was an attorney like Vivienne's mother, and her mother was an actors' agent. The three girls were inseparable in L.A., and Vivienne felt lost without them. She had met the other seven senior girls at Saint Ambrose, and they were okay, but seemed stuck up to her. She liked her L.A.

friends better. The girls at her new school seemed to be there due to force of circumstances. Three of them had divorced parents who couldn't agree on the custody arrangements, so boarding school was the simplest solution for their parents. Another one had begged to go to boarding school because she hated her new stepfather and wanted to get away. She said her mother acted like an idiot around him and agreed with everything he said. They were having a baby at Christmas, and she didn't want to be around for that, so she had opted for boarding school.

Two of the senior girls were new to the area, one with parents in Boston, the other in New York, and since they had to go to a new school anyway, they had agreed to try Saint Ambrose. One of them said she fought with her parents constantly about her boyfriend, and he got along just as badly with his parents, and they had sent him to boarding school nearby, so she agreed to go away too. She and her boyfriend were going to apply to the same colleges and hoped they would get in, so they could be back together again. They were nice to Vivienne, but she didn't feel close to any of them yet.

And none of the boys interested her particularly. Her mother had wanted her to come to New York with her and go to boarding school. Vivienne had wanted to stay with her father in L.A., but he had reluctantly agreed to let Vivienne go east for a year, for the experience. Her mother had convinced him that if she did well, the strong reputation of the school might help her get into a better college, so he had given in. But all Vivienne wanted was to go back to L.A. She was going to apply to UCLA, USC, UC Santa Barbara, and nothing further away from L.A. than San Francisco. She had no intention of staying in the East after this year. At least when she visited her father, she would see Zoe and Lana. She could hardly wait for Christmas vacation to see them and her dad.

Her parents hadn't told her the reason for the divorce, but the separation had been sudden and it was obvious that her mother hated her father now. Vivienne knew he must have done something big for her to react so vehemently. She had filed for divorce, quit her job at the law firm, found a position in New York, and they had moved away. Vivienne was disappointed that her father hadn't fought to make them stay. He called her every night, and she had told him she liked the school. She didn't hate it, but a lot of the kids seemed cold and snobbish to her. Most of them were from the East Coast, and all the senior boys she had talked to so far had been there for three years. The girls were new, like her, so at least she didn't have to fight her way in to a clique of girls who had been through high school together. Her mother had pointed that out as an advantage.

She had seen two boys she thought were cute the first day, Jamie Watts and Chase Morgan. They had invited her to sit with them at lunch, but she didn't want them to think she was panting after them. One of the girls had told her that Chase's parents were movie stars, but Vivienne didn't really care. There were lots of famous actors' kids at her old school. And she had met several stars at Zoe's house, since her mother was an agent. So she wasn't as impressed as the other girls about Chase's parents.

She thought Jamie was nice. He was in her first class that day, which was social studies. He sat down next to her, and walked her to her math class afterward. She liked him, and thought he was handsome, but she wasn't looking for a boyfriend. She had just gotten out of a relationship and wanted some time to breathe before she got involved again. She missed having a car, but there was nowhere to go here anyway. The school was in the middle of nowhere, from what she could see.

"Where are you from in California?" Jamie asked her. She liked his blue eyes and loose curly blond hair. He was warmer and friendlier than Chase, who seemed more aloof.

"L.A.," she said. He was easy to talk to, and she noticed others watching them as they walked along.

"Chase is from L.A. too. He's been here since freshman year," he told her, which she already knew.

"I want to go back after I graduate," she said simply. "I'm only applying to California schools."

"So is he, except for NYU. I'm going to apply for early admission to Yale. My dad will have a fit if I don't get in. All the men in our family have gone there."

"Are your grades good enough?" she asked, curious about him.

"Sometimes." He smiled, and looked like a kid when he did. She had already noticed that most of the boys looked younger than the girls. A lot of the boys still looked like kids; only a few looked like men. Jamie looked a little like her old boyfriend, but not enough to make a difference. She had gone with him for two years, and they had both been ready for a change. The relationship had gotten stale. From fifteen to seventeen was a long time. "Did you try out for any of the teams today?" Jamie asked her.

"I'm going for volleyball, tryouts are this afternoon."

"I'm on the swim team, and I want to try out for soccer with Mr. Edwards. He's a good guy. He started here last year."

She saw Jamie again in the cafeteria when she wandered in for lunch. They were on the same meal schedule, and she agreed to have lunch with him and Chase. She saw Chase looking her over during the meal, but he didn't say much. He was quiet all through lunch. Her next class was earlier than theirs, and she saw them talking animatedly after she left the table, and wondered if it was about her. She saw an Asian boy carrying a violin case join them, and then she went to her next class. She made the volleyball team when she tried out that afternoon. They barely had enough girls for the team, and added junior girls, which Vivienne didn't mind.

At the end of the afternoon, Simon Edwards ran into Henry Blanchard in the teachers' lounge. He was a fellow math teacher who had worked in co-ed boarding schools for most of his career. Simon walked over to Henry as soon as he came in.

"Okay, tell me the trick. How do I get them to listen to me? The guys in my class are mesmerized by the girls, they stare at them and into space. They don't listen, they don't hear me, they don't even look at the board." Simon was exasperated, and Henry laughed at him.

"Give it time. It's brand new. You're dealing with fifteen-year-olds. All they can think about is how to get their hands on those girls. Except if they actually did, they'd run like hell. It's all fantasyland for them right now. They'll get bored with it, and stop gawking at them. Eventually, they'll see them like anyone else. Give it a few weeks, maybe a month, and they'll hardly notice them."

"Right now, I could sing 'The Star-Spangled Banner' in my underwear and none of them would notice. I could be speaking Swahili or cursing at them."

"Try it. It might make you feel better. But whatever you do, in a few weeks they'll relax and listen to you again. Especially after a couple of lousy grades."

"I taught at a co-ed day school in New York and they never acted like this. Boarding school intensifies every-thing."

"That's because they don't get away from each other. They don't go home at night to parents, siblings, and other friends. We all live together. It's heady stuff for boys that age. It's all new to them. They'll get tired of it. Trust me. Just keep things light in class for a few weeks until they settle down." It reassured Simon somewhat, as he headed to his room in the dorm.

Both sexes wore a school uniform so it wasn't even as though the girls were wearing suggestive clothes, although he had noticed that they knew how to tweak it, and some girls wore their skirts shorter than others. Some of the ones who did wore shorts underneath their uniform. He noticed that the girls who rode to class on bikes did that. As he thought about it, Vivienne Walker raced past him on her bike. Her skirt fluttered in the breeze, and he saw the shorts she was wearing under her uniform skirt too, but what he saw mostly were her gorgeous long legs. For an instant, he forgot who and where he was, and suddenly he realized how his students were feeling. How could you ignore, or get used to, legs like those? Then he reminded himself that she was a seventeen-year-old student and he was a teacher and he had no business admiring her legs. But it was hard not to, with a girl who looked like she did.

It gave him new compassion for his male students, who were being taunted by a hundred and forty girls their age, living in the same place, in close proximity. He said something about it to Gillian, and she laughed and said she just wore them out, and kept them all so busy that they didn't have the time or energy to think about anything except practice when she had them. But if the junior and senior girls looked like women to him, it was no surprise they looked so enticing to the boys they were in class with.

There was an all-school picnic on Saturday, and Simon noticed very little mingling. He'd held the soccer tryouts two days before, and chosen his team. There was talk of starting a female soccer team, but too few girls had signed up. He noticed that the library was full all weekend, so they were actually studying. In spite of Henry's prediction that it would take several weeks, by Monday the male students were starting to act sane again. They were still ogling the girls, but they were paying attention to him in class too, which was a relief.

By the following Monday, a week later, everyone was back in the groove. Homework assignments were being turned in, and the students who had been chosen for sports teams were going to practice. A few had signed up for clubs. Others were still deciding. The new students were making friends, and more often than not, the boys hung out in clusters, and the girls kept to themselves too.

They hadn't really started to integrate yet. They were mainly observing each other from a distance.

But in spite of that, Simon saw Vivienne walking with Jamie on campus several times, just walking and talking, not holding hands. He saw her once with Chase Morgan too, walking into the library, which probably didn't mean anything. He hadn't seen any sign of romance on campus yet. It was probably too soon. They were just fellow students for the moment. The freshmen were shy, and the seniors were cautious. The sophomores were carefree and gregarious, and the juniors were worried about the year ahead and how it would impact the colleges they'd get in to, as juniors did everywhere.

By the end of four weeks, Gillian and her assistants were working hard with the male and female teams. Everyone attended when they competed against other schools. Vivienne was a strong player on the girls' volleyball team. She had been on the team at her L.A. school too.

Simon was already busy with the recommendation forms his senior students had given him to fill out for their college applications. All of them were nervous about which schools to apply to – even Chase Morgan – with a few exceptions, like Jamie Watts and Tommy Yee, who were sure to get in almost anywhere. It was an unsettling time for all of them. Simon was thoroughly enjoying coaching male soccer, and after his years in Italy and

France post-college, he was good at it. Gillian was grateful for his help. She had her hands full with all the male and female teams she was responsible for.

Much to everyone's surprise, by mid-October it almost felt as though they had always been a co-ed school. As Henry Blanchard had predicted, the students had stopped staring at each other all through class. The boys had stopped lusting after the cute girls long enough to listen to their teachers occasionally. The boys and girls had started joking around with each other in the cafeteria, around the campus, and in the gym, the way high school kids did and not like aliens who had just arrived from two different planets. Simon was enjoying teaching them. It challenged the students and added balance and reality to have boys and girls in the classroom. Gillian still said she loved her new job, and all was well in their world.

In the third week of October, they had their annual parents' weekend, and even the parents noticed how easily the kids were mixing, how at ease they seemed with each other, with genuine camaraderie, and how congenial the atmosphere was. Many parents tried to come but some couldn't, for valid reasons. It was always lonely for the students whose parents weren't there. Other parents tried to compensate for it, and included their children's friends. Neither of Chase's parents could make it, but he had known they couldn't. They were both on location, working on films. He and Jamie Watts hung out together, and the Wattses were happy to include Chase when they went off campus to dinner, which was allowed on parents' weekend.

Steve Babson's father hadn't come either. He never did. His mother said he was on call, but he always had some excuse. His mother came, and seemed nervous and shaky. She took Steve out to dinner, had three glasses of wine, and a cocktail first, and he drove her back to her hotel, since he had his license. He walked back to school, hoping no one at the restaurant had noticed how much she drank. It was the only nearby restaurant where parents could take their kids, and the place was jammed with students from Saint Ambrose and their families.

The Yees had come but always stayed separate from the other parents. They had a list of teachers they wanted to speak to, and managed to get a few minutes with each of them, although that wasn't the purpose of the weekend. Parents' weekend was to get a feeling for how their children spent their time out of the classroom. Tommy said that all his parents cared about were his studies and his grades, which were fine so far. But fine was never good enough for them. They expected him to be top of every class.

Gabe Harris's father came and had a long talk with Gillian about what teams his son was on and how he was doing, and if they were the right ones for him. His mother hadn't been able to get the day off from the restaurant she managed, and she had to stay with Gabe's younger siblings in New York. Gabe's father made no effort to meet the other parents, and felt out of place with them. He spent time alone with Gabe, talking about what colleges he was going to apply to, and which schools gave the best athletic scholarships, which he had thoroughly researched.

Both Russos were there in full regalia, dressed to the teeth, as loud and showy as they always were. Joe Russo was driving a new red Ferrari, and Adele was wearing a shocking pink mink jacket with jeans and high heels. Rick looked like he wanted to climb under a rock the entire time they were there. Joe made sure everyone knew how much he had donated to the school. They mortified Rick every time. He hated it when they came to visit, and that they flaunted their money in everyone's faces. Unlike them, he was always discreet about it, or tried to be.

Vivienne's mother drove up from New York, and her father canceled at the last minute. He'd promised to come from L.A., but a meeting came up that he couldn't miss. The atmosphere was tense between Vivienne and her mother, although she was very impressed with the school, and thought Chris would have been too. She was sorry he hadn't seen it. She didn't say anything overtly nasty about him, but Vivienne could tell how angry she still was, and how hurt. Nancy implied that the meeting that had kept him from coming was probably only an excuse, and more than likely he was with his girlfriend. Her father had been vague about her and Vivienne hadn't met her yet. The bitterness of their divorce in progress hadn't dissipated, and Vivienne doubted that it ever would, although her mother refused to discuss it with her. Whatever the reason, she was sad that he hadn't come. She wouldn't see him now until Christmas, since she was spending Thanksgiving with her mother in New York.

Several of the boys hovered around Vivienne, and she introduced Chase and Jamie to her mother. They were very polite. Chase said he was from L.A. too, and Jamie introduced his parents, who were standing nearby. They chatted for a few minutes, and Nancy questioned her daughter afterward, asking if she was interested in either one.

"They're just friends, Mom," Vivienne said with a dismissive look.

"They seem like they like you a lot," she teased, although she knew Vivienne had that effect on men of all ages, and was blasé about it. She had been faithful to her boyfriend for two years, but she didn't seem interested in either of these boys, and said she didn't want to get so deeply involved again.

"There are eight girls to a hundred and eighty-six

senior boys, Mom. They don't have anyone else to gawk at." She blew off their attention as without consequence, although her mother thought both were very good-looking, well brought up boys. And she was even more impressed when she heard who Chase's parents were.

There wouldn't be a full senior class of girls until the current freshman class graduated, and thereafter. For now, it was slim pickings for the senior boys, but Vivienne wasn't looking for romance. She was still adjusting to the school, and all she could think about was getting into college and back to California as fast as possible. She was working on her applications every weekend. She hadn't decided who to give her recommendation forms to yet. She wasn't close to any of her teachers, and had only met with her advisor, Charity Houghton, the headmaster's wife, once since school started. She was writing her essays, and wanted to be finished with the application process when she left for California for Christmas, so she'd have time to see her friends. Zoe and Lana couldn't wait for her to come and she still FaceTimed with them almost every night.

She'd made friends with one girl in her dorm, Mary Beth Lawson. She was from Washington, D.C., and her parents worked for the government. She was vague about what they did, and Vivienne wondered if they worked for the CIA. They visited each other in their rooms at night. Vivienne liked her, but they were still getting to know each other. It wasn't the same as Zoe and Lana, whom she had known since she was seven and had gone all through school with every day.

*

Adrian Stone spent most of the weekend in his room. Neither of his parents had shown up, as usual. They refused to be at the school at the same time, and they could never agree which of them should attend the weekend, so neither came. He didn't really care. He spent most of the weekend in the computer lab, or alone in his room. Everyone else was out, and it was peaceful. He didn't have to talk to anyone or make excuses for his parents, which he had to do all the time. No one noticed his absence, which was a relief. He was afraid he might get into trouble for not going to the big parents' lunch in the cafeteria on Saturday or the brunch on Sunday. He went down after everyone had left, said he had the flu and that his parents hadn't come, and the kitchen staff let him take a plate of food back to his room.

There was a tug-of-war on Sunday afternoon, with parents and faculty on one side, and students on the other. The students always won. Then everyone disbanded. The goodbyes seemed easier than they'd been on the first day of school. The students were going home in five weeks for Thanksgiving. They would have a full week at home, and were looking forward to it. Since his parents would both be on location then, Chase was going to New York with Steve Babson. He wasn't upset about it. It had happened before. His parents had an apartment in New York, but he wasn't allowed to use it when they weren't there.

By the time the parents left the campus on Sunday afternoon, they were satisfied that their children were well and happy, and the school as a whole had adjusted to a major change. Having girls there seemed to add a lighter, more festive atmosphere. The girls' parents seemed pleased that their daughters were being treated well. It had been a very good weekend. The leaves were in full flaming color, and the weather had been perfect. Everything had been just right.

"I'd say it was one of the best parents' weekends we've had. Great turnout," Taylor said to Nicole as they walked across the campus toward Taylor's house, which came with the job of headmaster. Charity had been busy with the parents all weekend too, and Ellen Watts, as the head of the parents' association, had tried to meet all the parents of the girls, so she would at least recognize their faces in future. She had enjoyed speaking to some of them a lot. It was true, having girls there changed things subtly. The school seemed more balanced somehow: even though there were fewer girls than boys, it was more representative of the real world now, with females in it. The all-male atmosphere previously had seemed more intense.

"You have a very impressive parent group," Nicole said to Taylor as they walked. She had enjoyed the weekend too. And she wasn't surprised by the racial disparity. She had been aware of it before she came to Saint Ambrose. It was true of her previous school too. There were about forty African-American families in the student body, all the parents doctors and lawyers and bank presidents. And that had only been true for the last twelve or fourteen years. Before that, there was no diversity at all at schools like Saint Ambrose. It was a fact of life in elitist schools of its kind. Saint Ambrose made no pretense of being anything other than an elitist school. And twenty years earlier, those forty families wouldn't have been a part of the school at all. One day it would be different, she knew, but they hadn't gotten there yet. Being assistant head-master as a female African-American was already a huge step for them, and the rest would come with time. Those forty African-American students were getting the best education money could buy. It was a beginning. Nicole was proud of being part of bringing women into the school.

They crossed paths with Larry Gray, walking home to his rooms in one of the older dormitories which had housing for heads of the departments. Nicole had her own house at the edge of the campus, smaller than Taylor's, but it was perfect and big enough for her. She was comfortable there.

"Great weekend, don't you think, Larry?" Taylor said, and Larry nodded with a cautious look.

"The year is young. Anything can happen." He saluted them and walked on, as Nicole and Taylor laughed.

"Ever the optimist," Nicole said to Taylor, who smiled and shook his head.

"I'd say we're off to a good start," he replied in a confident tone. "Whatever Larry thinks."

"I think so too. A very good start. Saint Ambrose is now officially a very credible co-ed school." It was only six weeks into the school year, but they were off to a very good start indeed. None of Larry Gray's dire predictions had come true. Nor would they, Taylor and Nicole were both sure.

Chapter Three

Halloween had always been one of Gillian's favorite holidays. There was a childish side of her she enjoyed allowing to come through. She had big plans for the gym on Halloween. Gillian enlisted the help of her two assistants, several of the teachers she had gotten to know, and a few seniors. The night before Halloween they worked like demons turning the gym into an enormous haunted house. Gillian had brought some of the supplies with her, and bought the rest in town. There were giant cobwebs hanging from everywhere and partitions created with bolts of black cloth. Giant rubber tarantulas were all over the place, and plastic skeletons, an oversized ghoul she'd had for years, witches, and goblins. She had a CD of ghostly sounds with screams. By midnight they had the gym ready to terrify and delight any willing student, and Gillian put a sign on the front door that read "Beware! Enter at Your Own Risk!"

They had no basketball or volleyball practices scheduled there that day, and the students were allowed to wear costumes after classes. Gillian had been told that the day had always been fairly lackluster before the arrival of the girls, who threw themselves into it heart and soul. She made an announcement in the cafeteria at lunchtime that there was a haunted house on campus, but only the bravest should enter, and be prepared to be terrified. She posted a few signs around. A willing crew of seniors showed up to guide the freshmen through. The costumes were varied and creative, everything from Superman and Catwoman to gladiators, Vikings, Julius Caesar in a bedsheet, and one freshman girl had brought a Minnie Mouse costume from home, just in case. It looked adorable. There were several Barbies, a Hello Kitty, Batman and Robin. The costumes were both bought and homemade. Several of the teachers showed up at the haunted house in costume too. Gillian wore a Frankenstein costume and had the height to look seriously frightening. Maxine Bell, the school counselor, came as the Bride of Frankenstein. There were several pirates, and many witches, and kids from every grade were thrilled to go through it, screaming at every twist and turn. Everyone had a great time, and Nicole smiled as she walked by on her way to a meeting with Taylor. The haunted house was a huge success, and the freshmen went through it again and again. Gillian had smoldering cauldrons, and giant bowls of candy which she handed out liberally. She was planning to keep it running until senior curfew at ten P.M. They could have fun with it for an hour on their own, after the younger students had to be in their rooms at eight and nine P.M. Her crew of willing helpers had agreed to stay as late as they had to, to help her take it down.

They had lots of visitors all through the afternoon and evening, before and after dinner. It was even scarier as the night got darker. Taylor and Nicole showed up and went through it too, and thanked Gillian for putting it together. Everybody loved it. Simon Edwards was working the door in a Darth Vader mask that said, in a robotic voice, "Don't make me destroy you!" which he had brought from New York, and worn at his previous school. Everyone had gone all out to make the haunted house a success, and it was the hit of the campus. One of the sophomores who had been there the year before —"B.G." as the kids were calling it, "Before Girls"—said that this was the coolest year ever, and Taylor and Nicole smiled when they heard him say it.

The seniors had gone through the haunted house trying to seem cool, but even they jumped and started and screamed, as witches, who were teachers with painted green faces, leapt out at them unexpectedly. Rick Russo and Steve Babson had gone through it together, with Gabe not far behind them. Rick whispered to Steve on their way out.

"Trick or treat," he said meaningfully. Steve frowned

at first, wondering what he meant, and then understood that Rick had something to share with him. They had split a pint of bourbon once, and a bottle of wine, and hadn't gotten caught. "Behind the tree line," Rick whispered again. It was where they had done it before, and Steve nodded, looking pleased by Rick's suggestion, as he helped himself to a handful of candy on the way out. There were miniature Snickers bars and KitKats, M&M's, Tootsie Pops, and Hershey's Kisses. The new athletic director had gone all out and spent her own money on the treats, as a gift to the kids.

Gabe came up behind them then, and Steve passed the message to him. "Behind the tree line." Gabe got it immediately, and the three of them headed toward a seldom-used path that was a shortcut to some maintenance buildings. It was more frequented this year, because it was also a shortcut to the girls' dorms, which some of them had discovered. But there was no one walking there now.

The trees provided a solid wall, beyond which there was a clearing, and a cluster of tall old trees with heavy roots. It was a secluded spot that no one ever went to. All three boys were strong enough to push through the bushes that reinforced the tree line, and with a few leaves sticking to them here and there, they walked into the clearing and laughed in anticipation of what they were about to do.

"So what's the treat?" Steve asked Rick, keeping his voice down, so no one venturing down the path would hear them. But the maintenance staff was off by then, and most of the girls seemed to travel the more obvious paths to their dorms.

"Courtesy of my father's bar," Rick said, pulling a silver flask out of his jacket pocket with a grin. He was wearing a black sweatshirt and windbreaker, and black jeans that had been part of his pirate costume a little earlier. They could see the flask clearly in the moonlight.

"What's in it?" Gabe asked, as Rick took the first swig himself.

"Vodka," Rick answered and handed it to him. Gabe took a swallow and handed it to Steve, who drank from it too.

"Trick or treat, gentlemen," Rick said and all three of them laughed, and then stood still and listened as they heard voices on the path. They were male voices, and they recognized them immediately. Steve ran over to the tree line, peeked through a narrow opening, and called through the bushes in a stage whisper.

"Hey!" Chase and Jamie were on the other side, and stopped walking when they heard him. "Trick or treat!"

"What are you, a freshman?" Chase said with a grin.

"Come on in," Steve invited them.

"What are you doing in there? We were heading there too." Without hesitating, Jamie and Chase pressed through the trees and bushes as the other three had, and looked at them, smiling. "You're having a party and didn't invite us?" Chase was carrying a backpack, and all five of them walked away from the bushes and went to sit under the enormous tree with the gnarled roots. Steve almost tripped over one of them, as the vodka started to take effect. They all sat down on the ground, and Chase set down his backpack as Steve handed them the flask. Both newcomers took a drink.

"Sissy stuff," Chase said as he handed back the flask, opened his backpack, and pulled out a full bottle, while the others' eyes grew wide. Rick slipped the flask back in his pocket.

"What is that?" Rick asked, intrigued at the prospect.

"Tequila. I figured maybe we could have a little fare-well party before graduation and it might come in handy," Chase said with a grin. "But we decided to have a few shots tonight. Looks like you had the same idea."

"And you had it in your room?" Gabe looked shocked. He wouldn't have dared bring alcohol to the school or hide it in his room. He thought Chase was gutsy to do it.

"Locked in my trunk. I carry the key. We figured we'd give it a try tonight and save the rest for later. Everyone's so busy with the haunted house, no one's going to notice anything." He and Jamie had talked about it before they left their dorm—their rooms were side by side—but they wouldn't dare drink it there. The clearing behind the tree line was the perfect location for a little mischief. Having a few drinks on Halloween sounded like fun to them.

Chase opened the bottle and handed it to Jamie, who took a drink and made a face as it seared his throat. It was the strongest drink he'd ever had, and a lot stronger than the vodka.

"Not bad, huh?" Chase commented. "I tried it last year when my parents told me they were getting a divorce." He looked serious for a minute, took a swig himself, and passed it to Rick, who took a longer drink and passed it around. It made him feel manly and confident.

"Wow, that's strong stuff," Steve said and took another swallow of the liquid in the bottle. It made the rounds again between the five of them. By their third drink of it, they were all starting to feel a buzz, and then stopped dead when they heard a high voice singing on the path.

"Shit, girls," Rick whispered, and they all sat quietly, waiting for the voice to pass, and then realized that it was a male voice singing in Chinese. They recognized it immediately.

"Tommy," they all said in unison and laughed as they ran back soundlessly to the tree line, peeked through the bushes, and saw him carrying his violin case.

"Hey, Yee!" Jamie said through the trees. Tommy nearly jumped a foot, and for a minute thought it was a ghost. He was on his way to practice at the music lab, since he had promised his parents he would every night.

"Who is that?" he asked, looking terrified, talking into the bushes.

"It's us, get in here," Chase said boldly, and they were all grinning. Tommy had gone through all four years with them and they liked him. Once in a while he hung out with them, when he wasn't studying. They pushed the bushes apart for him, and pulled him through, as he looked around the group and grinned. He saw that he was among friends.

"I thought you were a ghost," he said, smiling at them. "What are you doing in here?" But he could guess. He'd been at the wine party with them in the same place the year before. They only broke the alcohol rule about once a year, for a special occasion.

"A little trick or treating." They all went back under the tree and sat down. This time, Rick and Steve stumbled over the roots. The tequila had begun to give them a warm glow. It was a cold night and none of them cared. Chase handed Tommy the tequila bottle, and he looked impressed.

"Whoa, you guys have upgraded, that's strong shit."

"Try it," Chase said. Tommy took a cautious sip and made an awful face.

"I've got vodka if you want it," Rick offered. He held out the flask again, and Tommy took a sip of that too. They continued passing both bottles around between the six of them, but eventually they stuck with the tequila. It tasted worse, but the effect was stronger. They hadn't intended to get drunk, just to get a little buzz on, but, sharing it among themselves, they'd had more to drink than they realized. Rick was lying on the ground with his head on a tree root, grinning to himself and then at the others.

"Man, I feel great!" It felt like a rite of passage, now that they were seniors, to impress each other with how much they could drink.

"Yeah, me too," Gabe said, before he took another swig, and they passed it around again. Jamie was laughing to himself, and then they heard female voices, for real this time. It was a bunch of girls, taking the shortcut to their dorm. The boys waited silently for them to pass. It sounded like there were a lot of them, and they didn't want them to discover their secret hiding place. As far as they knew, no one else ever used it. There wasn't much opportunity to party at school. They were pretty well supervised, and none of the others would have dared bring alcohol to school. Jamie had been planning to save the tequila till graduation, and Rick had taken his father's flask when the opportunity presented itself.

They were about to start talking again after the girls had gone by, when they heard another female voice humming on the path. She wasn't talking and they guessed she was alone. Jamie went stealthily back to the bushes and peered through as best he could. The bushes and trees were thick, but he recognized who it was immediately. It was Vivienne Walker. She was wearing a witch's costume she had thrown together with a short black skirt, a big black sweater, and a witch's hat Gillian had loaned her to take the freshmen through the haunted house. She had on thick black stockings and flat black ballerina shoes. She still looked pretty even as a witch.

"Pssst!!!" Jamie hissed at her, and she turned with a startled look. He didn't want to scare her. "It's me, Jamie. Do you want to come in?"

"Come in where?" She looked confused.

"Back here."

"What are you doing there?" She looked suspicious and uncertain, but she was happy to see him. They were becoming friends in the past six weeks.

"It's just me and the guys, Chase, Tommy, Steve, Rick, and Gabe. We're trick or treating." It sounded so ridiculous that she laughed. He was slurring his words a little and she wondered if he'd been drinking, but she was flattered to be asked to join them, like being part of a secret club, or an initiation of some kind. It made her feel like "one of the guys."

"Okay," she agreed, and he parted the bushes for her and pulled her through. She had to grab her hat, and an instant later, she saw them all sitting under the tree, and walked over to them with Jamie, who was pleased to see her too. He liked her, but hadn't decided what to do about it yet. He wanted to ask her out, but didn't want to spoil their budding friendship. She had told him she had just broken up with a boy in L.A., and he thought it might be too soon. He was thinking of calling her over Thanksgiving in New York.

"If you tell anyone you saw us here, we'll have to kill you," Rick said, trying to look ominous, but he was already drunk and looked goofy more than scary. He seemed drunker than the others, but she could tell they'd all been drinking. She wondered if she should leave, but didn't want to seem like a sissy or a poor sport. And she and Zoe and Lana had gotten drunk once on a bottle of wine in L.A.

"I wouldn't tell. So where's the trick or treat?" For a minute she thought they had stolen a bunch of the candy from the gym, which seemed funny, and then Chase handed her the bottle of tequila and her eyes opened wide. "Oh, that kind of trick or treat," she said, startled. She made a quick decision and wanted to look cool. She liked the idea of being friends with them. They were the big stars on campus. She took a swig, which sealed their conspiracy if she was drinking with them. It burned like fire as it went down her throat and she made a face.

"*Yerghk,* that stuff is awful," she said about the tequila.

"We had vodka too," Rick volunteered, "but I think we're out." He checked the flask and it was empty. "We've only got tequila left." The boys had another swallow, but Tommy didn't. He was sitting slumped against the tree, looking glazed. The others still wanted to party, and Vivienne had just gotten there. It seemed too soon to leave. They handed her the bottle again and she took another fiery drink. If this was some kind of initiation into their friendship, she didn't want to flunk.

"That shit is strong," she commented, and already felt slightly dizzy. She hadn't had time for dinner and it was hitting her fast, faster than she'd realized it would. She'd never had anything that strong to drink before, and neither had they—except Chase, who'd tasted tequila that one time, but he'd only taken a sip then. That night they had all had a lot more, and the effect was more powerful than they'd expected, or even realized.

And then with no warning, as they all sat together, Jamie leaned over and kissed her. The amount of alcohol he'd consumed gave him the courage to do it, and it suddenly seemed like a good idea. It did to her too, and she kissed him back. Vivienne was glad he'd kissed her and she didn't see Chase staring angrily at them. His eyes looked huge and intense and he was furious at Jamie. Chase wanted her too and he didn't want Jamie to have her. He'd been thinking about her for a while. He gave Jamie a hard shove, and raised his voice.

"Why did you do that? She's not your girlfriend." And the next moment, Jamie took a swing at Chase and the two boys were wrestling on the ground. Vivienne wanted to stop them, but she suddenly realized she was too drunk to try. She felt unsteady on her feet. The other boys couldn't move at first either. They stood up unsteadily and Gabe and Steve tried to pull them apart. While they were trying to stop the fight, Rick staggered over to Vivienne, and before any of them knew what had happened, Rick had grabbed Vivienne, pushed her down, pulled her tights and panties down, opened his jeans, and plunged into her. She was too drunk and dizzy and shocked to make a sound. Tommy had his back turned to the whole scene and was throwing up, and didn't know what had happened. Steve saw it first and pulled Rick off her, while Gabe fought to separate Jamie and Chase. Steve took a wild swing at Rick and fell himself. Rick was already zipping up his jeans, and Vivienne had passed out. Jamie realized what Rick had done, when Gabe finally pulled him off Chase. Jamie took a swing at Rick too and landed a punch to his jaw. Chase looked at the scene in horror. Everything had gotten out of hand within minutes. Their harmless drunken Halloween night had turned into a brawl and a rape. None of them could believe what Rick had done. They turned on him and he tried to stagger away from them. He was crying by then, and shouted at Chase and Jamie.

"She'd never have wanted me if she wasn't drunk. She only wanted you two!"

"You bastard!" Chase shouted at him, as he tried to

land a punch in his face and missed. They were all too drunk to know what to do next, as Vivienne lay on the ground, deeply intoxicated from the tequila. The boys could barely stand up, only slightly sobered by the turn of events. The tequila was in full control by then, the bottle nearly empty.

"What do we do now?" Chase asked them, fighting back tears as he looked at Vivienne.

"We'll all go to prison," Gabe said with a look of terror, "we have to get out of here."

"We can't just leave her," Jamie said. He had pulled up her panties and tights, crying while he did it. He could see she was breathing, but she was deeply unconscious, more than likely from the tequila.

"Let's go back to our rooms and figure it out, we can call campus police and tell them we heard suspicious activity back here and they'll find her. I have a blocked number," Chase volunteered, despite the fog in his head. He could barely think straight and felt dizzy.

"Don't tell them it was me," Rick begged them, with tears streaming down his face. "I didn't mean to do it."

"But you did," Jamie said, almost sober for an instant.

"Get Tommy," Chase told Gabe, as they all gathered up their things and staggered toward the tree line. They all felt sick as they pressed through it. They had lost track of time while they were drinking, and it was two hours past curfew. Chase called campus police before they reached their dorm. He said he'd heard suspicious activity behind the trees and thought someone might be hurt, and had hung up, as they walked quietly into their building and went silently to their rooms. No one heard them. Rick went to the bathroom and threw up, as the others retreated. None of them had ever been that drunk. Chase passed out as soon as he sat down on his bed. The room was spinning as Jamie lay on his, thinking about Vivienne and what had happened to her. He felt even sicker when he thought about it.

The campus police had already found Vivienne by then and had called for an ambulance. There was no sign of the rape. All they knew was that there was an unconscious girl on campus. They didn't know if she was drunk, had fallen and hit her head, or been attacked by a stranger or someone on campus.

The six boys who knew what had happened, those who hadn't passed out yet, heard the siren of the ambulance ten minutes later. They were relieved that Chase had called for help. And the boys had promised Rick not to give him up, but they were all trapped in the nightmare with him. Their lives and futures had been thrown away with a single bottle of tequila and a flask of vodka if they got caught, and an innocent girl had been the victim of Rick's momentary insanity.

By the time the ambulance got to the hospital, all six boys were in a deep, drunken sleep, and Vivienne was still unconscious. And this was only the beginning. Their Halloween had changed all of their lives forever.

*

It was just after midnight when Adrian Stone, the resident geek, snuck back from the computer lab. He knew that everyone was busy with the haunted house that had stayed open late, and he crept into the lab sometimes. He knew how to work the lock, and he went there at night. He'd been doing it for all three years he'd been there and had never gotten caught.

He didn't know what they'd been doing, but he had seen the six boys stumbling and running after they came out from behind the trees. He had been hiding too, and he had an eerie feeling that something was wrong and they had done something bad. It was none of his business, but he was curious, and they were gone. They were all the big heroes on campus who didn't know who he was or that he was alive anyway. He liked watching them, wishing he was like them and that they could be friends one day, but he knew that would never happen. He wondered if they had a secret meeting place or a club of some kind, and he decided to slip through the trees and check it out before going back to his room. He saw the big trees and the clearing, and stumbled over the empty tequila bottle lying on the ground. And then he saw Vivienne, lying still in her witch costume. He knew who she was too, the most beautiful girl on campus. He approached slowly; she looked like she was sleeping peacefully. And then he thought he knew what had happened. They had killed her. He didn't know why they'd killed her, but they had. She was ghostly pale in the moonlight and she looked dead to him. Adrian didn't dare touch her to see if she was breathing, but he was sure she wasn't.

He didn't know if he was supposed to tell someone, but it didn't matter anyway. He was sure she was dead. She wasn't moving, and didn't make a sound. She was definitely dead. He saw the violin case leaning against a tree, and all of a sudden he felt a wave of terror wash over him. What if someone thought he did it? If someone had seen him the way he saw them, and later they said he had killed her. And if he told about anyone who had been there before him, they'd come back and kill him.

He backed out through the bushes from where he had come and ran as fast as he could all the way to his dorm. He was panting when he got there. He snuck in through a back stairway the way he always did, and slipped into the room he shared with two other boys. They never talked to him anyway and went to sleep early every night. They never knew when Adrian slipped out or when he came back.

Adrian climbed into bed with all his clothes on, shaking. By morning someone would find the dead girl, and whatever happened, he wasn't going to say a word. If he did, he was sure he'd get blamed and probably go to prison. He heard the ambulance siren five minutes later, and was glad he'd left as fast as he did, or they would have caught him at the scene and blamed him. He was sorry she was dead, but he didn't want to go to prison for it.

*

The campus police called Nicole Smith right after they found Vivienne behind the tree line. Nicole was asleep, but woke up and answered quickly.

"We have an unconscious girl on the grounds. She's alive, she has no ID on her. It looks like it could be alcohol." They told Nicole where she was and that they had called for an ambulance. "There was an empty tequila bottle on the ground under the tree." Nicole felt a shiver run down her spine. Alcohol and kids could be a lethal combination, and at some point had been a problem at every school where she'd worked.

"Oh my God. I'll be there in two minutes." She leapt out of bed, stepped into shoes, put a coat on over her pajamas, grabbed her bag and phone, and took off at a dead run across the campus. She was breathless when she got there, right after they put Vivienne in the ambulance. Nicole recognized her immediately. Nicole climbed into the ambulance with her.

They sped to the hospital with sirens shrieking. The paramedics said Vivienne was alive. They suspected alcohol poisoning. Nicole was sure that everyone on campus must have wondered what was going on when they heard the siren—that a teacher had had a heart attack, or a student had a burst appendix. She still had no idea what had happened or who was involved. The campus police said there was no sign of violence. She was just lying there unconscious, fully dressed, and they thought it unlikely she'd been drinking alone. For now, all Nicole wanted was for Vivienne to survive. Kids died of alcohol poisoning. It wasn't unheard of. They'd figure out later who else had been there, and left her passed out.

As soon as they reached the hospital, the paramedics ran her into the emergency room, and a team rushed to tend to her. They very quickly confirmed that she was dangerously inebriated and her blood alcohol level was high. They came to tell Nicole they believed Vivienne had alcohol poisoning and were going to pump her stomach. She could die of it, and still might. It had happened at other schools, but never at Saint Ambrose. And they said that, as a matter of course, to be thorough, they were going to examine her to see if she'd been raped. There were signs of intercourse when they undressed her. There was dried semen on her abdomen. The police had already been called by the paramedics and arrived ten minutes later. They were from the rape detail, and informed

Nicole that, given the circumstances, it was a possibility they had to consider. It could have been consenting sex, but she was a minor. And since she was unconscious, anyone could have raped her. A sergeant and two patrolmen had already been dispatched to tape off the area where she'd been found as a possible crime scene. Nicole felt as though she were living a nightmare, but if they were right, she thought it highly unlikely that any boy at the school would commit a rape. But it had happened at other schools, and anything was possible with alcohol involved.

They asked Nicole if she knew any of the details, and she said she didn't. The campus police had gotten an anonymous call from a blocked phone reporting suspicious activity and had found Vivienne when they checked it out.

"If she was raped, it could have been by an intruder, a sex offender in the area recently released from prison, a staff member, faculty, another student. We'll be able to narrow it down when we can talk to her." Nicole nodded and waited for the doctor to speak to her. She didn't want to call Taylor or Vivienne's mother and father until she knew more about Vivienne's situation.

It was almost an hour before the senior doctor in the emergency room came to talk to Nicole and report on her condition.

"She's stable, the alcohol level in her blood is

excessively high, and she did have intercourse. We won't know if it's rape or not until we talk to her. There are no obvious signs of violence. She may have been coerced or unconscious. Or she may have gotten drunk with another student and had consensual intercourse. Does she have a boyfriend at school?"

"Not that I know of," Nicole said somberly. She still couldn't believe Vivienne might have been raped. The alcohol she'd consumed was bad enough—it was almost enough to kill her and it still could. The ER doctors used the rape kit they kept on hand, so they had all the samples they needed if it turned out to be a rape. They preferred to assume the worst and prepare accordingly. Nicole couldn't believe it. They told her that the police toxicology and DNA units would analyze the evidence later. "She's sleeping off the alcohol now," the doctor told Nicole.

"Will she be all right?" Nicole meant would she die, but she didn't want to say it.

"Yes. We're watching her closely. She could have died if no one had called it in. Kids die of alcohol poisoning all the time. How old is she?"

"Seventeen." He nodded. He had a daughter the same age. "We have full authorization for her, do you want me to sign anything?" He shook his head with a serious look.

"We know the school. You can sign the admitting forms while she sleeps it off. She must have had quite a night. You'll call the parents?" Nicole nodded.

She checked on Vivienne before she went to call Taylor. Vivienne was still unconscious. One of the detectives left with the sperm and DNA samples for the police lab to keep for future identification, if it was a rape. She called Taylor immediately after, and woke him out of a sound sleep. It was almost two in the morning by then.

"I don't have good news," she said in a somber voice.

"It never is at this hour. I heard the sirens over an hour ago. I figured you'd call me if it was serious. We have a sick kid?"

"Worse than that. Vivienne Walker has alcohol poisoning and may have been raped. I'm at the hospital now. They're not sure of anything yet. She's alive. Thank God someone called it in, so campus police found her. We need to call her parents."

"Oh God." Taylor was wide awake now, and thought about the difficult calls they had to make. There was silence at his end for a few seconds while he absorbed it. "If she was raped, we'd better goddamn well hope there is a serial rapist in the area, or all hell is going to break loose if it was someone on campus." Nicole knew it too. If a faculty member, employee, or fellow student had raped her, it was going to be the scandal of the century, and terrible for Vivienne to have gone through, whoever it was.

"It may not even have been rape, it could have been consensual. There was no sign of violence or injury," she said. "We'll know more when she wakes up and can talk to us, if she even knows who did it, and remembers. She may have been so drunk, she didn't know what she was doing. She may not even have seen him, if it was a rape by a stranger. She may already have been unconscious. But let's not assume the worst here. Alcohol poisoning is bad enough."

"Poor kid. I'll call her parents." He had instructions to call both of them if there was an emergency. It was another messy divorce with warring parents. Her father had made it clear that he was not fully on board with Vivienne going to Saint Ambrose. Her mother had talked him into it.

Taylor called Nancy, her mother, first, and told her what he knew as simply as he could, without judgment. That she'd drunk to excess, and there was evidence of intercourse, but not of rape. Nancy burst into tears and then composed herself, and sounded intelligent. She asked him questions he had no answer to, and wouldn't until Vivienne was conscious.

"I'll drive up right away," she said, sounding devastated. It was a five-hour drive from New York, and she'd be there by morning. Vivienne might still be asleep when she arrived. Taylor told her how sorry he was. He had a feeling this was only the beginning. Whatever had happened, they would have a lot of explaining to do about how something like this could occur on campus. It was an ugly first for them, and a terrible way to start their first co-ed school year. He was thinking of the school, and all the staff members who had been worried about their going co-ed. And he hated to see Larry Gray be right. He hoped nothing terrible had happened to Vivienne before or after she passed out.

Taylor called Christopher Walker next, Vivienne's father. He cried like a baby. He asked the same pertinent questions, and said he'd be on the next plane from L.A. He also said that that did it for him. She was coming back to California to live with him. Taylor didn't get into it—the poor man was so distraught he was barely coherent. Her mother had been calmer, but both parents were heartbroken by what had happened to their daughter, even if it was "only" alcohol poisoning and she'd been left unconscious by whoever she got drunk with, and knowingly had sex with someone. She could easily have died after they left her, or even before. Both parents said the whole episode was so unlike her. She was a responsible person, had never gotten drunk before, and wasn't promiscuous. But Taylor also knew that parents didn't always know their children as well as they thought they did.

Nicole Smith stayed at the hospital all night, waiting for Vivienne's mother to come. She arrived at seven in the morning, and must have driven over the speed limit the entire way. Vivienne still hadn't regained consciousness. But she opened her eyes when her mother walked into the room, said a few incoherent words and went back to sleep. Nicole left the room quietly and took a cab back to school. They had lots to do that morning. Until they knew more, they would have to increase security to protect all the females on campus. If there was a rapist lurking somewhere, they couldn't take any chances with the girls on campus now. Although since Vivienne had been drinking, if she had been raped, it was more likely to be someone she knew, and not a random stranger.

As soon as Nicole got home, she sent an urgent email to all students and faculty. There would be an all-school assembly at nine A.M. Nicole wasn't looking forward to it. Vivienne's identity would not be revealed, but the entire school needed to move around the campus with extreme caution, in case Vivienne had been raped. When Vivienne didn't reappear it would be obvious she was the victim, but there was nothing else they could do. It was a terrible situation, and for Vivienne most of all. Nicole's heart ached for her, as she got into the shower, and let the hot water pelt her body. It had been a devastating night, and now they had to find out what had happened, and if she had been raped, who the rapist was. And if she had been coerced into having sex by someone who got her drunk, they needed to know who that person was too.

Chapter Four

When Taylor and Nicole stood side by side at the all-school assembly in the auditorium at nine o'clock that morning, it telegraphed immediately that something serious had happened, and the entire student body fell silent. A number of them had heard the ambulance sirens the night before, and wondered if they were about to be told that one of the students had died. For anything less than that, they would have heard by email or word of mouth. And until that moment, as far as they knew, Nicole and Taylor were the only ones aware of what had happened.

Nicole announced it to the faculty and student body as carefully and as simply as was possible in the circumstances. A female member of the student body had possibly been "assaulted" the night before. They chose the word carefully since they still didn't know if Vivienne had had intercourse willingly while inebriated, or even before, or if she'd been coerced and raped. No details were known yet, and she had survived. Her name was not mentioned, but ultimately, her absence would speak for itself. Taylor added that the police would be conducting a school-wide investigation. If anyone had any information, had seen anyone suspicious on campus the night before, or had any knowledge of what had happened, they were urged to come forward immediately, so as to help apprehend the perpetrator. No one was to be protected, no suspicions were to be hidden, no information withheld, Nicole said pointedly, as the entire student body sat silently, riveted in their seats.

Until more was known about the situation, all females on campus, both students and teachers, were to move around with caution, in groups or at the very least pairs. They were to go nowhere alone. All the outer doors of dorm buildings and classrooms were to be kept locked. And males and females alike were to remain vigilant. If they saw anything unusual, or any strangers on campus, they were to tell a teacher or a member of the administration immediately, and call security. She reminded them again that the school and the police needed everyone's full cooperation and all the information they had, in order to catch the culprit. Nicole also reminded them that the no-drinking-on-campus rule was a serious one, and they expected it to be obeyed. Not doing so would incur suspension and possible expulsion. The school had a zero tolerance to alcohol policy. Then she thanked them all and left the stage with a somber expression, and Taylor followed her.

Pandemonium broke out in the auditorium the moment the headmaster and assistant headmaster left. There was a loud hubbub of startled conversation, guess-work about who the victim was and what had happened. It sounded as though some students had been drinking and someone had gotten hurt.

Adrian Stone sat frozen in his seat as it went on around him. He felt as though everyone in the room knew he'd been there, and could see it in his eyes. At least they hadn't killed her, that was something. They had said the student was alive. And he didn't think he'd be accused of "assaulting" her. He still didn't know what had happened or what they'd done to her. But he was sure he'd go to jail for not revealing the identity of the six boys he knew had been there. They might not have done it either, and probably hadn't. But they had been there, and must have seen her too. And they had left in a hurry, running and stumbling and bumping into each other. And she was unconscious when they left. But Adrian wasn't going to betray them. He was going to leave that to someone else. Maybe the police would figure it out on their own. He wasn't going to be responsible for sending six boys to prison for assault. He slipped out of the auditorium with his heart still pounding and ran smack into Simon Edwards, nearly jumping out of his skin when he did.

"Hey, Adrian, are you okay?" Adrian looked panicked and very pale.

"I'm fine, Mr. Edwards. I thought I was having an asthma attack, but I'm okay."

"I know, it's very upsetting, isn't it? We don't know the details yet, but it sounds like some drinking went on and, and something went wrong. That's what happens. Drinking and breaking the rules is always a bad idea." In the auditorium was the first Simon had heard of it, although he had noticed the siren the night before, and wondered what it was for, but it was too late to call anyone to find out. He had never suspected something like this. He knew of stories like it before, at other boarding schools—binge drinking and even rapes—but he couldn't imagine it happening here. The students at Saint Ambrose were all good kids. He just hoped it wasn't one of them, and that if there was a crime, it had been committed by an outsider, a random stranger. It was Taylor's most fervent hope too. But when drinking was involved, there was no telling what even the best kids would do.

Adrian skittered away then, and said he was going to get his inhaler in his room. Simon didn't think he looked well, but he often didn't—he had allergies, asthma, anxiety, and every possible psychosomatic disorder, as a result of the constant strife between his parents and their endless battles over him.

The senior girls were talking quietly among themselves. Mary Beth had noticed in the auditorium that

Vivienne was missing, and checked her room when they went back to the dorm, to see if she was sick. Her bed was made and hadn't been slept in. As soon as she saw it, she felt sick, and realized that Vivienne must have been the victim. The other senior girls in the dorm figured it out too, and looked at each other somberly. But none of them were inclined to gossip about it. They felt terrible for her, if she'd gotten hurt. Secretly, they were each glad it hadn't been them. They made a pact with each other to move as a group, as they'd been told, until the assailant was caught. Mary Beth sat on her own bed and cried after she left Vivienne's room.

Gillian was silent and upset as she walked back to the gym, and Simon walked with her. It was unnerving to think that something bad had happened in this safe, peaceful place. Neither of them wanted to think that a rape could have been committed by one of the students. And "assault" was a broad term. All they could hope was that, if it was rape, it had been a stranger, and he would be caught soon, rather than it being a member of their own community. And they hoped the victim wasn't badly hurt. The administration was being mysterious about it, which was never a good sign, and led to everyone fearing and assuming the worst.

Simon didn't know for sure who the victim had been, but he could guess. He hadn't noticed Vivienne at the assembly that morning, and Gillian mentioned it too.

They were all badly shaken by what had happened, as well as by the warning, and the little they knew. They had been told that a member of the student body was in the hospital, but how badly injured she was they didn't know.

When Taylor got back to his office, the police detectives were waiting for him. He invited them into his office and called Nicole in from hers to join them.

"We have two detectives of the juvenile rape team coming in from Boston this afternoon," they informed him. "They're both certified sexual assault investigators. We've been gathering evidence in the meantime." The detectives in front of him were serious older men.

"Is there any evidence of rape and who it might have been?" Taylor asked them. "Has Vivienne *said* she was raped?" There was a pause in the room then.

"She told her mother this morning that she was raped. She was forced, against her will. That's rape," he confirmed, and Taylor felt sick. It was his worst fear.

"Was it someone she knew?" Nicole asked in a quiet voice.

"We assume so. I'm sure the drinking was part of it and got out of hand. She won't say who she was drinking with. She's protecting them."

"Was she raped by several boys?" Nicole asked in a choked voice.

"She says just one," the detective said seriously.

It was the kind of situation that every school dreaded,

where everyone got hurt in the end. They had an obligation to protect their students and all of them had a
right to be and feel safe. "Do you think she'll tell us who
it is?"

"Not yet." The chief detective looked chagrined. "The
DNA and bodily fluid samples from the victim will eventually tell us," the senior detective said. "And a few things
from the crime scene. An empty tequila bottle for one,
and a violin case with a violin in it, and a tag on it with
the name of Thomas Yee. We would like to speak to him
this morning." Nicole could guess that there were fingerprints on the bottle. It was going to be a long and
comprehensive investigation if Vivienne wouldn't tell
them who had raped her.

"Of course. I'd have a hard time believing Tommy Yee
is mixed up in this. He's one of our most diligent
students." Taylor looked pained at the very idea.

"He'll need to explain how his violin got there," the
detective said, and Taylor nodded.

"The tequila bottle is covered with prints, which may
make things easier. The victim's blood alcohol level was
extremely high when they brought her in. In other words,
she was drunk, to the point that it could have killed her.
Whoever she was drinking with may have raped her, or
she may have passed out and they were afraid to get in
trouble so they left her there and someone else raped
her. That's a possibility. She could have been raped by

someone entirely unrelated to the school, but it's not likely. Most likely it was a fellow student. Someone knows, and will talk eventually."

"We certainly hope so," Taylor said fervently, and Nicole nodded agreement. "We'll do everything we can to help you. We want to know too."

"We'll run the prints on the bottle through our usual sources, looking for known sex offenders, and men convicted of rape who've been released from prison and are in the area, just as a technicality. If we don't have any matches there, and I doubt we will, we may finger-print the whole school," the detective said calmly. "If there were other girls drinking with them, one of them may talk and tell us who was there."

"All nine hundred and forty students?" Taylor looked surprised.

"Yes, and faculty and staff. First we want to know who she was drinking with and what happened. If she remembers, that may lead us to the rapist. We're going to speak to her again in a little while. She feels the classic guilt of rape victims, and she also feels uncomfortable that she got drunk with them. It's not a smart thing to do, but kids do it, and so do adults. I've never seen one of these school situations where alcohol wasn't involved. They go crazy, sometimes a gang dynamic kicks in. But whatever happened, she had a right not to be raped." Taylor and Nicole both nodded, devastated that it had happened and sad for Vivienne. And they believed what she had told her mother. It did bring up the school's policy about drinking, though.

"We'll do everything possible to cooperate with you, Sergeant," Taylor assured him, and meant it sincerely. The detective said he would keep them apprised of whatever turned up. Taylor sighed and looked at Nicole after they left. "We're about to be hit by the shitstorm of all time," he said. "And sooner or later it's going to wind up in the press."

"I don't think there's anything we can do to stop that," Nicole said. "People love bad stories about fancy prep schools. It doesn't look good for us either, or for her, that she was drunk. That doesn't make it okay to rape her, but she put herself in a terrible, dangerous situation. And the sergeant is right, alcohol is always involved in these disasters."

"What the sergeant suggested is extremely possible. That a bunch of students left her there drunk, and someone else found her and raped her."

"I wish that was true," Nicole said sadly, "but I don't believe it. I think it was one of our boys. I wish we knew who so we could deal with it and bring him to justice, and not turn the whole school upside down."

"We should enforce the alcohol-expulsion rule when we find out who was with her when she got drunk," Taylor said.

"We can't," Nicole said simply. "We can't expel a girl who was raped when she was drunk. Maybe suspend or expel the others for drinking and give her amnesty if she tells us who, and above all who raped her. Whoever it was has to be punished and should go to jail." Taylor nodded. He knew what had happened was going to tear the school wide open. No one would be the same after this.

"This will frighten other parents too," Taylor said thoughtfully. "No one with a daughter wants them at a school where a student was raped."

"I didn't apply to Yale for that reason," Nicole commented. "They'd had a rash of rapes on campus when I was applying. I didn't even look at the school. I went to Harvard instead."

"It's a second-rate school," he teased her, "but you did all right."

"My point is that it's hard to sell ourselves as a co-ed school if our female students aren't safe. We're going to have to be very sensitive to that. Particularly once it hits the press. You don't know what they'll do with it. They'll probably crucify us, and say we're to blame, for inadequate supervision or lax practices. But kids are kids and some kids have ways to break the drinking rules; in other schools too. And it doesn't have to result in rape."

"This is going to be brutal," he said unhappily.

"It was for Vivienne," Nicole said quietly. She was just

grateful Vivienne had survived the excess of alcohol and hadn't died. And they had the rape to deal with now. She agreed with the sergeant that alcohol was always involved and made these situations worse, especially with teenage kids.

He called Shepard Watts as soon as Nicole left his office, and told him what he knew, which wasn't much. That there had been a drinking episode, a female student had been drunk to the point of alcohol poisoning, and nearly died, and had been raped, most likely by one of their students. Shepard was deeply upset and said he fervently hoped it wasn't one of those horrendous stories where one group of boys watched another group rape an innocent girl. It had happened at several of the finest prep schools in recent years. A gang mentality took over, as the detective said, and lives were ruined, the victim's, the perpetrators', and those who watched.

"I can't even remotely imagine that happening here," Taylor said. "I think we need to reach out to the parents quickly though, before they hear it some other way. I'm going to draft an email today, and promise to keep them informed."

"It will cause an uproar," Shepard said, sounding doubtful.

"Trying to hide it will be worse. The kids know, they'll tell their parents immediately. They need to hear from me, and even from you as a parent and the head of the board."

"I think we should keep it quiet as long as we can. Did you really have to tell the students?"

"Of course. We have to protect the women on campus. We can't hide something like this from them. They have to know so they can be cautious and protect themselves. After something like this, every female on campus is at risk."

"Have you talked to Jamie about it?" Shepard asked him. "Maybe he's heard something. He would tell us if he has. He knows right from wrong."

"I haven't seen any of the students since it's happened, except at the assembly this morning. But we didn't stop to chat. I'm sure if he knows or hears anything, he'll tell us. The police are talking about fingerprinting the entire school. They want to know who she was drinking with before it happened, and see if they'll talk and identify the rapist, since she won't."

"She sounds like a troublemaker, or a drunk," Shepard said, annoyed. "This really is a headache we don't need. I was just about to start another capital campaign. I can't do that with a rape hanging over our heads."

"I don't think she's a drunk, Shep. She's a seventeen-year-old girl. I don't kid myself that they don't try to put one over on us now and then, especially seniors. They're under a lot of tension, and they're tired of being treated like children. They're ready to fly. They do it at home when they can get away with it, and they try to do it here. A year from now, they'll be getting drunk with their pals in college. The seniors are always a hard group to rein in. You see that in every school. But you don't see rape at every school, and I don't want to see it here. We need to deal with this quickly and hard. We won't tolerate this at Saint Ambrose. Vivienne has our full support," Taylor said to Shep.

"Well, I'm not going to be able to get you another ten million dollars, if we have shit like this happening." He was frustrated, but Taylor smiled.

"Call Joe Russo. He'll probably write you a check for five."

"I think he maxed out at one. Well, keep me posted. And I'm not thanking you for the bad news."

"You had to know."

"Yes, I did," Shep agreed, but he didn't like it.

"They're sending a juvenile rape team in from Boston later today. They're going to go over us with a fine-tooth comb, to flush out the rapist, and they have my full permission. We owe Vivienne that, and all our female students and faculty."

"Let's just get this behind us as fast as we can. Find out who the rapist was, send him to prison, and send the girl back where she came from before she gets drunk again."

"It's never as easy as that," Taylor said calmly.

"It should be," Shepard said, sounding impatient, and a minute later, they hung up.

Charity went to Taylor's office between classes.

"How are you holding up?" she asked her husband with a sympathetic expression. This was stressful for him too, as the headmaster.

"This is going to be a hell of a mess, isn't it?" he asked his wife with a worried look.

"Yes, it is," she didn't deny it, "and it's going to get worse before it gets better, but we'll deal with it, and eventually it will go away, once it's handled." She sounded certain and calm, which was one of the many things he loved about her.

"Do you think it will destroy the school?" he asked her, putting words to his worst fears.

"No, I don't. I'm sure that in its hundred and twenty-two years, the school has been through things just as bad, or worse. Things happen. The school will survive it, and so will you. And so will Vivienne, with therapy. The boy who did it needs to be punished."

"Do you think it's because we went co-ed?"

She shook her head with a smile. "Stop second-guessing yourself. You've been talking to Larry Gray again. It was right for us to go co-ed. This was just very bad luck, for Vivienne, and the school."

"I haven't seen Larry since the news of this broke this morning, thank God. He must be dancing a jig in his office, and putting up banners that say 'I told you so.' He predicted something like this," Taylor said, discouraged.

"She may have been raped by someone who has nothing to do with the school. You're going to have to stay calm and ride the wave on this. It may be a rough ride for a while."

"It already is, the poor girl. Shep was fairly harsh about it. He's pissed because he says it'll affect his next capital campaign."

"So tell him to wait six months. You didn't plan this, for heaven's sake."

"No, I sure didn't," he said, and kissed his wife, before starting to draft a letter to the parents. He wanted to be careful how he phrased it. But he was grateful for Charity's support.

The police waited until eleven to talk to Vivienne again. She was awake by then, and had a headache from the hangover, but the doctors said she was able to speak to them, and her mother remained in the room while they did. She looked fiercely protective of her, and Vivienne looked like she'd been hit by a bus, exhausted, hungover, and upset. Drunk or not, she'd been through a terrible experience for any woman, and she was only a young girl.

"Do you remember anything about last night, Vivienne?" the senior detective asked her, and she hesitated before she answered.

"Some of it. Not much."

"Can you tell us what you do remember?"

"I went drinking with a group of girls after we left the haunted house in the gym."

"Do you remember their names?"

"No, I don't," she said quietly. "They weren't in my grade, and I didn't know them very well."

"Can you tell us how many there were?"

"Two . . . four . . . maybe six . . ."

"Do you remember what you were drinking?"

Vivienne nodded. "Tequila."

"That's a pretty stiff drink for girls." He looked surprised, although he knew it already from the bottle they had as evidence and were checking for prints. "Did you bring the tequila?"

"No. One of the girls has a fake ID and she bought it in town. It was supposed to be kind of a Halloween party." That much was true, but not much else, and the detective sensed it.

"And what happened after you drank with the girls?"

"I don't know. I remember being on the ground with a man on top of me. And then I passed out. And I woke up here this morning." She looked all innocence, and had on her Alice in Wonderland face.

"And you don't remember who the man was? Or anything else about the rape?"

"Nothing in detail, I just remember him on top of me, and then I passed out."

"Did you know him? Had you ever seen him before? Was he a student you've seen at school?"

"No." He could tell from experience that she was lying, but didn't call her on it.

"Was he drinking with you?"

"I don't think so."

"Is he a student here?"

"I don't know. I don't remember what he looked like. He pushed himself inside me and then I passed out." She looked troubled as she said it, and the detective watched her face.

"Did you see any men or boys lurking around while you were still conscious?"

"No, it was just the girls, I think."

"You're not giving us much to go on, to find who attacked you," he said gently.

"It's all I can remember," she said, as she leaned back into her pillow and closed her eyes as though she was in pain, and then opened them again. "I never saw anyone, no men or boys at all, just the one on me when I passed out."

"All right." The detectives stood up, thanked her, and left the room. The senior detective in charge waited until they were in the elevator before he spoke to his partner with a chagrined look.

"She's lying through her teeth. She's protecting whoever did it. Maybe a boyfriend. And if I asked her about a boyfriend, she'd deny that too. I'm going to leave her to the Boston team. They're pros at this. I can never get a damn thing out of teenage girls, not even my own. I want to make one stop on the way back to the office."

"What's that?" his partner asked. It was rapidly becoming a difficult case. With no cooperation from the victim, they were going nowhere fast.

"I have a yen for a shot of tequila to start my morning off right, don't you?"

"While we're working?" He had never known his sergeant to drink on the job, but he didn't say anything while they drove into the town nearest Saint Ambrose, and stopped at the only liquor store in town. He walked in and asked where the tequila was, and the clerk shook his head. "I had one bottle, and sat on it for four years. Nobody drinks tequila around here. I think it's more of a West Coast thing. I haven't carried it in years."

"Sorry to hear it," the detective said with a smug expression.

"Can I help you with anything else?"

"Not today, but thanks." When they left the store, he looked at his partner. "She's lying about that too. Wherever they got the tequila, it wasn't here with a fake ID. I don't think there's a single word of truth in what she told us. She wasn't drinking with girls, or not only girls. She didn't pass out and wake up in the hospital this morning with a headache. I think she knows what happened to her, and she isn't going to tell us. She's either afraid of the rapist, or she's protecting him because she knows him. There's a lot more to this than meets the eye."

They drove back to the office then, and when they got there the first computer runs were on his desk. They had run the prints on the empty bottle. There were seven sets of them, and one of them was hers. She'd been finger-printed at the hospital the night before when she was unconscious. The other six weren't a match with any known convicted felons or sex offenders nationally, in the state of Massachusetts, or any of the New England states. So it wasn't a known con, or a serial rapist who had wandered into the area. Six people had shared the bottle of tequila with Vivienne, and the sergeant was almost sure they weren't girls. His best guess was that they were six male students, one of whom had raped her, and they went to her school. They were going to have to fingerprint every student at the school, and maybe the staff too. They had their work cut out for them. After lunch, they were going back to the school to talk to Tommy Yee, the owner of the violin they'd found under the tree at the scene of the crime. He was the only boy they could tie to this event so far, and even if he hadn't raped her himself, the detective was hoping he knew who did.

*

When Tommy Yee woke up the morning after their drunken binge, he had a blinding headache and still felt a little drunk. He made his way unsteadily to the bathroom, as scenes of the night before darted through his mind like a horror movie he had seen. The memories were disjointed and all of them were equally upsetting, and as he stared at himself in the mirror, wondering how it could have happened, a wave of panic rushed over him. He darted back to his bedroom, glanced around the room and knew instantly what was missing. His violin was gone and he knew where he had left it. In their haste to leave the scene and flee before they were discovered, he had left it in the clearing. So whoever found Vivienne eventually would find his violin, and the case had a tag with his name on it.

As he realized it, he knew two things for certain. That they were going to be able to tie him to what had happened to Vivienne, and blame him for it. And his parents were going to kill him. His violin had cost his grandfather almost a hundred thousand dollars, an insane amount of money. They would never forgive him for this. It was unthinkable that he would lose it, and even more unthinkable that he had raped a girl. He could suddenly imagine himself going to prison. If he'd lost his violin, he might as well be dead. He thought of going back to the scene of the crime to look for it, but they'd probably arrest him then and there, since they had found her. How could he have been so stupid, to drink with them, to get so drunk, to be there at all. He didn't even know Rick had raped her until the others told him. And now he was part of it, and sworn to silence to protect Rick, who wasn't even a close friend. He hadn't seen Rick do it.

He saw the email about the all-school assembly then, and knew what it had to be about. And as he left his room to attend the assembly, he felt naked without his violin case in his hand. He prayed she hadn't died, after they left her unconscious in the clearing. They had called the campus police. Or Chase had. Tommy wished he hadn't joined them, but it was too late now. He was one of them, and would probably end up in prison with them. He wished he was dead and hadn't gotten so drunk, but he had.

Chapter Five

The two detectives appeared in Taylor's office while he was eating a sandwich at his desk, and he felt a knot form in his stomach the moment he saw them. Nicole was just leaving. She had asked all the school counselors to check in with their counselees, to see how they were reacting to the news of the rape. The word was out. The student who had been "assaulted" had been raped. And the search was on for the rapist.

"We're here to see Tommy Yee," the sergeant explained, and Nicole doubled back to discuss it with them. "We can take him with us, or talk to him here. We might get better results at the station," he said practically. Tommy was the only human link they had to the crime, and they wanted as much information as they could get from him, particularly since Vivienne was so uncooperative. And since Tommy's violin case had been found at the crime scene, he had probably been there at some point that night. They wanted to know what he'd seen.

"I'd like to make something clear," Nicole said to them. "He's an only child from an extremely traditional Chinese family, and probably our best student. If he feels that he has disgraced his family in any way, he instantly becomes a prime suicide risk. If you take him with you, and keep him for any reason, I want a suicide watch on him 24/7. Can you assure us of that?" Taylor hadn't thought of it, but he was grateful Nicole had.

"We can talk to him here, if you think it's that risky," the sergeant said quietly. The situation was serious enough without adding a suicide to it.

"We'd appreciate it," Nicole said, and Taylor nodded. She went to get Tommy herself. She found him leaving the cafeteria after lunch. He was alone, although she usually saw him with two or three other seniors. She thought he looked tired and pale, and unusually tense. He didn't talk to her on the way to Taylor's office when she told him, as gently as she could, that the police were waiting to talk to him there. He didn't say a word. She couldn't imagine him raping anyone, and he looked as though he was going to cry when he walked in and saw the two detectives waiting for him. He shook hands politely with them, and sat down in a chair.

"Do you know why we want to see you, Tommy?" He nodded, and then shook his head. "We found your violin at the scene of the crime, where the victim was raped. We want to know what it was doing there, and where you were last night."

"I went to the haunted house in the gym after dinner,

and then I went back to my room and went to bed. My violin was stolen yesterday. I went to the haunted house in the afternoon too. I left it outside and it was gone when I got back." The sergeant nodded.

"Did you report it stolen?"

"Not yet. I was going to today. I was hoping someone would find it and give it back. It has my name on it." He spoke in a soft voice and seemed calmer once he was talking. He had spent hours trying to figure out how to explain where his violin had been found. He had gone back early in the morning to find it but the area was surrounded by yellow crime scene tape, and his violin was gone. He had guessed it had been taken by the police.

"We checked. It's a Gagliano violin. That's a very expensive instrument. It sells for about a hundred thousand dollars. I'm surprised you didn't report it right away."

"People are very honest here, and I have my name on the case."

"That's how we knew it was yours." The sergeant paused for a moment then, and looked Tommy in the eyes. "Do you know who raped her, Tommy? We won't say you told us if you do. It's very important that you help us find who did it. Did you see anything last night, or hear anything?"

"No, I didn't," he said in a choked voice. "I don't know anything." And then he started to cry as Taylor and Nicole watched him intently and wondered what he was going to say next. "I didn't rape her . . . I didn't, I swear." He sat there and sobbed for five minutes as all four adults focused on him, and then he regained his composure.

"I believe you," the sergeant said seriously. "But do you know who did?" Tommy shook his head miserably in response.

"No, I don't."

"If you hear something, or remember something, will you let us know?" Tommy nodded and wiped his eyes.

"May I have my violin back?"

"I'm afraid you can't. Even if it was stolen from you, it was found as part of the crime scene, and it's been logged in to evidence."

"My parents will be very angry. My grandfather bought it for me. I can't practice now."

"We can lend you one, Tommy, not as fine as yours, but maybe it will do for now," Nicole said gently. "One of our alumni donated a Gustave Villaume." She knew from talking to the head of the music department. It was a fine violin, but nowhere near the quality of the one he'd just lost.

"Thank you," he said, looking devastated and frightened of what his parents would say.

"You can go now," the detective said, and Tommy nodded, thanked them and left the room, as the sergeant sighed and looked at Taylor and Nicole. "That's two for two so far. The victim is lying to us too. I don't believe his violin was stolen. With something that valuable and important to him, he wouldn't have let it out of his sight for a minute, not a conscientious kid like him." Nicole could recall seeing him with it all over campus, even in the cafeteria. "And the girl lied to us this morning about the tequila, and said she was drinking with a bunch of girls. We checked out part of her story, and it was a bald-faced lie. She's either afraid of whoever raped her, or he's a friend of hers and she's protecting him."

"That makes no sense," Taylor said impatiently. "Why would she protect anyone who did something like that to her?"

"Kids have strange loyalties. We've seen it before. And I don't believe for a minute that she was drinking with a bunch of girls. I think Tommy knows something too. I don't know why, but I believe him when he says he didn't rape her. But maybe he watched them do it. That happens sometimes in schools like this. A bunch of guys go off the deep end together, and do things they would never do on their own. I'm sure you know that too." Taylor nodded; he couldn't deny it, particularly when alcohol was involved. It altered behavior and upped the ante dramatically.

"We have a strong moral system here, based on family values. Our students don't go around raping each other," Taylor said, looking tense.

"You've never had girls here before," the detective

reminded him. "I'm sorry to say it, but we need to finger-print the whole school. We need to find who she was drinking with. There are six sets of prints in addition to hers. We need to start there. And it may end there. I'm willing to bet Tommy Yee is one of them. I didn't want to push him over the edge, given what you said." He looked at Nicole. "He can be printed with the others. We start tomorrow. I want a full set of prints on every-one, kids, faculty, gardeners, whatever you've got. Even girls, if their prints show up on the tequila bottle, so we know who she was drinking with. We'll set up tables with some of our off-duty patrolmen and run through the lot." Taylor nodded, looking unhappy, but he could see where the problem lay if no one would talk.

"We'll be ready for you," Taylor said quietly. "Should we notify the student body?" Taylor asked Nicole after they left. She shook her head.

"Let's not. I'd rather surprise them. I don't want the guilty party, whoever he is, skipping out."

"Do you really think one of our kids did it?" Taylor asked her, obviously worried. She hesitated before answering.

"I think it's possible. Anything is. And I agree with the sergeant. I think Tommy knows something. I don't think his violin was stolen. I see him with it everywhere. He wouldn't have left it outside the haunted house. He's too responsible to do that."

"All right. We'll tell them tomorrow morning about the fingerprinting. Let's run them through class by class. We can start with the seniors and work down." She nodded and went back to her office.

Taylor was still thinking about it when the sergeant called him back an hour later.

"We got a match from the violin and the tequila bottle. The same prints are on both. I was right. So Tommy was part of the tequila party that probably led to the rape."

"Are you going to arrest him?" Taylor sounded shocked.

"Not yet. The Boston team is taking over for us this afternoon. We'll give them what we've got. It's up to them. And he's not going anywhere. Let's see what turns up when we print the whole school."

"We're starting with the seniors, which may be more useful to you."

"Thank you. I appreciate it. I'll probably come by tomorrow to see how it's going."

"Thank you, Sergeant," Taylor said and then hung up. He was dreading what would come next.

*

Chase and Jamie had lunch together in the cafeteria as they always did, but spoke very little to each other. They both had massive hangovers after the night before, and felt sick. Neither of them could understand what had happened or why, what had gotten into Rick to do something so terrible. And both boys were embarrassed to have gotten into a fight with each other over a girl. That wasn't typical of them either. They didn't say a word about it, but they both felt bad. They picked at their food. The others didn't come near them.

Jamie had seen Nicole Smith come looking for Tommy and they wondered what that was about. Steve, Rick, and Gabe had eaten with other people. And Gabe said something to Chase on their way to a math class they took together.

"You okay?" Gabe asked him.

"Yeah, of course. Fine," Chase said tersely, and sat in the back row far away from him. He looked tense, and tried to pretend he wasn't. They were all wondering what would happen next, but Chase was sure that none of them would give it away. Not even Tommy. He hadn't done anything anyway, except throw up and cry at a distance from them. They had told him what Rick had done. He hadn't seen it himself.

It was as if the tequila had made them all crazy. Chase wanted to talk to someone about it, but he couldn't, and Jamie had looked like he was on the verge of tears all day. All he could think about was how Vivienne had looked when he kissed her, before it all started. And then seeing her lying there, pale and unconscious on the grass. He wanted to go and see her at the hospital, but he knew he couldn't. They weren't even supposed to know who the victim was. It would be instantly suspicious if he went.

Gabe caught up with Chase again after class. "Do you think we should send her flowers in the hospital or something?" he whispered to Chase, who looked like he was about to hit him.

"Are you insane? They'd trace it to us. Leave it alone, man. It's over. It's done. We have to live with it now, and just hope to hell she'll be okay in the end and no one talks." They were furious at Rick for what he'd done, but they didn't want him to go to prison. In fact, he had jeopardized them all with his insane behavior.

"No one will talk," Gabe said, hoping he was right. "I just thought . . ."

"Don't think. It's too late for that," Chase said angrily, and walked away. He knew at that exact moment, cold sober, that none of them would ever be the same again. Nor would Vivienne. Every time he thought of her now, he felt sick. He should have protected her, and seen what Rick was doing instead of fighting with his best friend in a jealous fit because Jamie kissed her, and he had a crush on her too. He should never have lost his temper. If he hadn't, he might have been able to stop Rick. He would never be able to forgive himself for that—that he had seen it too late, and hadn't stopped him.

*

When Chris Walker entered his daughter's hospital room, Vivienne was sleeping, and her mother was dozing in a chair. He stood looking at Vivienne, thinking of what had happened to her, and tears slid down his cheeks. He wanted to be angry at her about the drinking, but he was too upset about the rape. As though sensing him in the room, Nancy opened her eyes and she saw the man she'd been married to for twenty-two years. All she could think of was that she wished he wasn't there. Just seeing him again was a knife in her heart.

Their eyes met for a moment, and neither of them spoke. Then, finally, Chris knew he had to deal with her. Nancy had been avoiding him for months. She had refused to meet with him before she filed for divorce. He knew he deserved it, but it hurt anyway. She was a hard woman, with a soft side he had always loved, but she wouldn't let him see that side of her anymore. All that was left between them was the pain he had caused her, and their wonderful daughter. He would always be grateful to her for that.

"How is she?" He had caught the first plane out of Los Angeles that morning, rented a car at the Boston airport, and driven two hours to the hospital.

Nancy pointed to the door and he followed her into the hall. They could talk more freely there.

"About the same. She's very shaken up, understandably. She won't talk about it, even to me. She says all she remembers is a guy on top of her she'd never seen before, and then she passed out. I think she's ashamed of having put herself in that situation, by drinking and getting so drunk. She could have died if someone hadn't called the campus police. Her friends just left her there, unconscious. The psychological damage from all this will be huge," she said sadly. It was every parent's worst nightmare for their daughter, and Chris started to cry again.

She let him sit alone for a few minutes, and came back with a cup of coffee from the machine, with just the right amount of cream and sugar, which she handed to him. He was startled by the kind gesture, but she felt sorry for him. He adored his daughter, and had always been a wonderful father to her. She knew how upset he'd been when she took Vivienne to New York and sent her away to school. But she didn't want Vivienne in L.A., spending time with the twenty-five-year-old he was living with now, and had been sleeping with for two years before Nancy discovered the affair. She had walked in on them, in their home, in her bed, when she had come home early from a business trip, and Vivienne had been away for spring vacation with friends. It was obvious that Kimberly, the twenty-five-year-old, had been there before and was very much at home in their house.

Nancy had flown to New York a week later, found a job at a law firm, quit her job in L.A., applied for certification, took the Uniform Bar Exam to allow her to practice in New York, and filed for divorce. Two months later, as soon as school ended in June, they had moved. She had since received her certification to practice law in New York. Chris had moved Kimberly in as soon as they left. Nancy was currently demanding that he sell the house and pay her her half of it. She didn't want Kimberly living in the home she had loved and made into a wonderful place for the three of them. If she had to start over, so did he. He was fifty years old and she was forty-two, old enough to be his girlfriend's mother, which made it sting even more.

He had begged Nancy to stay in L.A., or leave Vivienne there with him for her last year of high school, which was what Vivienne wanted too, but Nancy wouldn't allow it. He had finally conceded. She'd enrolled her in Saint Ambrose, which seemed even more cruel to him. She had deprived him of his daughter, and wasn't even with her herself, and now this had happened. He wanted to take her back to L.A. when she got out of the hospital. He was even prepared to ask Kimberly to move out and get her an apartment until Vivienne started college. He wouldn't do it for Nancy, but he would for his daughter. He wanted to do all he could to help her get past what had just happened to her.

"Do they have any idea who did it?" he asked Nancy as they sat in the hallway side by side, waiting for Vivienne to wake up. Nancy shook her head in answer.

"She says she got drunk with a bunch of girls and then passed out. She remembers a man on top of her. The other girls left her there. She's not even sure if the other girls were still around when it happened. She thinks they might have left before. She doesn't know."

"That doesn't sound like her. I thought they had strict alcohol policies at the school."

"They do, but kids get by with things even in the best of schools. The police think she's lying to them." She hesitated for a minute. "I think so too. They think she's protecting the boy who did it and she knows who he is."

"Why would she do that? That makes no sense."

"Maybe they were friends, and she got drunk with him and his friends and things got out of hand. So far, they have no clue who the kids are, girls or boys. Viv says she can't remember the girls she got drunk with and doesn't know their names. None of it holds together, and I think the police are stumped. There's a team from the rape detail coming in from Boston sometime today. They're used to working with juveniles, and the school is doing everything they can to cooperate with the police. The police told me this afternoon, they're going to fingerprint every student in the school tomorrow, male and female. They have prints on the tequila bottle they found at the scene. Viv's prints are on it too. They took hers last night."

"Will they send the boy to prison if they figure out who did it? They usually don't in these kinds of schools.

They're a bunch of spoiled rich boys and their parents get them off." He looked angry as he said it.

"There are a lot of rich kids at the school," she conceded, "but they've had scandals like this at other important prep schools, and the press have crucified them. I don't think Saint Ambrose wants that, particularly in the first year of going co-ed. No one would ever send their daughter there again."

"Why did it have to happen to our daughter?" he said, his eyes bright with tears. He had cried the whole way east on the plane. He was terrified she'd never recover, and be emotionally scarred for life, which was a possibility. Nancy had been talking about it with Vivienne all afternoon, telling her that she couldn't let this stop her or make her frightened and bitter. She had to get past it, whatever it took. Taylor Houghton had already called Nancy and told her that the school would pay for all of Vivienne's medical expenses, and whatever psychiatric counseling she needed later. It was the first thing Chris had heard about the school that he liked. Chris had grown up poor and was a self-made man, and had a visceral dislike for the kind of spoiled, entitled snobs that he felt came out of schools like Saint Ambrose. Nancy had tried to assure him that there was a decent mix of people at the school, and that not all of them had been born with a silver spoon in their mouths and with fathers who had gone to Princeton and Yale, although many had. He'd had a chip on his shoulder about that all his life. He had worked his way through college at night, and made a great deal of money by his wits and business sense, without the benefit of Harvard Business School.

They saw the light go on over Vivienne's door then. She had rung for the nurse. She was awake. Nancy let Chris go in first. She knew how happy Vivienne would be to see her father. They both burst into tears when they saw each other, and he held her in his arms, and gently stroked her long golden hair, just as he had when she was a little girl. It made Vivienne cry harder when he did it. She felt as though she had let him down by getting drunk the night before, and everything that had come after. She knew better than to get drunk with a bunch of boys, even though her father didn't know she'd done that.

"I'm going to take you back to L.A. with me, if your mom will let me," Chris told her. As usual, he dealt with their daughter directly, without asking her mother first, which was how he operated. He took charge of everything, but not anymore. As much as she had once loved him, Nancy had come to hate him, and now he was just a relic of the past. Everything she had felt for him had turned to ashes. It was six months since she had walked in on him in bed with Kimberly, and in two months, their divorce would be final, and they could put it behind them. But she knew she'd never forgive him.

"Can I go back to L.A. with Dad, Mom?" Vivienne's

eyes had lit up when he said it, and she asked her mother as soon as she walked into the room.

"The police may need you here," Nancy said practically. She was the dreary naysayer in Vivienne's life now, the one who had dragged her to New York, and then sent her away to school. But Nancy thought it would be good for her to be away from both of them during the divorce. She had never told her daughter that she had walked in on her father with a woman, or that he had been cheating on her for over two years. Nancy was a hard woman at times, but she always played fair, and she didn't try to poison Vivienne against her father. She didn't want to see him anymore, and now here they were together, facing a crisis. She had hoped never to lay eyes on him again. They only spoke to each other now if it was absolutely necessary, and couldn't be handled by lawyers or in emails. She wanted as little contact as possible with him. It was over for her.

After they'd talked for a while, Chris went out to get dinner for them at a nearby restaurant, and Vivienne looked peaceful and happy now that she'd seen him. She always looked that way when he was around.

"You're still really mad at him, huh, Mom?" Nancy didn't answer. She didn't want to get into it with her. "Is it about the girl he started dating after we left?" Nancy wasn't going to tell her it had been going on for years.

"It's about a lot of things. It just stopped working for

us. We ran out of gas." No matter how much she hated him now, she refused to malign him to their daughter. She wouldn't stoop to that.

"I don't believe you. You loved him, Mom. And all of a sudden you hated him and made us move away. You must have had a reason for it." Vivienne had been trying to guess what it was for six months. Neither of them would tell her. Her father was too ashamed, and her mother determined to be fair and generous to him, and to take the high road.

"You should ask your dad about it," Nancy said quietly.

"He won't talk about it either. He just says he made some very big mistakes and you won't forgive him for them. Can't you at least be friends?"

"Maybe in time," she said vaguely. "Sometimes it takes a long time for things like that to go away." She changed the subject then, and looked at her daughter. "Viv, you've got to tell the police everything you remember about what happened. Were you really drinking with a bunch of girls, or were there boys there?" Vivienne looked away and spoke softly.

"There might have been one or two," she said, "but I didn't know them. I don't remember anything else." But her mother could see it in her eyes: she wasn't telling the truth.

"Are you afraid you'll be blamed for some of it?" Vivienne didn't answer her, and with that Chris walked in with spaghetti and meatballs and pizza from an Italian restaurant, and he handed Vivienne and Nancy theirs. They had a nice time together despite the circumstances.

"How long do you have to stay in the hospital?" Chris asked her.

"We don't know yet," Nancy spoke for her. "They wanted to observe and examine her and make sure the alcohol is out of her system. And she needs to be available for the police." He nodded. He was planning to work from his computer for as long as he could and take her back with him, if Nancy would let him. She wasn't going back to Saint Ambrose in any case, and he wanted to get her back into her old school in L.A. All she had to say was that she didn't like New York or boarding school. She didn't need to say anything to her L.A. friends about what had happened, and getting raped. He didn't think she should. He wanted to discuss all of it with Nancy in the next few days. He wanted to get Vivienne as far away from what had happened as possible.

She had a pounding headache that night, and they gave her something to help her sleep. Her parents left the room while she was dozing off and they promised to come back the next day. Nancy thought that she and Chris should take turns. She didn't want to spend hours at the hospital with him. It was good that they were being civil, but every time she looked at him, she saw his face again when she had walked in on him, and it made her want to close her eyes and run away. She said good night to him in front of the hospital. He offered her a lift but she said she wanted some fresh air and was going to walk. She had left her car at the hotel. She was staying at the one closest to the school, a quaint New England inn, and he had found a motel a little further away. She was relieved that they weren't staying in the same place. She had loved him for a long time, but she didn't anymore. There were some things you just couldn't forget or forgive. He had done them all.

Chapter Six

Gwen Martin and Dominic Brendan had been partners on the rape detail of the Boston Police Department for almost seven years. They were both from big Irish families, and had grown up in the same neighborhood. Gwen was thirty-seven years old, and had four older brothers, three of whom were cops and one was a priest, and her father and grandfather had been precinct sergeants. Being a policeman was the only thing she'd ever wanted to do growing up. She had worked vice for a while, as a decoy, and had somehow wound up in the juvenile rape detail instead, filling in, and had stayed because she felt as though she was making a difference in the world. It broke her heart to see what happened to some young girls. Some of them were raped by fathers or brothers, or hoodlums in the slums where they lived.

Dominic Brendan was the oldest of seven children, and had been responsible for his younger siblings, when his father, also a policeman, had been shot in the line of duty. As a result, he loved his nieces and nephews, but he had never wanted to marry or have kids of his own.

"I gave at the office," he always told his siblings when they nagged him about when he was going to get married. At forty-six, he loved being single, did what he wanted with his spare time, and enjoyed his job. He told Gwen that listening to her complain and spending five days a week arguing with her was close enough to being married. They had never dated each other, but made a great team, and he had a magical touch with kids of all ages. His mother still regretted that he hadn't become a priest.

They had spent the previous afternoon going over the evidence in Vivienne's case with the local police. It was still pretty thin. They had seven sets of prints on the tequila bottle, five of which they couldn't tie to anyone yet, and a victim who claimed she remembered almost nothing of a heinous crime and didn't know her assailant, and had admitted to being drunk at the time. The local detective on the case was convinced she was lying, either out of fear of retaliation by her attacker, or to protect him if they were friends. Either way, she was no help at all, which wasn't entirely unusual. And they had a boy with a violin case, whose prints were on the bottle found at the crime scene and whom they suspected was lying too, but were almost convinced wasn't the rapist. Ultimately, DNA tests would tell.

"So where do you want to start?" Gwen asked him. "They're fingerprinting the whole school today. That should keep the local guys busy. Nine hundred and forty students, not to mention faculty and other staff." And the hospital was running all the DNA and semen tests from what they had taken from the victim when they brought her in. "Sooner or later, they're going to get a match. It's going to be the scandal of all time at a school like this. I worked one of these fancy prep school rapes when I started. Six boys raped a freshman girl, and seven others watched. They practically sold tickets. And the parents were so rich and important that no one went to jail. The judge gave them all a break. They got six months' probation, and they blamed the girl. That was ten years ago. It doesn't work like that anymore. At least not in the real world." They both knew that the Massachusetts rape shield laws prevented defense attorneys from attacking a victim on the issue of consent. But they could attack her on other issues, like sexual history or reputation, which scared some victims off from reporting a rape. And there was still the possibility that Vivienne knew the boy and had consented to have sex with him, but the local detectives didn't think it likely, in the drunken condition she was in.

Dominic glanced over at Gwen. She had bright red hair and freckles, and looked more Irish than anyone he knew. "Their parents are still going to fight like lions if any boy at the school is convicted and sentenced to prison. Saint Ambrose is about as fancy as it gets. Kids like that always make me nervous. They're so smooth and sophisticated, they always make me feel like I'm not good enough." He was a little rough around the edges, but the smartest cop Gwen had ever worked with. Their professional relationship was based on unspoken affection and profound mutual respect.

"Good enough for what? To send a kid who raped a girl to jail? You're good enough, Dom. You're plenty good enough for that."

She was wearing jeans and sneakers and looked like a kid herself. She didn't want to scare them. As a policewoman, she wanted them to talk to her. She liked to hang out and get the lay of the land when they started a case as confusing as this one. Vivienne should have been desperate for them to find her attackers, but she wasn't. She was reticent and uncooperative, which wasn't unusual, but made the case harder. She wasn't their ally, yet.

Gwen was startled when they parked in one of the school lots and she saw that the students were all wearing uniforms—the boys in blazers and ties, the girls in plaid skirts, with white blouses or navy sweaters and blazers too, with the school emblem on it. It was a *very* traditional school.

"Shit, maybe I should have worn a dress and heels." Dom laughed at her as they got out of the car and looked around. It was a beautiful school. "It looks like Harvard," she said, impressed. It was hard not to be.

The two detectives headed toward the administration building to meet with Taylor and Nicole, and were shown into the headmaster's wood-paneled office. Nicole was there, going over schedules with Taylor. Classes were going to be disrupted all day, with the fingerprinting going on. Both detectives introduced themselves, and they sat down on two couches in front of the fireplace with Taylor and Nicole, who looked harassed and worried.

"Things are a little chaotic right now," Taylor said somberly. "We're all unnerved and devastated by what happened." Gwen nodded and felt a little foolish in her kid-friendly clothes. She hadn't realized that the school would be this formal and sedate. Nicole was wearing a dark gray suit and heels, which she did on most days. Taylor's secretary came in to tell him that Joe Russo was on the phone and it was urgent. He excused himself and left Nicole to talk to the detectives and bring them up to date on what was happening at the school. No new evidence had surfaced, and no one knew anything about what had happened that night. No one was talking.

"It's still early," Gwen said to her. She liked Nicole immediately. She seemed like a smart woman and a straight shooter. "There's always a kid around somewhere who knows or saw something and eventually squeals. They can't help it. They have to. It's too heavy a weight for them to carry. Sooner or later, they talk. Somebody must have seen something that night, or heard it."

"There's no sign of it yet. We just told the seniors that they're going to be fingerprinted today. It made more sense to start with them since Vivienne is a senior. It's unlikely she was raped by a freshman boy." Dom didn't comment.

"When are they starting?" Gwen wanted to know.

"The police got here half an hour ago. They've already started. They have a hundred and ninety-four kids to get through."

"They should be able to do that pretty fast." However Gwen often found that away from the cities, the police were understaffed and sometimes slower than she liked. But they were caring and methodical too. They had handled the case efficiently so far and hadn't missed any important steps in their initial investigation. Nothing had been overlooked, and the school was cooperating fully.

"We'll bring the juniors in as soon as they're ready for them," Nicole confirmed.

"I'd like to hang around where they're doing it, and see if we hear anything or if anyone will talk to us," Gwen said thoughtfully.

"We've told them that Vivienne Walker has been sent home with mono. But they're not stupid, and I think they all figured out yesterday that she was the victim, when she wasn't here. But we can at least do that for her," Nicole said and Gwen nodded. The senior girls had guessed but hadn't said anything and were protective of her.

While they were chatting, Taylor was trying to calm down Joe Russo, who was livid that his son was about to be fingerprinted like a common criminal, as he put it. Rick had called and told him, and his father was outraged. He was threatening never to make another donation to the school if Taylor didn't pull him out of the line immediately.

"You know I can't do that, Joe. We have to cooperate with the police. There can't be exceptions. If we refused to let them fingerprint him, it would implicate him. And we owe this to the victim and her parents. If she were your daughter, you'd want everything possible done to find her attackers too. They're going to print me, for heaven's sake, and the entire faculty. And I didn't do it. They're fingerprinting the whole staff and everyone on the grounds, women too."

Joe was slightly mollified when he heard that. "Rick said it was just seniors." He sounded confused.

"This morning. After that, we're fingerprinting all students, and everyone else. We're just starting with seniors. We had to start somewhere."

"I guess that's not quite as bad, but I don't know why you bother with kids you know as well as Rick, Jamie,

Chase, the star students of the school. Are you finger-printing Chase too, or is he getting preferential treatment?" It always irritated him that Chase's parents were famous movie stars, and he had a chip on his shoulder about them.

"Of course he isn't getting special treatment. Why would he? No one is. His father being an actor doesn't make him exempt from what happens here." And Chase's parents hadn't asked for it either, if they even knew about it. But they never asked favors of the school.

"I just wondered," Joe said gruffly. "It's a hell of a thing to happen," he admitted, shaken by it too, and he felt sorry for the girl and her parents.

"Yes, it is," Taylor agreed with him, as his secretary slipped him a note that Shepard Watts was on the phone, and he nodded to indicate that he would take the call. "I've got to go now. There are two detectives here who came up from Boston, from the juvenile rape detail. Keep in touch."

"Yeah, I will," Joe said, sounding off balance after his initial attack, and Taylor hung up, and switched to the line Shepard was holding on.

"Hi, Shep. It's crazy here. What can I do for you?" Before he could say another word, Shepard unleashed a torrent of fury into his ear. How dare they fingerprint his son? He was the head of the board, Jamie was their best student, and finest athlete, Taylor knew the whole family, they were friends, what the hell was wrong with them, didn't Taylor have any notion of propriety and courtesy? Any loyalty to them? His son wasn't a rapist. The idea that his son was being fingerprinted had driven him into a frenzy, and Taylor spent fifteen minutes calming him down, and finally had to cut it short. He got back to the two detectives with Nicole, looking harassed and even more stressed than before, after talking to Gwen and Dom about what lay ahead.

"The parents are starting to call and complain about their kids being fingerprinted," he said, looking tired. Charity was right, it was getting worse before it got better.

"I guess everyone here thinks they're special," Gwen said quietly. "That must be hard to deal with at a time like this." Taylor nodded agreement.

"They're all special, but no one gets special treatment. It wouldn't be fair to the others." Listening to the headmaster, Dominic decided he liked him. He was conservative and traditional, but he seemed honest and sincere, and genuinely wanted to find the rapist, whatever it took.

"Why don't I take you over to where the seniors are now," Nicole suggested, as much to give Taylor a break as to accede to their requests.

The police had set up shop in the auditorium, and there were three long lines of seniors waiting for their turns, talking quietly among themselves. Nicole left the detectives to their own devices then, and went back to her office.

"You know where to find me," she told them before she left, and Gwen noticed a number of the students staring at them, wondering who they were. The process was moving relatively quickly. The policemen filled out a card with their name and date of birth, their class at Saint Ambrose for reference, fingerprinted them, and they were done. It was a painless process, but the implication of it was unpleasant: that among them was a rapist, whom the police were determined to find. And for lack of information, no one was above suspicion.

Jamie passed Chase in the line on his way out. They had gone in separately, and had made a point of not spending too much time together for the past two days. Chase had already asked him what had happened to the bottle, and neither of them could remember. No one knew, except Taylor and Nicole, that it was in the hands of the police, and they had lifted prints from it. Chase and Jamie were extremely nervous, and Rick had said earlier that he had been throwing up for two days. He didn't know if it was alcohol poisoning or stress. When Jamie turned to leave, he saw Gwen Martin watching them and he had no idea who she was. She didn't look like a cop, but she didn't look like a teacher either. She looked out of place in her jeans, sweatshirt, and sneakers. And the man with her was badly dressed and looked bored.

Gwen wanted to ask someone who the two handsome blond boys were, but there was no one around to question. She would find out from Nicole later. They were distinctly good-looking and confident. She watched the lines continue to move forward, and by lunchtime, they were finished with the seniors. The juniors were going to be told after lunch that it was their turn.

Gwen and Dominic stayed until after lunch, and then Gwen told her partner she wanted to drop in on Vivienne.

"Is she up to a visit?" he asked her.

"I think so. She talked to the local guys yesterday. Let's find out."

They drove the ten minutes to the hospital, and when they got there, the nurse at the station on her floor pointed to her room just down the hall. Her parents weren't there, which was convenient. The nurse said they had left for lunch. Vivienne was awake when Gwen knocked and walked into the room. She left Dominic in the hall. Vivienne looked startled to see her. She didn't know who Gwen was. Gwen gave her a sunny smile to put her at ease. "Are you up to a visit?" She wasn't sick or injured, but she was still a little under the weather from the effects of the alcohol poisoning.

"Sure." Vivienne smiled back at her. She thought she was a worker from the hospital, or maybe another shrink. She had already seen one that morning.

"I'm from the Boston Police Department," Gwen said

as she sat down, and Vivienne's face tightened immediately.

"I talked to the police yesterday," she said in a plaintive tone, and suddenly acted as though she was in pain. "Actually, I have a headache."

"I'm sure you do. So do we, Vivienne. We want to help, but we don't have much to go on. Do you think you can jog your memory a little, and try to remember something, anything that happened that night, even way at the beginning of the evening, someone you saw hanging around?"

"I told them yesterday, I drank a lot of tequila and passed out."

"But you don't remember who you were drinking with?"

"No, I don't. I didn't know them well. What difference does it make? I was just drinking with a bunch of girls." She had come up with a great cover story. She was too drunk to identify them, didn't know the boy who raped her, and passed out while it was taking place. "My mom and dad will be back in a minute," she said, as though that would put Gwen off, but it didn't. Nothing ever did. She was dogged in her pursuit of the truth.

"I'll just keep you company till they get back." And then Gwen had an idea. She wanted to know anyway, and Vivienne was as good an information source as any. "I was watching them fingerprint the seniors today," she said casually, as though it was an everyday occurrence, like PE.

"They're fingerprinting them?" Vivienne looked surprised.

"They're fingerprinting the whole school, it's just routine in a case like this. Even the headmaster." Vivienne smiled at that. "I noticed two really handsome tall blond boys in the line of seniors. Friends of yours?"

Vivienne shrugged in answer as though it wasn't important, but her eyes said something different; they were suddenly wary.

"Yeah, I know who they are. The one with the curly hair is Jamie Watts, his father is head of the board, and the other one is Chase Morgan. His parents are Matthew Morgan and Merritt Jones. They're both away making movies, his dad in Spain and his mom in the Philippines." She seemed to know a lot about them. But there were only two hundred in the class, so it wasn't hard.

"They must be the big guys on campus, good-looking dudes."

"I guess. They're just boys." She acted as though she didn't care.

"Have you ever dated either of them?" Gwen sounded as though it was just idle girl talk but she could see that Vivienne didn't trust her. She remained guarded at all times.

"No, I haven't dated anyone since I've been here. I think it would be weird, living at the same school."

"Or convenient." Gwen grinned and Vivienne smiled. Gwen had an easy way about her.

"Maybe. The boys here aren't that cool. They're cooler in L.A."

"That's probably true. They're not cool in Boston either. You should see my work partner. He looks like he gets his clothes from Goodwill." Vivienne laughed at that. "So what happens now, Vivienne? What do you want to happen?" It was a seemingly innocent question, but Vivienne fell right into the trap. Gwen knew exactly where she was leading her.

"I just want to forget what happened the other night," she said, looking pained, and Gwen nodded.

"The night you don't remember, right? What is it you want to forget, if you don't remember?"

Vivienne caught herself quickly. "Getting drunk and everything that's happening now. The fuss everyone is making about it. Police, fingerprinting, trying to get me to remember what I told them I don't know. I don't remember what happened, except that I got drunk with a bunch of girls. I don't even think they were seniors and I can't remember what the boy looked like." None of it was true. Gwen could sense it and see it in her eyes.

"Yeah, getting drunk like that can kill you. And nothing good ever happens when you add alcohol to it. That's true for adults too. But whoever the boy was, he needs to be accountable for what he did. You can't just let that go by, Viv, or he'll do it to someone else. A lot of high school boys get drunk, but they don't rape girls when they do. This boy did. That's a terrible crime, and he has to be punished for it. We have to find him, we can't just give him a pass. That wouldn't be fair to you."

Vivienne looked sobered by what she said. "What if he was drunk when he did it?"

"That's not an excuse. There is no excuse for what he did. Did you know him, Vivienne?" Gwen asked gently, and Vivienne looked scared and angry.

"I told you I didn't know him. He must have been a stranger on campus. No one at Saint Ambrose would do that."

"Maybe they would," Gwen said kindly. "Whoever he is, he needs to be stopped and brought to justice for what he did to you." Tears sprang to Vivienne's eyes and she nodded.

"He probably won't do it again," she said, as though she knew him. Gwen watched her closely.

"You can't be sure of that. You don't even know who he is. There's something wrong with him to want to rape you like that. Good guys don't rape women." Vivienne nodded and then looked panicked, as though Gwen already knew too much.

"My head really hurts now," she said, in a thin whiny voice, like a child.

"I'll leave you so you can rest. I'll come back another

time," Gwen said gently and stood up. Vivienne didn't look happy to hear it, and Gwen left the room, so Vivienne could lie quietly and mull over their exchange. She had a lot to think about, and Gwen was better at this game than she was. Vivienne couldn't stay in hiding forever. Sooner or later, Gwen knew she would talk. She had to. She was carrying too heavy a burden to hold on to it forever, and Gwen could outlast her, however long it took. She wanted the boy who had raped Vivienne Walker caught. She wasn't going to let it go until he was.

*

"How was she?" Dominic asked Gwen when she came out, and they walked down the hall together. Gwen was pensive, thinking back to what Vivienne had said.

"Scared," she said finally. "I'm not sure of what yet. The boy who did it, herself, us. Maybe she's afraid she'll get painted as a slut if there's a trial, and that she'll get blamed somehow. That's what usually happens. There are some powerful parents involved. I spotted two boys on the fingerprinting line this morning. She says one of them is the son of the head of the school board, the other one is Matthew Morgan's son. People like that aren't going to take it lying down if their son is accused of rape. We're going to need some pretty solid evidence if this case goes that far and we finally get a perp."

"We've got the medical evidence," Dominic reassured

her, "and the prints on the bottle, of the people she was drinking with."

"The two may not necessarily be the same, according to her. According to her, the prints on the bottle were a bunch of girls'." It was why the girls at the school were being fingerprinted too, to see if that part of the story held up. Out of nine hundred and forty students, someone got drunk with Vivienne. Gwen knew she wasn't wrong to be nervous about that part of the story. Defense counsel would make mincemeat of her for being drunk, so drunk she barely remembered being raped, according to Vivienne. What kind of girl would do that? She had backed herself into a serious corner with her story, which Gwen suspected wasn't true anyway. She was protecting someone, and Gwen wanted to know who. And even a girl blind drunk off her ass on tequila had the right not to be raped. Maybe she was just afraid of having everyone know she got drunk and was raped, and was afraid of what people would say.

"I don't know," Gwen said to Dominic with a sigh, as they got into the unmarked police car they had driven up from Boston, "there are pieces of this case I just don't like."

"Like what?" He always trusted her instincts, and had learned to listen to her theories. They were usually sound, even when they seemed crazy to him at first.

He used to argue with her when she told him what she was thinking. Now he paid close attention. She'd been right too many times and had an incredible instinct for kids.

"I don't know. Everybody's scared for one reason or another. She's scared, although we're not sure of what. The school is scared. The other parents are going to go crazy if their kids are implicated in some way, or accused of rape. This won't be easy to bring to justice, especially if she won't cooperate with us. It serves everyone's best interest to put it behind them and try to forget it, except that's not right, and it's not how we work. We have a victim and a heinous crime, and they all want us to forget about it, even the victim, the school, the guy who did it, parents. We're swimming upstream here, Dom, against strong currents." She looked serious as she said it. In most cases, they got more support than this. And Gwen sensed clearly that Vivienne wasn't on their team. They had to get her there.

"This isn't the first time," her partner reminded her. "We're not always the heroes in the piece." This was especially true when a victim got torn to shreds on the stand, and was made to look guilty in some way. It could happen to Vivienne with an unsympathetic jury and they both knew it. She was new to the school, and had admitted to being drunk to the point that she passed out, and her blood alcohol level had been sky high. If she hadn't been raped, she'd have been expelled by then, according to the school's "one time you're out" drinking policy, which seemed a little extreme to Gwen for kids that age. Apparently schools of this caliber didn't want drunks in their student body, although she was sure that some of the parents were. But the school had zero tolerance for alcohol.

Vivienne could get on the stand, if they got that far and found the boy, and she could be made to look like a drunk, and maybe even a slut. That was how many rape cases used to work, but not anymore. The tides had turned and were now in Vivienne's favor, but only if they found her assailant, and she cooperated with them. The world was listening to women now, but she had to be brave enough to speak up. Gwen wanted to help her do that, and stand up against a crime that violated her as a human being. All they had to do was convince her of that, which was no easy feat. The attitude about men raping women had changed. It wasn't tolerated anymore, at any age. The courts were more savvy now, and tougher than they used to be. But Gwen still had no idea what had really happened here and what they were dealing with, and she intended to find out.

"Do you think they'll try to drop the case—the girl and the school, I mean?" Dom asked her. He had just thought of it for the first time. It had sounded like a straightforward case at first, but it wasn't. A recalcitrant victim was a major problem. They couldn't help defend her if she wouldn't ally with them and help herself.

"They might," Gwen said thoughtfully. "But it's not up to them. The police have it now, and if they want to pursue it, they will. It will depend how ballsy they are. A school like Saint Ambrose is a big dragon to take on. There will be lots of fire-breathing on the cops. It depends too what happens when the press gets hold of it, and they will, for sure. Somebody in town will call them, or a disgruntled parent, either way. I'm surprised it's not on the news yet, and the TV crews aren't parked outside. I'd say they may get another day or two of grace, and then it'll be the latest hot story. Schools like this always get national attention when something major happens." Dominic nodded agreement. A lot was going to happen in the next few days, on every front. They just had to wait and see what turned up, and what came out of the fingerprint matches. That would tell its own story, and it might force Vivienne to tell them the truth.

"Let's go get something to eat, I'm starved," he suggested. "Then we can check and see what's happening with the seniors' fingerprint matches."

"Yeah, I'm starving too," she agreed.

"Now I know you're worried."

"How do you know?" She grinned at him.

"Because you only eat when you're worried about a

case. The rest of the time a hamster couldn't survive on what you eat." Gwen was small and had a thin frame, which made her look younger than she was. She could almost pass for a kid sometimes, which was one of the reasons why they related to her. Dominic was a big man, and carrying fifteen or twenty pounds more than he wanted to. But he liked to eat, especially when they were working on a difficult case.

They went to a coffee shop he had spotted earlier near the hospital. They sat down in a booth and she ordered a hamburger, and he the meatloaf special with mashed potatoes and gravy.

"If I were married to you, I'd put you on a diet," she said while they waited for their food.

"That's why I'll never be married to you," he said happily. "Or anyone else. Freedom is happiness."

"Yeah, whatever," she said and listened to her messages. She had twenty-two of them, all about new cases. She was going to have to refer them to someone else on the detail for now. They had work to do at Saint Ambrose, and had only just started.

*

Taylor and Nicole were discussing the issue of the press, and how to handle it, at that exact moment. They were both amazed that the media hadn't contacted them yet, but they knew they were on borrowed time. Taylor would have liked to talk to the head of the board about it, but after his unpleasant conversation with Shepard Watts that morning, he wasn't eager to call him. But they were going to have to make some fast decisions once the media got wind of the story.

"We don't know where this is going yet. For all we know none of our boys were involved in it. And even if they drank a bottle of tequila with her, that doesn't mean they raped her. It's going to take more than that," Nicole said hopefully. "We'll have to see what the DNA matches tell us. It's early days, Taylor, don't panic." They wanted to bring Vivienne's assailant to justice but they wanted to protect the school too, and the two goals might not be compatible. Vivienne's needs had to be served first. But, if the parents weren't happy with how they handled it, it could cost Taylor's and Nicole's jobs, and they knew it.

"I'm not panicked, but I'm getting there," Taylor said honestly. He hadn't seen Larry Gray yet in the two days that they'd been dealing with it in crisis mode, but he knew he'd have plenty to say about it. "Let's sit tight for another day or two, if we get away with it, but we'd better have a statement ready when they call us. I want to write to the parents too, but I'd like to wait till we hear what turns up in the fingerprints before I do that. I've already had calls from parents, particularly the girls' parents. I've assured them that we've increased security, the police are on campus, and we've instituted the buddy system.

But the parents of the whole student body need to hear from me soon," he said and Nicole nodded. "I've got the letter ready to send."

"I'll start drafting a media statement. That may be more pressing," she suggested. They were in full agreement, and he was discovering that she was a great person to have on hand in a crisis. She was levelheaded, smart, discreet, loyal, brave, and honest, which was an unbeatable combination, and she was unfailingly clear about her allegiance to the school, although she'd only been there for two months. She and Charity were proving to be an invaluable support system, although the final responsibility for all decisions rested on him. "The police said we'd hear from them by tonight if they come up with any matches from the bottle. They're going to run it all through a computer in Boston, which is faster and more state-of-the-art than anything they have here." He nodded and Nicole left a few minutes later. Taylor sat at his desk, staring out the window, and he suddenly felt a deep compassion for the captain of the *Titanic*. They had hit the iceberg, and he just hoped that Saint Ambrose wasn't going down. It was the most potentially explosive situation he had dealt with in his entire career, and he hoped that they'd all come out of it in one piece— students, faculty, the victim, and the school. He had the weight of the world on his shoulders, and looked it.

*

Steve Babson and Rick Russo came to Jamie's dorm room after class that afternoon, and he looked shocked to see them.

"What are you doing here?" he whispered. "Together."

"We just had to see you," Steve said miserably. "I've been on academic probation for three years. If our prints turn up if they find the bottle, I'll be kicked out in five minutes, for the alcohol rule, if nothing else."

"Are you fucking kidding me?" Jamie said in a low voice with a look of anguish. "You won't have to get expelled. We'll all go to prison, for what Rick did and our knowing about it and not reporting it. We're all accessories. And maybe we deserve to go to prison," Jamie said, thinking of Vivienne. But they had promised Rick not to give him up, and all felt honor-bound to stick by him, out of loyalty and friendship, even if what he had done was wrong. But there was risk in it for them too.

"My father won't let that happen," Rick said more confidently than he felt. "He'd get us out of it somehow. He says money always wins the day in the end. Why the fuck didn't any of us remember to take the bottle with us?" It bothered Jamie that Rick was showing no signs of remorse, only terror for himself.

"We were out of our minds that night, and we panicked," Jamie said about the bottle. Chase heard them from next door then, and came to see who was visiting Jamie, and looked angry as soon as he saw them.

"What are you idiots doing here? We agreed to stay away from each other," he whispered.

"They have our prints now," Steve reminded him. "If they found the bottle, they'll know we were drinking with her."

"It's not our prints we should be worried about," Chase said with a dark look. He had been tortured since it happened, and looked like he'd lost five pounds in two days, and probably had. None of them looked well. They felt sick and hadn't been sleeping, thinking of Vivienne. And Chase was tormented by what Vivienne must be going through, and so was Jamie, but they didn't talk to each other about it. They couldn't. Some kind of absurd male rivalry had suddenly exploded between them, and the match to the dynamite fuse was the tequila.

"They've got to have the bottle by now," Steve said anxiously.

"Fuck the bottle," Chase reminded them, "they've got Viv. If she talks, we're dead. And she has every right to blame us, and Rick."

"I don't think she will," Jamie said quietly.

"They have Tommy's violin case," Rick told them. "I saw him yesterday. He left it there, but that doesn't prove anything either. That's circumstantial evidence. It wouldn't hold up in court." But it wasn't good news either. Tommy was afraid to come near any of them, and was staying well away from all of them. He had his own terror to deal with. "He told the police it was stolen when he went into the haunted house. He says they believed him."

"Who knows what they really believe," Chase said cynically. "You guys should go. We just have to wait and see what happens with the fingerprints they took today. Have you talked to your parents yet?" Steve shook his head. That was the last thing he wanted to do, in his case. Talking to the police was easier.

"Have you?" Steve asked him, and Chase shook his head too. They were still on location.

"I have," Jamie spoke up. "I called my dad, he had a fit that they were going to fingerprint us. He called Houghton about it. He said everyone on campus is being fingerprinted, the girls too, staff, faculty. My dad said he couldn't stop him."

"My dad called him too, Houghton told him the same thing," Rick added.

Rick and Steve shuffled toward the door, and the four of them looked at each other, wondering how it had ever happened. None of them could stop thinking of Vivienne and how she had looked when they left her. No matter how drunk they were, some of the worst memories of that night were still vivid, especially when they realized Rick had raped her, while Jamie and Chase were fighting.

"See you guys," Rick said as they left, and he and Steve parted company outside the dorm.

*

Adrian Stone was in the infirmary at that exact moment with his second severe asthma attack in two days, and Betty the school nurse had just called the doctor. His inhaler no longer seemed to be working.

Chapter Seven

After Steve and Rick left, Jamie wandered into Chase's room. The two boys looked at each other, and Chase pointed to his bed, asking if Jamie wanted to sit down. Chase was sitting at his computer. Both boys were silent for a long time.

Jamie spoke first. "What do you think is going to happen?"

"We could go to prison if they find out. We probably would, as accessories," Chase said soberly. "We were there and we couldn't stop him. And now we're not co-operating with the police."

"Do you think we should confess to what happened that night?" Jamie whispered. He had closed the door on the way in. It felt good to talk to someone. He had been going round and round in his head for two days, trying to figure out what had happened, why, and what to do next. He still couldn't understand what madness had gotten into Rick.

"I've been asking myself the same question, but they'll send Rick to prison for sure then. I don't feel like I have a right to take everyone down, but we owe Vivienne something too. I wish I could talk to my dad about it," Chase admitted, "but there's no cell service where he is, he's on some remote mountain filming, and they can only reach him by radio in an emergency. I can't tell him this over a radio. I have to wait till he's back." He looked at Jamie seriously then. "I'm sorry I fought with you that night. It was crazy. I think she likes both of us. She's a terrific girl. I didn't want you to have her." He looked morbidly depressed over it and so did Jamie. "I feel so stupid about it now. And if we hadn't been fighting and drunk, we'd have seen Rick and been able to stop him. It makes me sick thinking about it. I want to kick his ass every time I see him."

"Me too. None of it would have happened if we weren't drunk," Jamie commented.

"I brought the fucking tequila," Chase said mournfully, consumed with regret as he brushed a tear off his cheek. "Shit, I wish I could take it back and do it all again. I wish we hadn't partied that night. It sounded like fun at the time. Rick took it to another level." A level none of them could take back now and they'd all pay a price for.

"I think if we go to the police now, it will only make it worse," Jamie said. "We have to ride it out. And we promised Rick. He'll go to prison for sure, if we talk. And she's not talking so she must not want the police to know what happened either."

"Yeah, I know," Chase agreed with him. "Christ, my father will kill me if this ever comes out."

"So will mine," Jamie agreed. "Do you think Rick's dad can really get him off with some big fancy lawyer?"

"I don't know," Chase said, "I think my dad would expect me to take my punishment for what I'd done."

"I don't know what mine would do, kill me maybe," Jamie said. Protecting Rick now was a heavy burden for both of them, and went against what they felt they owed Vivienne too. It was an intolerable conflict.

Chase looked at him ruefully. "This would kill my dad. I hope it never comes out, for everyone's sake. It sucks for Vivienne, though. I wish we could make it up to her."

"Do you think she'll be okay?" Jamie asked, as tears crept down his cheeks too. They were both crying silently as they sat there, but it felt better to be together than alone. They were in this together, and had been friends before, although Jamie knew he would think of that night now whenever he saw Chase. But he had no one else to talk to that he could be honest with. The memory of what had happened, and their silence now, was irrevocably intertwined with their friendship.

"I don't know," Chase said. "How could she be okay? She'll probably be a mess for a long time. I keep thinking we should confess, but I don't want to send all of us to prison, it'll ruin our lives if we do."

"Maybe we deserve that. Maybe that's what justice is all about," Jamie said softly.

"If she wanted us to be in jail, she'd tell the police what happened, and she hasn't, or we'd be in jail by now, and they wouldn't be fingerprinting half the world, including the headmaster and the maintenance guys. She hasn't told them, and I don't think she will." Chase was almost sure, but not quite. And he was having a hard time deciding what was right. There were so many people involved who would all be impacted by any decision he made.

"Maybe she's embarrassed too, for being with us and getting so drunk. But what Rick did is a hell of a price for her to pay for getting drunk. She didn't deserve that. No one does." Jamie was groping for understanding of something neither of them could explain.

"It's not right for Rick to get away with it," Chase said solemnly. "I wonder what my dad would do. He's the most honest man I know."

"We'll always be a terrible memory for her now, and always will be. Why do you think she hasn't told the cops?" Jamie asked him. He had wondered a thousand times.

"Scared to maybe," Chase answered. "Even if it's our fault, they could rip her to shreds in court, and make her look bad. The lawyers our fathers would hire would sacrifice her to save us. Or maybe she's just a decent human being and doesn't want to ruin our lives, although we ruined hers." They were quiet again for a long time, thinking about it, and then Jamie stood up. He felt a thousand years old. "We'll see what happens with the prints tomorrow," Chase said, and Jamie nodded, and went back to his own room to lie on his bed and cry, thinking about Vivienne. He felt the weight of the world on his shoulders, and all the remorse Rick should have and had shown no sign of.

*

Detective Brendan called Taylor at nine o'clock that night. "We've got the preliminary report on the seniors," he said in a neutral tone.

"Any matches with the prints on the bottle?" Taylor asked, silently praying the answer would be negative, even if it was a futile hope. He didn't want any student to be guilty.

"All six of them, and Vivienne's," Brendan said in a somber tone. "We need to bring them in for questioning, and we're going to run them over to the hospital for cheek swabs, for DNA matches with the semen samples. We're getting down to serious business here. We can call off the rest of the fingerprinting now. We have what we needed." It was a very important first step and successful from a police perspective.

"Are you going to arrest them?" Taylor asked in a hoarse voice.

"It depends where we go from here, what they tell us, if one of them confesses to the rape, what the DNA match is. Right now we have them located at a crime scene, drinking tequila. That's not a felony, they're minors drinking, possibly in the wrong place at the wrong time. We have to take this one step at a time. If none of the DNA samples is a match, they're your problem, as to how you want to handle the drinking. We're not going to arrest them for underage drinking. If one of the DNA samples is a match with what we got from the victim, that's a whole different story, and you know what comes next. We want to find the man who raped Vivienne. If these boys are her friends, that may be why she wouldn't tell us anything, and cooked up a story about drinking with a bunch of girls she can't remember. I have a hard time believing she'd protect a boy who raped her, unless she's in love with him, but you never know with kids. They have strange loyalties for odd reasons, and a rape trial will be rough on her. The others would be tried as accessories if they were at the scene when she was raped, and for obstruction of justice for not reporting it, and possibly for lying to us, in Tommy Yee's case. It will also depend on what the boys say now, if they lie to us or tell the truth, and what Vivienne corroborates. They're all minors, so we'd get a closed courtroom for a trial, but at seventeen, these boys may not be tried as minors if it involves a rape case, and if one of them committed the rape, he may be tried as an adult and get an adult sentence and go to prison as an adult—that could mean five to eight years in prison. I know that some of these prep school rapes have gotten a lot of media attention, and the boys involved have had some pretty light sentences. I don't think most judges are willing to do that anymore. It brings a shitstorm down on them in the media for giving hard sentences to ordinary folk, and six months' probation to rich boys, and the public doesn't like it. The courts are taking rape cases very seriously these days, more so than ever. So if one of them is charged with rape, I don't think he'll get an easy ride on this. But we're getting ahead of ourselves. We want to pick them up in the morning for questioning, and I'd like you and Miss Smith to be present in lieu of their parents when we question each of them. I don't want you to warn them before we come to get them. We don't want anyone slipping through our fingers tonight."

"Of course. I understand. Can you tell me now who they are?" Taylor could feel his heart pounding and was wondering if the stress was going to kill him.

"I'll tell you if you treat it as confidential. I'd prefer if you don't notify their parents until we've brought them in. We'll have a better idea what we're dealing with then, and after the DNA matches, but you'll want to notify their parents tomorrow once they've been questioned."

"I'll have to."

"I don't envy you," Dominic said sympathetically. "That can't be easy, particularly in a school like this." But they both knew that any parent in any social stratum would have been terrified for their child in a situation like it. And at least most Saint Ambrose parents could afford powerful lawyers, which others couldn't, although some Saint Ambrose parents couldn't either, like those of the scholarship kids. "We've got six sets of prints that are a match with the bottle, other than the victim's. James Watts, Gabriel Harris, Steven Babson, Richard Russo, Thomas Yee, the boy with the violin, and Chase Morgan. Those are the six." Taylor was sitting with his eyes closed, feeling sick as he listened.

"Those are some of our best kids. Our three top students in fact, and Chase is the son of Matthew Morgan, the actor, which means we'll have national media coverage if it goes farther than underage drinking at a crime scene, and even that will drag all the press here for weeks. We're in for a tornado, Detective Brendan."

"We might be. It could turn out to be a tropical storm, not a hurricane. Let's hope so. Is eight A.M. too early for you?"

"We'll be ready for you. And thank you for calling me first. See you in the morning."

"We'll run them in to the hospital first, it'll just take a few minutes. It's a cheek swab. Do you have a vehicle for them?"

"We'll bring them in one of our vans."

"Detective Martin and I will follow you. Good night."

When Taylor hung up, his hands were shaking. Charity walked into his office, where he'd taken the call, and saw the look on his face. She walked over to him.

"What happened?" She was worried about him. He was deathly pale. This was one of the greatest challenges he had faced in his career, or even in his life.

"Six senior boys are a match with the fingerprints on the tequila bottle found at the crime scene. Some of our best boys." His lip was trembling as he said it and there were tears in his eyes, thinking of what lay ahead if it turned out to be more than drinking on campus on Halloween. If the DNA matched one of them, the boy would be prosecuted, and if convicted, he would go to prison. He couldn't even imagine it at seventeen. He looked at Charity then. He trusted her completely with all his secrets, even this one. "Steve Babson, Rick Russo, Gabe Harris, Tommy Yee, Jamie Watts, and Chase Morgan."

"Oh my God," she said and sat down next to him. "Are you going to call their parents tonight?"

"I've been told not to. They're taking them in for questioning and DNA tests tomorrow morning. They asked me to wait to call the parents until after that, since Nicole and I will be there with them in loco parentis."

"Should you call Shep as head of the board?" She looked worried, for all of them.

"I can't. I have to follow what the police want. They're afraid that they'll run. And I agree with them. I think some of them would. And Nicole is worried about Tommy Yee. We don't want a suicide here on top of it. I think after tomorrow it's going to be open season in the press. I just hope we come through it, and the boys will be okay. Whoever committed the rape deserves to be punished, but the others could be prosecuted too."

"You just have to ride the wave now. It's all you can do." She kissed him, and they walked slowly to their bedroom together. She put him to bed like a child. She knew he'd have to be strong tomorrow, and she was willing her own strength into him. He cried in her arms, and she held him tight.

*

Adrian Stone was in the infirmary that night. Betty Trapp wanted him where she could keep an eye on him in case he had another asthma attack. The doctor had prescribed some pills to take along with his inhaler, and Maxine Bell, the school counselor, had dropped by to see him. He was happy and relaxed, watching TV and eating dinner on a tray.

"How is he?" Maxine asked the nurse when she came in, before she went into the other room to see him.

"He seems okay. He was very agitated when I saw him earlier, and he seems anxious."

"Have his parents filed any new court orders against each other? That usually does it to him."

"Not that I know of. I asked if he'd heard from them recently, and he said not since school started."

"That was two months ago," Maxine said with a frown. "Wonderful, concerned parents," she said to Betty in a whisper. "They drag him into court every chance they get, in order to punish each other, but they don't call or write just to see how he is. Did you call them today after his attack?"

"I have orders only to text them, so I did. I texted them both. I said he was doing fine, told them about the medication Dr. Jordan added, but neither of them responded. I guess they figure he's okay, and we're watching him here." Maxine nodded, and went in to visit Adrian, who seemed fine. He was a slight boy, short for his age, and had been too thin since he got there. In his pajamas he looked more like twelve than sixteen, and had barely gone through puberty yet. He had the faintest shadow of fuzz on his upper lip and nothing more, and his long hair made him look younger too. Some of the boys in his class already shaved.

They chatted for a little while. Maxine didn't want to interrupt his show, and left him to have a cup of tea with Betty, who was happy for the company. Betty had come to be the nurse at the school when her husband died. She had no children, and it seemed like a perfect solution to her new situation. Maxine had never been married, and had enjoyed working in boarding schools for thirty years. Both women were in their fifties and had become good friends, and both were dedicated to their jobs, and the children at the school.

"I got an email a few minutes ago that we don't have to be fingerprinted tomorrow. Anything new there?" Maxine asked her.

"I got it too. There was no explanation, it just said it was canceled."

"I hope they figure it out soon. All the kids are tense right now, and a lot of the girls are scared." They talked of other things then, and Maxine went back to her suite of rooms near her office on campus a little while later. They had already agreed to spend Thanksgiving together and were going to New York for the weekend, for the theater, as they'd done before. It would be good to get away.

*

Vivienne lay in her bed at the hospital after her parents went back to their respective hotels, and she thought about what Gwen had said to her, about making the boy who'd raped her accountable for what he'd done. And she hadn't lied about her headache, it really was worse. She believed that if she told the truth and made all of them accountable for their part in it, especially Rick, their lawyers would somehow make her look like a slut in court, and her parents would be ashamed of her. She knew she'd been wrong to be drinking with the boys, but she had never expected it to turn out the way it had. For just a minute she had liked the feeling of both Chase and Jamie wanting her, and then Chase had gone crazy, he and Jamie got in a fight, and everything got out of control when Rick had forcibly had sex with her, and after that she passed out.

She liked most of them, especially Chase and Jamie, but she felt uncomfortable with them now and knew they could never be friends after what had happened. But she didn't want to ruin their lives and get them expelled for drinking, and she didn't want it to be her fault if Rick went to prison. It was too much responsibility for her. What he did was wrong, but ruining his life wouldn't make it any different. She was confused about what to do, and had no one to talk to about it. She didn't want to talk to her parents, and she thought of everything Gwen had said. Sending Rick to prison for years seemed too harsh, but so was what he'd done to her. She wondered if any of it was her fault, for drinking with them and getting drunk, or if she'd encouraged Rick in some way. But even drunk, Chase and Jamie hadn't raped her. And once she told the truth, she couldn't stop what would happen to them. A jury and the courts would decide, and no one would listen to her. It still seemed better not to say anything at all, and do her best to forget it. The consequences for speaking up were so extreme.

She hadn't texted Lana or Zoe or any of her girlfriends in L.A. since it happened, or answered their texts or requests to FaceTime with her. She didn't know what to say to them. The rape wasn't her fault, but she was ashamed anyway. Too ashamed even to tell her mother. They were already upset about her breaking the rules and drinking.

Lana and Zoe had asked her how her Halloween was, but she didn't answer them. She didn't want any of them to know what had happened to her. They would never look at her the same way again. If she told them the truth, they'd think it was her fault because she'd been drinking in secret, alone with the boys after curfew, and got so drunk. They might think she was a slut too. Maybe everyone would if they knew.

Vivienne lay in bed and cried until the sleeping pill they'd given her took effect and she fell asleep. All she wanted to do now was go home to L.A. with her dad, to turn back the clock and climb back into the womb of her past life. Maybe she wouldn't even see anyone while she was in L.A. She couldn't face Lana or Zoe. But at least she'd be there, in her own house, with her dad, where she knew she was safe. After the rape, by someone she knew, she didn't think she'd ever feel safe again. She had never expected Rick to rape her, or for a night of drinking tequila with the boys to turn out the way it had.

Chapter Eight

Nicole arrived at the cafeteria at a quarter to eight the next morning. She and Taylor had decided that her presence would be less noticeable at that hour than his. He was waiting in the van outside, and the two detectives from Boston were due at eight o'clock, to escort them to the hospital and the police station.

She spotted Jamie and Chase first, having breakfast together, as they often did. They were eating steaming bowls of oatmeal and they both looked tired. She stopped to speak to them quietly, so no one else would hear her.

"I'm sorry, boys. We need you to come with us this morning. We've got some business to take care of. If you'd head out now, the van is outside." They both looked startled and scared for a minute, and then covered it with false bravado, as they stood up, cleared their dishes and dumped their unfinished breakfasts, and walked outside. They barely had time to whisper to each other on the way out.

"Fuck, what do you think it is?" Jamie said to Chase.

"Nothing good, I suspect. Be cool. Don't talk," Chase

instructed him, and Jamie nodded as they both saw the headmaster waiting for them in the van. A few students noticed, but most hadn't paid any attention. They were in a hurry for breakfast before class.

Steve Babson and Gabe were together, and looked like they were having an argument about something. Nicole rounded them up. Rick was just coming through the line with a tray laden with food he hadn't touched yet. She asked him to go outside too. Then she had to look for Tommy Yee, and was concerned that she couldn't find him. Then she saw him dash in with his violin case, the violin he'd borrowed from the music department. He grabbed a banana and was about to leave when Nicole caught up with him, and escorted him to the van to meet the others. By then Detectives Martin and Brendan had arrived. Their car was parked off to the side. It was eight o'clock sharp. The two detectives got into their car, and followed the van off the grounds. Not a word was said in the van as Nicole drove. She didn't explain where they were going, and no one dared ask. They were sure they were about to be arrested, and several of them had gone pale when they got into the van and said good morning to the headmaster sitting in the front. He greeted them politely but made no attempt at conversation with them. He was going to leave the explanations to the detectives, and didn't want to say too much. He didn't want any of them bolting from the van.

All six boys looked surprised when they stopped at the hospital, and they wondered if they were being taken to be confronted by Vivienne or accused by her in person. Instead Dominic and Gwen led them to a lab on the ground floor, where the insides of their cheeks were swabbed and they were told it was a DNA test. Chase finally had the guts to ask them what it was for.

Gwen answered him simply and clearly for the benefit of all. "It will clear you of any involvement with the rape of Vivienne Walker, which would be a very good thing. And in any case, the police are requiring it as part of their investigation. The full results will take several weeks, and we'll have a preliminary report in a few days."

"Why us?" Rick asked, trying to look surprised and unconcerned.

"We'll talk about that when we get to the police station," she said, as she shepherded them back to the van. Detective Brendan brought up the rear.

Once at the police station, the boys looked wild-eyed and silent. None of them had ever been to a police station before, or been arrested.

"Are we being arrested?" Jamie wanted to know.

"No. We brought you here for questioning," Gwen said, as she and Dominic led them into a conference room, and Nicole and Taylor took their seats at the far end. They invited the boys to sit down around a large scarred-up table. The police station was in ill repair, and there was a jail next to it, for drunks and those who had committed minor crimes. The station was noisy and bright with fluorescent lights. There was nothing welcoming or attractive about it, and all six boys looked terrified.

"You're here, boys, because a tequila bottle in the location where Vivienne Walker was raped had seven sets of fingerprints on it. The bottle was nearly empty. One set of prints belonged to Vivienne Walker, and the other six sets of prints were yours, which potentially puts you at the crime scene the night it happened. The bottle was fresh, so at some point that night the six of you polished off that tequila with her. What happened after that, we're not sure. This is your chance to tell us the truth. Tell us what you know, what you saw, what happened, whether or not things got out of hand, what time you left, when you last saw her, and what condition she was in. Generally speaking, if you lie, someone will talk eventually, some piece of evidence will lead us to the truth. I strongly urge you to level with us. It's going to go a lot better if you do. We'll talk to each of you separately, and if the stories don't match up, then we'll know you're lying to us. For the moment, you're not under arrest, unless you make a full confession today. But you are under investigation. You can't leave the area—in your case, the school. I can't stress strongly enough how important it is to be honest with us. Things are going to go a lot better if you are.

Even if your friends don't tell the truth, you'd be a lot smarter to be truthful with us. Loyalty among friends is a wonderful thing, but not when it comes to breaking the law. I think your parents would tell you the same thing."

She called in two sheriff's deputies then to sit with them, and instructed the deputies that the boys were not to converse with each other. And with that, she and Detective Brendan took Steve Babson into a room behind the conference room and told him to sit down. The detectives asked Nicole Smith to join them, and she quietly took a seat.

"Tell us what happened on Halloween night, Steve." Gwen wasn't harsh or threatening with him, but it was clear that she represented law enforcement and the spotlight was on him. She turned on a tape recorder, advising him that she was doing so, and he could feel his body shaking and his heart racing as he answered. "When did you meet up with your friends, did you have a plan, and how did Vivienne happen to be with you?"

"We all went to the haunted house, the guys did. And we decided to have a little party afterward. We knew that spot behind the tree line. Nobody ever goes there. We meet there sometimes."

"Have you ever partied there before?" He hesitated, and then nodded.

"Once, maybe twice in three years," Steve said, and she believed him.

"Who was there on Halloween night?"

"Me, Gabe, Rick. Jamie and Chase came a little later."

"Who brought the tequila?" He hesitated for a long time and looked at her.

"I can't remember." He remembered, but wasn't going to sell out Chase.

"Did you?"

"No," Steve said clearly.

"Was Vivienne with you?"

"No."

"Do any of you date her, or have gone out with her?" He shook his head, as both detectives watched him. He looked like a nervous kid, and he was visibly scared.

"No. Girls just started at Saint Ambrose this September, so we don't know any of the girls that well. But she's nice. We've talked to her in the cafeteria. We've seen her around."

"Why did you guys invite her to the 'party'?"

"We didn't. We heard her on the path on the other side of the bushes, she was singing. So we invited her in."

"Had you already been drinking by then?" He nodded. "A lot?"

"Enough."

"Were you drunk when she joined you?"

"Kind of. But not too drunk. Just a little. Oh, and

before that, Tommy came down the path and we invited him in too."

"Were there other girls there?"

"No, just Viv."

"Why Viv?"

"She came by when we were there. She's pretty, really pretty, and nice." Gwen watched his eyes carefully. For her, the truth was always there. So far so good. And Dominic was making his own observations of body language and gestures, the speed of Steve's speech when he got nervous.

"Did she drink with you?" She knew the answer to that, but wanted to know what he'd say.

"Yes, we passed the bottle around."

"Once, twice?"

"A bunch of times. I don't know how many."

"And she kept drinking with you? Did any of you stop at some point?"

"I think Tommy did. Vivienne didn't. She matched us round for round."

"Did she seem really drunk, like out of it drunk?"

"She was drunk, but no more than we were."

"Did she pass out?"

"No."

"And then what? You kept drinking? You stopped? What?"

"We finished the bottle, and we left. It was after curfew, and we didn't want to get caught, so we left."

"Were you falling down drunk, or just kind of drunk on the way back?"

"No, we were cool."

"And where was Vivienne? Did she leave with you?"

"No, we left her there."

"In the clearing? Why?" He nodded and she saw his eyes become wary.

"The girls' dorms are the other way from ours. There's a shortcut from there."

"And you just left her? Did you see her leave?"

"No. We just left. And I guess we figured she'd walk back on her own."

"How did she look when you left her?"

"She looked okay, about like us. I figured she'd just go back to her dorm. Maybe somebody jumped her after we left, but she looked fine when we took off."

"Was she waiting for someone? Did she say anything?"

"No, we just said bye. I think she was still standing there when we left. Maybe she was waiting for someone, she didn't say." He was talking faster as he said it, which Gwen noticed too.

"And then?"

"That was it. We went back to our rooms and went to bed."

"Anything else you can tell us, that you saw, that she said? Did you notice anyone else on the path when you left?"

"No. It was past curfew for the younger grades and for us too. It got later than we thought."

"Do you remember what time it was?"

"No."

"You saw no workmen, no strangers, no adults when you left?" He shook his head again.

His story was straightforward and plausible if it was true, but she wasn't sure it was. Where it fell apart for Gwen was why they would just walk off and leave a girl they'd been drinking with, knowing that she was fairly drunk. Or maybe they were too drunk to care. But his story had them just marching off and ditching her.

"Did you call the campus police that night?"

"No, I didn't." It was true. Chase had. If his story was true, the question was what had happened between when they left her and when the campus police had been called. Gwen had the feeling that Steve was lying to her.

"Was she conscious when you left her?"

"Yes. She was about like us."

She thanked him and led him back to the conference room and asked Rick Russo to come in. He looked calm and confident when she escorted him into the smaller room. She expected to go over the same details with him, and was startled when she asked the first question and he looked her in the eye, smiled at her, and spoke clearly.

"I'm sorry, Detective Martin, but my father has advised me not to answer any questions until I have an attorney present. I have a right to an attorney to be questioned, or one of my parents with me."

"That's true, you do. Ms. Smith is standing in for your parents today. You also have an obligation to cooperate with our investigation to get to the bottom of this, since your fingerprints on the bottle place you at the crime scene that night. And when did you contact your father?" she asked him, annoyed.

"I texted him on the way over in the van. He can arrange to have an attorney come up here whenever you want."

"Fine. Arrange it. Soon." Rick looked relieved as she walked him out of the room, and the others looked surprised. She had exchanged a biting look with Dominic, who raised an eyebrow. They were a sophisticated group, or watched too much TV, in his opinion. Nicole remained silent in her seat and didn't comment, but it didn't surprise her.

Gwen brought Gabe Harris in next, and his story was much the same as Steve's, with a few variations. He didn't think any of them were excessively drunk, and Vivienne seemed fine to him when they left. It didn't seem odd to him either that they had left her there, drunk, and walked off, if what they said was true. If it was, chivalry was clearly dead. Gabe had added that he thought she had said something about meeting friends there after they left.

"After curfew?" she asked Gabe carefully, watching him closely. "You said that all of you were there after senior curfew and it was late. Was she planning to stay out after that?"

"I guess so," he said, looking very blithe and somewhat cavalier. "But she seemed fine. None of us were worried about her."

"That's not saying much," Gwen commented, somewhat caustically. "She told us that she got so drunk with friends that she passed out, so she has no idea what happened after that. And you're telling me she was perfectly okay."

"Well, a little drunk, but not really passed out."

"What does 'not really passed out' mean? She either was or she wasn't. Was she unconscious?"

"No, she wasn't. She was fine."

"And you didn't see her leave?"

"No, but she would have gone in the opposite direction from us, down the same path." So none of them had seen her leave. Gwen let him go then, and brought Jamie in, and he pulled the same stunt as Rick Russo had. He said he wouldn't speak to her without an attorney present. He was very polite and respectful about it, but very firm. He said his father had told him not to answer questions without his attorney present. He had texted his father from the van too. And when she brought Chase in, he did the same.

"My parents are out of the country on location," he said quietly, "but they wouldn't want me interrogated without their attorney present." She was irritated by the end of it, when she brought Tommy Yee in. He looked visibly frightened, and fidgeted the entire time. He had a tissue in his hands which he shredded as she asked him the same questions. His version was slightly different. He admitted to drinking with the others, but he said he thought Vivienne had drunk very little of the tequila, and she left before they did, and by the time they left, she had gone back to her dorm. Gwen had no idea why he varied the story, but she wound up with two different versions of the end of the evening, and half the boys wouldn't answer a single question without an attorney to represent them. She wondered if their stories would be different too. All of their accounts of the evening were different from the victim's. She didn't know yet what to make of it, except that obviously some or all of them were lying, including Vivienne.

She addressed them all as a group in the conference room before they left, with Taylor and Nicole. She spoke to them more sternly than she had in the beginning.

"I want to remind all of you again that now is the time to make a clean breast of things, not do a lot of fancy footwork and embroidery. If you tell us the truth, or even confess to something you wish had never happened, it's going to go a lot better for all of you in the end. If you lie to us, and we discover it, through evidence, or because one of you decides to confess, or someone comes forward who saw what actually happened, you're going to have a much harder time dealing with the law." They all nodded like obedient children as they listened to her. "And I want to tell you again that the matter is still under investigation. You may not leave the area under any circumstances. You have not been cleared. You're not being charged with Vivienne Walker's rape *yet,*" she emphasized the word, "but you're not off the hook either." She looked pointedly at Nicole and Taylor too, and reminded them that the boys were to remain on campus until the investigation was concluded. Both the headmaster and assistant headmaster said they understood, as did the boys.

When they left to go back to the school, Gwen sat down in the conference room with Dominic. She wasn't sure what to think.

"So what did you get out of all that, Dom?" she asked him.

"Some of them are damn good liars, though not as good as they think. And they're clever little bastards, refusing to talk without a lawyer present. That's a real rich kid move. No 'normal' kid would even think of that. They got off the hook nicely with that bullshit. I'll tell the headmaster they have three days to reappear with an attorney and respond to us, or we'll put them in a juvenile facility, pending further investigation. We couldn't hold them for more than a couple of days, but it would scare them. And we have three different versions of the end of the evening—two of theirs, and the victim's. They walked off and left her, and she must have left after they did, but no one knows. She stayed waiting to meet up with other friends, *after* curfew—why would she risk that? And she left before they did according to the Yee kid. So what's true? They were all drunk as skunks but she was 'fine'? And she says she was so drunk she was unconscious, and never met up with them at all. They're full of shit, Gwen. But maybe it doesn't matter. The answer is going to be in the DNA matches. If one of them raped her, the rest of the story will come out. If we get a match on the samples they took today, these six boys are going to be one sorry lot of liars and up shit creek without a paddle. I think they'll all tell us the truth then. Right now, I don't believe a word of the end of their story, any of them, and the victim's version least of all."

"I want to go see her again," Gwen said, looking intent on it.

"When?"

"Now." She was determined, and he groaned.

"Shit, you never let me eat."

"I'll feed you after we see her." He agreed grudgingly,

and while she got her purse, the boys were riding back to the school in silence. They seemed relieved and more relaxed than they had when they'd left school that morning. Jamie had sent each of them a text in the van to meet in his room. Since they were interrogated together, he didn't see why they couldn't get together. Instead of going to lunch, they went to Chase and Jamie's dorm.

"So how did it go?" Chase and Jamie asked the others, once they were in Jamie's room. Only three of them had answered the questions; the other three had dodged it.

"You didn't have to talk to them," Rick pointed out. "You had a right to a lawyer."

"I can't afford one anyway," Gabe said simply. "If we go down for this, I'll wind up with the public defender." But they all hoped it wouldn't come to that.

They rapidly discovered that they had offered different endings to the evening and Jamie groaned. "So now they know we're lying."

"They're not stupid," Rick commented. "They probably know that anyway."

"Did you tell them I brought the tequila?" Chase asked them, and Steve said he had told Gwen that he didn't remember who brought it.

"Thank you," Chase said, relieved.

"She said that Vivienne says she was so drunk she was unconscious the whole time, and we all said she looked fine." They remembered what she had really looked like when they left and they all shuddered. "Why would Viv say she was unconscious?" Gabe asked, looking puzzled.

"So she can't identify us as she never saw us," Chase said, looking touched. "She's trying to save our asses, even after what Rick did to her, which says a lot about her. What happens if one of us confesses?"

"We all get fucked," Rick said clearly. "Why would you do that?"

"Do you feel right about what we're doing? Lying about it?" Chase asked him.

"Hell, yes. I'd feel a lot worse going to prison." Rick sounded very sure.

"I've thought of confessing too," Jamie chimed in.

"Don't do that," Steve begged them, looking panicked. "Nothing about this is going to be better if we all go to prison."

"We're all liars," Chase said, looking depressed. Now that he needed a lawyer, he had to tell his parents. They all did. This was too serious now.

Taylor was already dealing with it. He made Shepard, Jamie's father, his first call as a courtesy, and Shep went through the roof.

"They're interrogating Jamie? Taylor, why haven't you stopped this?" He blamed the headmaster that it had gone this far.

"Shep, I can't stop it. Their fingerprints were all over a bottle of tequila found at the crime scene. They were there. What happened before, after, and during, no one knows. But they were there for part of the evening and she was with them, and by the end of the evening she was raped and half dead from alcohol poisoning. They're not off the hook yet. This is not in my control, or yours, or even theirs at this point. It's a criminal investigation. I just pray that there are no DNA matches, because if there is one, that boy will go to prison."

Shepard shouted into the phone at that. "Over my dead body."

"And nearly hers," Taylor reminded him quietly. "We're in it, we just have to ride the wave now. And you need to encourage Jamie to tell them the truth."

"Are you saying my son's a liar?"

"I'm saying what we all already know. Something terrible happened that night, and we don't know who did it. Anything is possible. The DNA matches are going to tell us the whole story."

"The girl is probably some kind of whore." Taylor winced. They were friends, but he couldn't believe Shep's attitude about Vivienne's rape. He would do anything, honorable or not, to get Jamie out of trouble. Taylor knew how much he loved his son, but this had gone far beyond that. A girl's life had been impacted forever by a terrible act, and he couldn't take that lightly, neither as a human being, nor as headmaster, no matter how fond he was of Shepard and his family. He hadn't spoken to Ellen since it began, only to Shep, in his role of father and head of the board. He had no idea what her take was on it.

"You need to get him a lawyer, Shep. They want him back for questioning within three days, with his attorney, since he refused to be interrogated today."

"Can't you do something to stop this? Call someone? Pull some strings?" Shep was exasperated and furious with him.

"I have no strings to pull. The police are in charge here. A shocking crime was committed. Now it's up to the police. They're trying to find the man who did it."

"Well, my son isn't the one."

"I hope not," Taylor said sincerely, and after they hung up, he called Joe Russo and told him essentially the same thing. He needed to find an attorney for Rick. Joe went through the roof much the way Shep had. They were not men who were willing to bow to anyone, not even the law, and would do anything to protect their sons. It didn't surprise Taylor about Joe Russo, but it did about Shepard, and disappointed him. He was even willing to vilify the innocent victim to shield Jamie.

The only way Taylor could reach the Morgans was by email, since call service was unreliable in both locations where they were. He told them that Chase was safe and well, but a serious situation had arisen at the school that required communication with them immediately. It was an urgent matter. From experience, he knew he would hear from them within a day. In fact, Matthew called him an hour later, from a landline in Spain, and Taylor explained the situation to him. He was appalled and devastated to hear about Vivienne. He said his manager would send a lawyer up for Chase as soon as possible, and he should go back to the police and answer their questions. Taylor advised him that he and Nicole had been in the room when Chase was questioned, in lieu of parents. Taylor thanked him for his help. He really appreciated it and his compassionate attitude about Vivienne, which neither Joe nor Shepard had demonstrated.

"I hope he had no part in it," Matthew said in a voice full of emotion.

"So do I," Taylor said sincerely. "I'll let you know if anything else develops."

The Harrises were devastated when he called them. Gabe was their great hope for the future, and they had invested everything in him, money, time, love, support. The whole family was backing him, and had for three years, and they had deprived everyone else to do it. It was heartbreaking, and would be even more so if he went to prison. Mike Harris cried when Taylor told him Gabe was under investigation, and he promised to keep him well informed.

Bert Babson didn't take his call, predictably. His nurse said he was in surgery, but Jean, Steve's mother, called him twenty minutes later, and Taylor explained the situation to her. She said she would come up immediately to see Steve, and she thanked Taylor profusely for his help. She actually sounded sober, intelligent, and coherent, even if very shaken by the news.

The hardest call of all was to the Yees. He called Tommy's mother at her accounting firm. She was businesslike and cold. She was very proper and formal on the phone, but Taylor could tell that she was horrified, and he had a feeling that Tommy would be severely punished by them, whatever happened, for being implicated at all. They were extremely tough on him, and he agreed with Nicole's concerns about Tommy's reaction.

By the time he hung up after speaking to Shirley Yee, Taylor felt as though he had been squeezed like a lemon and thrown away.

*

Gwen was with Vivienne by then, and very gingerly explored with her the stories that the boys had told them.

"Why were they interrogated at all? I said I wasn't with them that night," Vivienne said, looking shaken.

"You lied to us, Viv. Your fingerprints and theirs were on the tequila bottle."

"Is that why you fingerprinted the students?" she asked in a frightened voice, and Gwen nodded.

"You have a right to be protected, valued, and vindicated. Do you want to tell us the truth now?" Vivienne didn't answer her for a minute.

"I don't want them to get in trouble because of me," she said in a small voice.

"Why not, after what one of them did to you? If it was one of them."

"Maybe some part of it was my fault. Maybe I did something wrong or gave them the wrong impression. And besides, I got drunk with them." She was willing to admit that much now. She had no other choice, since the boys had talked about it and the fingerprints on the bottle were undeniable.

"Every rape victim in the world says what you just did, and thinks it. It doesn't matter what you do. I don't care how short your skirts are, or how drunk you get, you have the right to wear whatever you want and not be raped." Gwen sat in silence for a minute, letting her words sink in. "Viv, are you going to tell me what happened?"

Vivienne shook her head and then slid deep into her bed. "No, I can't. And I didn't say any of them did it." But Gwen knew one of them had, and she knew that Vivienne remembered what had happened.

"Are you in love with one of them?" It was the only

other reason Gwen could think of that she would protect them.

"No. I like them all . . . and I like two of them a lot. Maybe I could have fallen in love with one of them, but now it will never happen."

"No, I guess it won't. So you let them all go scot-free, no matter what?"

"Their lives will be ruined forever if they go to prison."

"And yours?"

"I'll be okay," she said, in a small childlike voice, but she was having nightmares about it, and head-aches.

"You'll remember it forever, and that you did nothing, and you'll regret it one day. I want you to think about this, Viv. Hard. You have a responsibility to yourself, the community, and even to them." Vivienne turned her face away then and ignored her.

"My head hurts," she said in a whisper.

"I'll go. Call me if you want to talk . . . and tell me the truth about what happened." She left Vivienne alone in her room then. Her parents had been out somewhere, and Dominic was waiting for her in the car in the hospital parking lot. She slid into the front seat next to him and looked at him in frustration.

"Well, did she tell you the truth this time?"

"More or less. One of them did it. But if I try to get a statement out of her, she'll deny it. She doesn't want to send them to prison. She's afraid she might have caused it to happen, and I think she had a crush on two of them. Shit, teenage girls are complicated."

"So are grown women. Now feed me for chrissake. We can talk about it again after lunch."

"Okay, okay, take me to your diner." She smiled at him and they drove away, as she thought about Vivienne and what a devastating experience she'd been through. It tore at Gwen's heart yet again.

*

Adrian Stone went to his advisor that afternoon, as he'd been instructed to do if he needed advice or assistance. He said he wanted to call his court-appointed lawyer, and he wanted to use her phone to do it.

"Is something wrong, Adrian? Have you had a problem with your parents?" She was all too familiar with his history with them.

"I have a legal problem," he said seriously, sitting on the edge of his chair.

"What kind of legal problem?"

"It's confidential."

"All right. You can use my phone. I'll leave you alone for as long as you need." She left the room and went to get a cup of coffee in the teachers' lounge.

"Thank you," he said. He dialed the number in New York. It was an emergency cellphone number he'd been given by the attorney, and the lawyer picked it up on the first ring.

"Mr. Friedman, this is Adrian Stone, at Saint Ambrose," Adrian said in a strong voice.

"Are you okay? Are your parents filing court orders again? Have they come up to see you?" He hadn't been notified of any recent motions.

"No, it's not about them this time." He sounded businesslike and very adult. "I think I've committed a crime, and I could go to jail. I'm having anxiety over it, and my asthma is back. I need to see you."

"What kind of crime?" The lawyer sounded shocked. Adrian was the meekest kid he'd ever met.

"I'd rather tell you in person. I need your advice. I don't know what to do. Do you think you could come up to school to see me?" There was something about the orderly way he said it that convinced the attorney it was important. He glanced at his calendar and almost groaned. He had back-to-back appointments and court appearances for the next month.

"Can it wait till Friday?" the lawyer asked, curious about what his client had gotten into. Adrian was a good kid with terrible parents and he wanted to help him.

"I think it can." But he wasn't sure. It meant waiting three days.

"Then I'll be there. If things get rough before that, call me."

"I will. And thank you. You're a very good attorney."

"Thank you, Adrian." Sam Friedman smiled and promised to be at the school on Friday afternoon after lunch. He was going to drive up from New York.

Adrian looked a thousand percent better when he hung up, and he was proud of his decision. He knew it was why he was having the asthma attacks. He could hardly wait to see his lawyer on Friday. He thanked his advisor when he saw her in the hall, and left, feeling relieved.

Chapter Nine

To his credit, Larry Gray had made himself scarce during the harrowing days after the Halloween night rape, as the students and faculty were now calling it. He hadn't shown up to gloat in Taylor's office, for which Taylor was very grateful. Their paths crossed finally as Taylor walked across the campus to see Maxine Bell and get her opinion on counseling for the students about what had happened. It was constantly on everyone's mind now and the freshman teachers had reported to him that their first year girls were still frightened that it could happen to them.

He stopped when he saw Larry and braced himself for a barrage of "I told you so"s, which didn't happen. Instead he was deeply sympathetic.

"I'm sorry, Taylor. If there's anything I can do to help, let me know. I've left you in peace for the past few days, because I figured you were swimming through a tsunami."

"That's about the right image. It's been incredibly difficult, trying to find the perpetrator, calming the students down, calling parents, worrying about the media."

"You'll get through it. Remember what they say, neither misery nor happiness lasts forever." Taylor laughed. It was such a Larry thing to say.

"I'll try not to think of that the next time I'm happy, but I don't think there's any risk of that at the moment. This has been a real beast to deal with, and the victim didn't deserve it. No one does."

"Everyone will settle down," he said confidently. "Is Shepard giving you a hand with it?"

"Not really. In the end, the buck stops here. You know how that is. Charity has been great, though. Are you okay?"

"Happily buried in my little fiefdom. I've introduced the freshman girls to Jane Austen. They love it. Take care of yourself. Call if you need reinforcements."

Taylor patted his shoulder, and went on to meet with Maxine. This was one of the reasons why he was deeply fond of Larry. He could be an immense pain in the ass at times, and a stubborn, irascible opponent, but underneath it all, he had a good heart and was dedicated to the school, devoted to his students and colleagues, and always loyal.

Taylor ran into Gillian Marks and Simon Edwards that afternoon too, coming back from a boys' soccer game on their farthest playing field, and both had expressed their sympathy. It was comforting to know he had the support of the faculty. There were silver linings in the cloudy sky after all, although very few.

That night, while trying to relax and unwind with Charity, he got a call from the father of a graduate of the school. He had an important position at NBC, as a producer, and he called Taylor to give him a heads-up.

"You're going national on the eleven o'clock. You've got a hell of a problem, Taylor. They got a hot tip from someone and followed it up. I tried to find out the source, but I couldn't."

"How bad is it?" Taylor looked grim, but wasn't surprised.

"Not as bad as it could be, but that can change pretty quickly. I gather you've had a rape on campus." There was no point denying it. "They're saying that a number of students are under suspicion, but the perpetrator hasn't been identified yet."

"There goes Shepard's capital campaign. That's what he was afraid of."

"They're making a big point of saying that it's your first year as a co-ed school, and obviously you weren't prepared for it. These days with social media, there are no secrets. Is the girl all right? That's the most important thing."

"I hope she will be. She's still in the hospital recovering, emotionally more than physically. It's been a bitch of a week, for everyone."

"I'll give you any storm warnings as I hear them, but with it being reported on the eleven o'clock news, you should be prepared for TV trucks camping out on your doorstep by breakfast time tomorrow."

"You're right. I'll take care of it," Taylor said, sounding grateful and exhausted. He called Nicole as soon as he hung up, despite the late hour, and warned her. Then they both watched the eleven o'clock news in their respective houses. Taylor wasn't thrilled with it, but it could have been a lot worse. Someone had informed them that a number of male students had had DNA tests and been interrogated by the police that day. Obviously they had inside information, but you couldn't hermetically seal off a situation like this. There were bound to be leaks from any number of sources. Taylor guessed that a medical technician at the hospital had tipped them off, or even a cop. But if they hadn't, someone else would have. It was to be expected. His phone rang seconds after the news ended. It was Shepard.

"So, we're off and running. Do you have a statement ready?" He sounded tired too. He had spent two hours on the phone with Jamie that night, berating him for getting drunk on campus when he knew the rules, and reminding him that he could still get expelled, although what he was facing was so much worse, if it went badly. He had asked Jamie to be honest with him, and he had sworn to his father that he had had nothing to do with the rape of Vivienne Walker, and he had no idea who did. It made his father all the more determined to get him out of the heat of it, whatever it took, and he still wanted Taylor's commitment that he would help him do it. It turned into another bitter argument before they hung up. Shepard felt that Taylor was being extremely uncooperative and disloyal to their friendship.

"This can't be about friendship, Shep. I have two hundred male seniors to worry about, and if the police get a DNA match on any of them and can tie them to the victim, this is going to be a tragedy, even worse than it already is."

"I don't want my son to be that tragedy," Shepard said, sounding desperate. He and Ellen had been fighting about it all night. She had heard him tell Jamie on the phone to lie if he had to, and she asked Shep what kind of values he was teaching him. She said that if Jamie had had any part in it, he had to face the music like any other student. He couldn't lie his way through life, and pay no penalties for the mistakes he made. That wasn't who Jamie was or who she wanted him to be.

"And do you want him to be writing to you from prison, while you share your morality with him?"

"If he raped a girl, then that's what he should do. What if someone rapes one of the twins one day?"

"Jamie didn't rape anyone!" he shouted at her, then slammed the door in her face, and locked himself in his study. Now Taylor was telling him what he couldn't do to help him. He didn't care if he had to cut an arm off, or move to get Taylor fired, he was not going to let this disaster hit his son and wreck his life. And the girl shouldn't have been drinking tequila with a bunch of boys in the first place. What kind of cheap slut was she? She had probably had sex with them willingly, and then changed her mind afterward. He said as much to Taylor in a subsequent call later that night, but Taylor disagreed with him.

"You're wrong on that, Shep. She's a good girl from a nice family. Her parents are in the midst of a divorce, but they're both fine people and so is she. She didn't deserve this. No woman does. And calling her a slut does not make rape acceptable. Men can't get away with that today. Rape in *any* form is *never* okay, no matter who the rapist is. This should never have happened."

"Well, it looks like the press will be all over it tomorrow. I hired a lawyer today, he's the best criminal lawyer in New York. I'm coming up with him to talk to Jamie in the next day or two, as soon as he has time to do it." Taylor almost groaned, realizing how disrupted campus life was going to be for the next many months, with TV trucks and cameras in their faces, parents coming any time they wanted, lawyers for the boys who were involved to whatever degree, and additional counseling for the students. How were the kids ever going to focus on their studies, and in the seniors' case, apply to colleges? If the worst happened, there would be no college for the boy who had raped her, or anyone involved, or even high school graduation. They would have to get their high school diplomas in prison.

"Let me know when you're coming up," Taylor said, trying to sound calmer than he felt.

The next day, when he woke up, Taylor looked out the window and there were trucks and camera crews from every network in their parking lot. Reporters were walking around the campus, describing it to their viewers and showing glimpses of it on TV. They had no permission to do so, but the parking lot was open. It had never been a problem before.

Taylor and Nicole circulated among them a little while later and gently asked them to disturb the students as little as possible and remain in the parking area. When asked to identify the boys who were currently being investigated, they refused to name them.

"That wouldn't be fair. No one has brought charges against them. In this country, we're innocent until proven guilty. So far, no one has pressed charges against a single Saint Ambrose student." Taylor set the record straight on national network TV.

By that afternoon, everyone was sick of the cameramen and the reporters, but there was nothing anyone could do about them, and if they chased them off the property, it would look like they were hiding something, which was the last thing they wanted. The media was determined to make it one of the biggest stories of the year.

With bad luck and bad planning, Joe Russo, Mike Harris, and Shepard Watts all showed up to see their sons on the same day. Joe and Shepard had brought the lawyers they'd hired for their sons with them. Taylor gave them both conference rooms at Saint Ambrose to meet with their sons, so they'd have privacy. The attorneys were high-powered criminal attorneys, and Mike Harris told Taylor, with tears in his eyes, that if charges were brought against Gabe, he'd have to be defended by the public defender. He couldn't afford to hire a lawyer for him. He assured Taylor that Gabe had his family's full support and they would always be there for him. When Gabe came to meet him in Taylor's office, Mike held him in a powerful embrace and cried like a baby, while Gabe choked on sobs, and told his father how sorry he was that the police were investigating him, and that their stupid Halloween "party" had turned into this. And he said he deeply regretted drinking on campus and had written a letter to the headmaster to that effect.

Joe Russo had the opposite reaction, and right in front of Taylor's entire office staff and whoever was standing there at the time, he hauled off and slapped Rick so hard across the face that Rick fell backward and almost hit his head on a table. His cheek was bleeding where he'd been hit, and then Joe grabbed him by his shirt and almost lifted him off the ground. He was a powerful man and bigger than his son. Taylor intervened immediately. Joe was shaking with rage.

"Listen to me, you little shit. If you *ever* get into this kind of trouble again, I'm going to kill you. Do you understand me?" Rick nodded and looked terrified, and then Joe hugged him and told him that he loved him, and they disappeared into the conference room with the expensive criminal lawyer he'd hired. Joe swore he could get any man off, even if he'd pulled a gun and shot someone in front of twenty witnesses. None of the boys had been charged, but with the police conducting in-depth investigations, both Shepard and Joe wanted to be ready if things went against their sons. And if their sons had committed the crime, both fathers swore they would do anything they had to to get them off. They made it clear that *their* sons would *not* go to prison.

The lawyer Shep had hired was extremely well known and had defended numerous politicians, important people, and celebrities. He looked a little slick to Taylor, but he had a big reputation for success, which was what Shepard wanted, and he was willing to pay any price for it, and so was Joe Russo—they could afford it.

The Yees had sent their lawyer up, an excellent Chinese-American lawyer, and he was very competent.

This time the Morgans couldn't leave the films they were working on, but they'd had their manager hire a very well-known attorney, who was the criminal lawyer to the stars, and Matthew had promised Chase he would come up as soon as he could leave the picture, and the lawyer would come up to attend the police questioning with him.

Bert Babson had refused to hire a lawyer or come up to see his son. He disowned him over the telephone, and said he wanted nothing more to do with him. He told Steve he was a "worthless piece of shit like his mother," and would turn out to be a drunk like her one day, which was how Bert Babson had always treated both of them. He had been physically and verbally abusive to both of them for as long as Steve could remember, and he was afraid of his father. He had seen him beat his mother on several occasions.

The day after Shep and the others had come up, Jean Babson had come to school to see Steve and brought a very serious-looking young attorney with her. She was crystal clear, and made perfect sense when Taylor talked to her. She said Steve had her full support. And when they left, she hugged her son and told him how much she loved him and had faith in him. She whispered to him that she had started going to AA again and already had a sponsor. She'd tried it before and it had never worked, but Steve hoped it would this time. He really needed her to be on point and there for him. She also told him that she had made a decision, which she said was long overdue. She and his father would be getting a divorce. The same attorney she had brought along for Steve was filing it for her. Steve smiled broadly at that piece of news.

"Good for you, Mom! You should have done it years ago."

"It's never too late," she said in her gentle, sweet way. She was only sorry it had taken her so long to do it, and that Steve had seen so much dissent and abuse at home while he was growing up.

Taylor felt like he'd been running a circus all week, or a reality show. He knew that Jamie, Chase, and Rick had gone to the police for questioning with their attorneys.

Through it all, the press was constantly lurking in the background, either in the parking lot or just off school property. Campus security insisted that they keep their distance from the students. In spite of that, Taylor had a flood of calls from assorted parents complaining that their children's privacy was being invaded and studies disrupted by ongoing media coverage on the campus. Several times they had seen their children in the background, or their sports practices recorded, when they watched the nightly news and the continuing drama at Saint Ambrose was reported.

Gillian was being heroic, trying to keep everyone busy and acting normal in the midst of chaos, in an attempt to distract students from the tension and keep everyone's spirits up.

"Where did we hire her from?" Taylor said to Nicole at the end of a particularly harrowing afternoon. "We should have hired two of her, and five of you," he said gratefully. Nicole had been remarkable at sharing the load with him, and he didn't know what he would have done without her, or Charity's discreet support at night, while he tried to catch up on work and she corrected history and Latin homework sitting in his office.

*

Detective Brendan had called to report to Taylor that the remaining three boys had been questioned in the presence of the attorneys their parents had hired, which had mostly amounted to a lot of fancy legal footwork to block any of the relevant questions that he and Detective Martin needed to ask them.

"We pretty much got nowhere," he told Taylor. "Chase Morgan's attorney was semi-reasonable, although he's a superstar and has defended damn near every athlete and movie star who ever got arrested for a felony. The Russo kid's lawyer is lucky Detective Martin didn't shoot him. He is the biggest sexist I've ever met, and treated us like dirt. And Jamie Watts's lawyer made everything as difficult as he possibly could, which I guess is what Jamie's father paid him for. It doesn't make the case any easier.

We're just trying to get to the bottom of this, we're not trying to persecute them."

"I'm really sorry," Taylor apologized. "Fortunately, the boys are a lot easier to deal with than their fathers, although the Morgans are very reasonable people."

"But the kids won't talk to us without the attorneys their fathers hire. We'll get there, it just slows us down a little." They'd been driving Gwen Martin crazy for the past two days, trying to block the investigation at every turn.

*

Vivienne and her family were having their own dramas. Vivienne had made it clear to her mother that she wanted to go back to California with her father as soon as she got out of the hospital. They were keeping her there to rest, get counseling, and avoid the press. Nancy looked hurt when Vivienne said it. She had already arranged to take time off so she could be with her, and had set up an appointment with a trauma therapist in New York who was supposed to be excellent, and specialized in rape victims.

"I want to go home, Mom," Vivienne said firmly, sitting in her hospital bed. And home to her was still L.A. They wanted her to stay for the rest of the week, and then they were planning to release her. She wanted to fly straight to L.A. with her father.

"Home is where we live, Viv," Nancy said sadly. The move to New York had not been a success from Vivienne's point of view. Especially after this. She would always remember with horror her first school experience in the East after they moved.

"Home is our old house and Dad's still living there," she said stubbornly.

"And what about . . ." Nancy glanced at Chris. She didn't want to mention Kimberly's name in front of Vivienne, although she knew he'd been seeing someone, she just didn't know it had been going on for almost three years, and that it was why they'd left and her mother was divorcing him. He had refused to stop seeing Kimberly. Nancy would have taken him back even after finding him in bed with her, but he had said he wasn't ready to give her up. So Nancy had filed for divorce and moved to New York. Out of respect for Chris as Vivienne's father, Nancy had never told her any of it, and Vivienne blamed her mother for the divorce since she filed it.

"I've taken care of it, for the time being," Chris said cryptically, and Nancy nodded.

"I'm not five for heaven's sake," Vivienne said to both of them. "I know you're dating someone. I want to meet her." He wasn't just dating her, they were living together. But he had rented a furnished apartment for her so Vivienne could come back to L.A. with him and recover at their home. He didn't want Kimberly living in the house while Viv was there. Kimberly wasn't pleased about it, but she'd agreed, and the apartment he'd rented for her was fabulous. She could hang out at the house with him when Viv was busy with her friends, and more once she and Vivienne got to know each other. He was hoping they'd become friends.

"And what about school?" her mother asked her. "Do you know what you want to do?"

"I'm done here." Both her parents nodded. They didn't disagree. It would have been too depressing and even traumatic to stay at Saint Ambrose now, with the memories she had there. "I don't want to go back to school for a while. I can catch up in January. I think I want to go back to my old school." However, she hadn't contacted any of her L.A. friends and didn't want to. She didn't want them to know what had happened at Saint Ambrose.

"And stay in L.A.?" Her mother looked disappointed when she nodded. It was a victory for Chris, and what he had wanted in the first place: for Vivienne to stay in L.A. with him until she graduated. And she wanted to apply to college in the West—USC, UCLA, Stanford, UC Berkeley, and UC Santa Barbara.

"I'm sure they'll make allowances for what she's just been through, if she gets behind in her work," he said. To him, it was a done deal. He and Vivienne had been talking about it for the last few days, without her mother present. She wanted Nancy to send her favorite things to L.A., which meant she wasn't planning to come back. It cut Nancy to the core, but she wanted what was best for her, especially now.

"Do they have to know what happened at my old school?" Vivienne asked her father, looking upset.

"Maybe not," her father said vaguely, although he thought they should, so that they'd accommodate her if she was disoriented at first, or her grades fell, which wouldn't be surprising.

"I want you to see a therapist who works with this kind of thing," Nancy said firmly, and looked pointedly at Chris. He wasn't good about following up on psychological issues. Nancy was. And the therapist in New York had said that Vivienne needed to deal with it while it was fresh, and not let it sit and fester or let the nightmares she was having grow steadily worse. "You need to keep up with some school work when you feel up to it, and get all your applications in, or you'll wind up missing your first year of college and have to defer it," her mother warned her, always the unwelcome voice of reason, to her and Chris.

"Maybe she should defer it," Chris suggested, and Nancy glared at him. She could see that he was planning to indulge her and let her sit around the house. With what had happened, Vivienne might get depressed. Her old friends in L.A. would be in school, and she didn't want her to give up college next year by default, by not sending her applications in on time. She needed structure and a routine to follow.

"Let's take this one step at a time, and then see how you feel," Nancy said, trying to slow things down. "Why don't you spend two months in L.A., now till the end of the year, and then make a decision about what you want to do. That gives you two months to hang out with Dad and feel better and start to recover before you make any major decisions. It's too early to decide any of it now." It seemed like a reasonable compromise to everyone, except Vivienne, who said she wanted to stay in L.A. for the whole school year. Chris loved the idea, but he wasn't sure how long he could keep Kimberly at bay in a furnished apartment now that she'd been living in the house with him since June, and loved it. She was already feeling displaced by Vivienne, who was only eight years younger than she was. He felt like he was going to have two daughters on his hands. Both were very vocal about what they wanted. "What about Thanksgiving?" Nancy asked cautiously. Vivienne had already been planning to spend Christmas with her dad, and Nancy had rented a ski house in Vermont with friends for two weeks, but Nancy had been looking forward to Thanksgiving with her daughter.

"If we go when I get out of the hospital, I don't want to come back right away. Can I spend it with Dad?" Vivienne asked innocently, not wanting to upset her.

Nancy reluctantly agreed. She was getting the short end of the stick here, but at seventeen, and after the trauma she'd just had, Nancy was willing to indulge her and do what Vivienne wanted. She wanted her daughter to be happy, and she had uprooted her very quickly when they left in June. She had talked her into coming to Saint Ambrose, and that had exploded like a suicide bomb in their faces now, so she felt obliged to give in to Vivienne to some degree, even if it was hard for her and would leave her alone without family for both of the holidays. Nancy had no family other than Vivienne, and neither did Chris. But he had a girlfriend, and Nancy had no man in her life, only her daughter. But the focus had to be on Vivienne now, and not her parents. Their plans were going to leave Nancy alone for both holidays. Neither Vivienne nor her father was thinking about that, however, and as always, Nancy had to be the bigger person and the adult. She was willing to do it again now, after what Vivienne had been through. She wanted Viv to get over what had happened, whatever it took.

"I think you should try to go back to school in January, and stay on track for college. That's an important goal." She said it to both of them, but she wasn't sure they were paying attention. She was always the voice of reason, duty, and responsibility, which weren't Chris's strengths, but Nancy wanted them to be Viv's, although she was willing to give her a pass right now. She decided to leave them alone for a little while after that, to celebrate their victory: Vivienne would be going back to L.A. with him, which was what both father and daughter wanted. Nancy went to lick her wounds quietly in the hall. She ran into Gwen Martin as soon as she stepped out of the room. She looked tired and exasperated, and Gwen smiled at her.

"Are you all right?" she asked Nancy. "You look sad. Is she doing okay?"

"Pretty much. Some days are better than others. She's been having nightmares, which is to be expected. She's decided to take some time off from school and stay with her father in L.A. for a while, over the holidays too. I just hope she gets back on track in January. I don't want to see her miss a year of college too because of this." Gwen nodded, thinking that the boy who had raped her was going to miss out on college forever. If he went to prison, he might never go back to school, and none of the kind of colleges that any of the boys had planned to apply to would accept them after this. Harvard, Princeton, Yale, MIT, and all the best colleges in the country, which had been a foregone conclusion for all of them, would be out of the picture, if any of them were convicted of rape. The rapist, whoever he turned out to be, would be getting a high school equivalency degree in prison and, if he cared, taking classes online and working in the prison laundry or machine shop. And spoiled rich boys were not popular in prison. The rapist would have hard years ahead of him, in exchange for a night of insanity. But Vivienne would pay the price for it for the rest of her life too, and it wasn't her fault, however much Vivienne doubted herself and blamed herself now, and questioned her own actions, getting drunk with the boys that night. But the boy who had raped her had thrown his life away.

"If the state brings charges, we'll need her back for the trial," Gwen told Nancy, "but that won't be for about a year. She won't have to go to the defendant's routine court appearances before that, unless he pleads guilty, but I don't think that's going to happen. All of the boys' lawyers have been telling us what good boys they are. They probably were, until one of them went nuts on Halloween night, and they all went crazy on tequila."

"Do you really think one of them will be charged with rape?" Nancy asked her. It was hard to believe one of them had done it, given who they were and their flawless histories.

"I don't know. It depends on a lot of things. Whoever is guilty should go to prison. I believe in crime and punishment. They won't learn otherwise, and they'll think they can do whatever they want for the rest of their lives. That's not a good thing." Nancy nodded agreement, thinking about Chris. He had cheated on her and broken her heart, and she had punished him too, by taking his daughter and moving to New York. Now Vivienne wanted to go back to him. So he wasn't punished after all. She had wanted to get as far away from him as she could and start a new life, but Vivienne hadn't been ready for that. Now she had been punished too. Nancy felt terrible about it, and regretted her decision to send her to Saint Ambrose. "I hope everything works out for her," Gwen said gently. "She's young and strong and smart and a nice kid, with good parents. I think she'll be okay."

"I hope so," Nancy said softly.

"Is she with her dad?" Nancy nodded. "I'll come back tomorrow. It wasn't important. Take care of yourself," Gwen said, and meant it. She felt sorry for Nancy too. What the boys had done during their foolish night had broken so many hearts. Almost too many to count with their own families in the mix. They'd never thought of that.

Chapter Ten

When Sam Friedman came to see Adrian, he was sitting in front of the school on a bench waiting for him. It was a beautiful autumn day, and the sun was out, though it was cold, and he'd been sitting there for an hour so Sam would see him as soon as he showed up. Sam had to sign in at a visitors' desk to meet with Adrian, and as soon as he had they went back outside.

Sam was a forty-year-old child advocacy lawyer who did a lot of work for the court, and in the three years he had represented Adrian, he had really come to like him. He was a funny, awkward, incredibly bright kid, and he looked hardly any different than he had at thirteen, although he was now sixteen. His bad luck was that he had crazy parents, both of them shrinks. Spending an hour with either of them was enough to drive Sam insane. He couldn't even imagine growing up in a house with both of them. But fortunately for Adrian, they had very little interest in their son, except to enhance their battles with each other, and they never showed up to see him. He had spent the Christmas holidays with Sam once, because he had nowhere else to go, and Sam felt sorry for him, and got permission from the court and his parents to take him home for a week. They'd had a good time together. Adrian said it was the best Christmas he'd ever had, which seemed pathetic to Sam. He liked him, and thought he was a wonderful boy, but his parents were living proof that even money and education didn't make people good parents.

They walked slowly along a path that wandered through the campus, and sat down on another bench, with no one around to hear them.

"Okay, so tell me what's going on. What's this crime that you committed?" Sam wondered if he had hacked into some major organization or corporation, or even a government agency on the Internet. He could see that happening, but not much else. And if he had done that, he would have done it for fun, not profit. He was an honest kid.

"We had a rape on campus on Halloween," Adrian explained to him, and Sam nodded.

"I know. The whole country knows. It's been all over the news. Please don't tell me you've become a serial rapist." Sam tried not to smile at him.

"No, but I saw them, Sam." His eyes were huge and serious.

"Who?"

"The guys who did it. At least I think I did." Sam was

instantly serious too. This was not a laughing matter, by any means.

"Were they students or people from outside?"

"Seniors."

"Do you know them?"

"Kind of. They don't know who I am. Most of them are the big guys on campus who everyone knows. They're big deal athletes too, some of them. I was at one end of the path, behind the gym. I was sneaking back from the computer lab at midnight. I let myself in. There's a line of trees behind the path, and I saw them all come through the bushes. They were crazy drunk, or very drunk—they kept stumbling and falling and pushing each other, and they were in a hurry to leave. I wondered what they were doing. I don't know why, I was curious, so I shoved my way into the bushes after they left. There's a clearing on the other side, and some big trees. I saw somebody lying there. I thought she was dead. She looked it. It was her. The girl who got raped, Vivienne Walker. I guess she was unconscious. I looked really hard and she wasn't moving at all, I thought she wasn't breathing. I thought they killed her. Then I realized that if anyone saw me there, they'd think I killed her. I didn't touch her. I didn't touch anything. But since I was sure she was dead, I figured it didn't matter if I didn't tell anyone, because she was dead anyway, and I knew someone would find her sooner or later. So I pushed back through the bushes, and ran back to my dorm. It was past curfew for me anyway, and I didn't want to get in trouble. I thought about what I should do, but I was sure they'd find her. And then I heard an ambulance siren a few minutes later.

"The next day we had an all-school assembly, and they said one of the female students had been assaulted. Later I heard she'd been raped. I wasn't sure if it was her. It could have been something else and they didn't find the body yet. Or maybe it was her. And they asked anyone to report it if they'd seen or knew anything. I didn't. I was too scared. I was sure someone would blame me, and if I told anyone about the guys I'd seen, I thought maybe they'd find me and kill me. They're almost all big guys, a lot bigger than me.

"The place where I saw her has been taped off as a crime scene ever since that night, so I guess she's the one who got raped and she wasn't dead. She sure looked it, though. But I do know something. I know who those guys are. If I tell someone now, I'll probably go to jail for withholding information, or obstruction of justice, or something like that. If anyone saw me there that night, the way I saw them, they'll probably arrest me for being at a crime scene, and not getting any help for her. I feel really bad about that. But I thought it was too late, so it didn't matter. She looked really dead, Sam. I promise."

"I believe you, Adrian. First of all, you're not going to jail. Next time you see something like that, you should call 911 and report it no matter what. You could save a life. But she wasn't dead, thank God, and she didn't die. What's important is that you may have seen the guy who raped her, if it was one of them. Maybe they only saw her and thought she was dead too, or they may have been involved in the rape, which is more likely, and you shouldn't withhold information like that."

"That's what I've been thinking, and I wanted to tell someone who they were, and that they were there that night and so was she. But I thought I'd get arrested if I told the police."

"No," Sam confirmed again, "they won't arrest you. And you may help them solve the case, which would be a great thing. Even without my help, you could tell the police, and they are *not* going to arrest you. But I can negotiate this for you. We can tell them that you want anonymity before you tell them, so the seniors won't know that you spoke to the police. I'll go to the police with you. I'm glad you called me. This is really important, you were right about that." He was stunned by the story Adrian had told him. He hadn't expected anything like this.

"They're not going to be mad at me for not telling them sooner?" Sam shook his head firmly. "You don't think they'll accuse me of raping her or trying to kill her?"

"Definitely not. Why don't you let me call the police

and we can go to see them together. They're going to be very grateful for the information. They've been asking for anyone to come forward right on TV."

"Would you do that for me? Call them, I mean? I think I should tell them who the guys are."

"I think so too." He was vastly impressed by what Adrian had said, and his very lucid description of what he'd seen. He had a tendency to get confused sometimes when he was excited, or maybe only when dealing with his parents. But there was nothing confused about what he'd described, and Sam had no doubt that Adrian had seen the rape victim, and possibly one of the boys he'd seen had raped her.

"I was so upset about it that I was sick for a few days, and I've been having asthma attacks again. I really think I'm supposed to tell them, even if I waited a long time. I think the campus police found her, or something like that. They said she was almost dead when they took her to the hospital. So someone saved her. I'm sorry I didn't. I'll know what to do next time."

"That's all that matters, and that you tell them what you know now." Adrian nodded and had looked enormously relieved ever since Sam had assured him he wouldn't go to jail. He believed him. Sam had never lied to him. He was a good lawyer and an honest man.

Sam took his phone out of his pocket then, called information, and asked for the number of the local police station near the school. Then he said "Connect me," the phone rang, and a police officer picked up.

"Hello, I'm Sam Friedman. I'm an attorney. I have a client in the area who has information about the rape case that occurred at Saint Ambrose school on Halloween. May I speak to the officer in charge of the case, please?" He paused then, while the officer gave him the direct phone numbers of the detectives in charge. Sam jotted down two numbers and then called the first number, and a woman answered. She had answered as "Detective Martin," and Sam hoped she didn't think it was a prank. But he continued anyway, after he told her why he was calling. "My client wants a guarantee of anonymity. Are you willing to grant him that?" She hesitated for a minute and then agreed. She was curious who his client was but didn't ask. "Can you see us now?" Sam asked her. Then Adrian heard him say, "That's fine." He repeated his name again because she'd asked him, and he hung up and looked at Adrian. "She said to be there in ten minutes. Do you know where the police station is?"

"Yeah. I think I can find it." They'd driven by it on school outings, although he'd never been inside.

"Then let's go." They both stood up, and Adrian followed him to his car. Adrian debated about telling someone at the school where he was going, but decided not to. They might not give him permission to go, and they would definitely want to know why he was going to the police.

"Will you get in trouble for going off campus without permission?" Sam questioned him, and Adrian shrugged.

"Not really. No one pays attention to what I do. I float all over the campus all the time. And I've been sleeping in the infirmary since my asthma came back, so they don't miss me in the dorm."

"Maybe it will go away again now," Sam said gently. This had obviously been weighing heavily on him. Sam was glad Adrian had called him. He wouldn't have dared go to the police alone. And Sam knew what he'd seen was important.

They found the police station easily and Adrian followed Sam inside. The station was busy, and when Sam asked for Detective Martin, a small woman in jeans and a plaid shirt came out and looked at them. She had wondered if some kid was playing a trick on them, but they were there and Sam looked respectable. He was wearing a suit and tie, since he'd had a brief court appearance before he'd left New York. He had short dark hair and serious, sympathetic gray eyes. There was nothing pompous about him. He seemed warm and sincere, and concerned with Adrian's well-being. He explained that he was a child advocacy attorney in New York and Adrian was his client.

Gwen led the way to the office she was using while

they were there. It was small and cramped, with a pile of files on the desk, and she smiled at Adrian.

"I think I've seen you at school," Gwen said. Adrian nodded; he had seen her too. Sam spoke for him, and said he was a court-appointed attorney and had been assigned to represent Adrian for the last three years on family matters. He handed Gwen his card, and she placed it on her desk.

"Adrian wants to know that he has complete anonymity. He doesn't want to be identified as an informant, but I think he has information you'll be interested in. He's concerned that he didn't report it earlier. He was afraid to, so he contacted me, and I came up from New York. I normally handle family court matters for him, so this is unusual for both of us. It might be new information for you or corroborate the evidence you have." Gwen liked him immediately. Sam was smart and to the point, and she could see that Adrian was terrified. His eyes were huge in his small pale face, and he took a puff on his inhaler while Sam talked. She could also see that he trusted Sam and how kind the lawyer was to him.

"You have asthma?" she asked Adrian directly, and he nodded. "Me too. It's a pain in the ass. I hate it," she said, and he laughed. "Mine got better when I grew up. Yours probably will too."

"Mine gets really bad when I'm anxious," he explained.

"Well, you don't need to be anxious here. We're

grateful for any help you can give us. And I understand if it took you a while to tell us. It's scary coming to the police with information like that. Why don't you tell me what you saw." She was very relaxed as she talked to him, and Sam observed how adept she was with kids. She put Adrian at ease in about two minutes, with an air of kindness and a gentle, friendly way of speaking to him. Sam liked her style.

"I thought you were going to put me in jail because I didn't tell you right away," he admitted, and she smiled at him again.

"No way. My name's Gwen, by the way." Sam noticed her freckles and green eyes and was touched by how warm she was with Adrian.

"I'm Adrian." He sat up a little straighter and felt important and respected in her presence.

"Are you a senior?" He was flattered, and pushed his mop of hair out of his face so she could see him better. He had big sad eyes.

"No, a junior," he corrected her, and then he told her everything he had told Sam, and a few additional minor details. Gwen listened intently the entire time. He gave her all six boys' names. They were their prime suspects, but it corroborated what they already believed, and gave them a witness at the scene at the time of the crime, or just after. It was strong evidence against them. It confirmed to her that Vivienne had not been "fine," as

they claimed, when they'd left. She was deeply unconscious and had already been raped, since the ambulance
came minutes later. And they had left her unconscious
and in extremis. All they needed now was the DNA match.

"This is exactly what we need, Adrian. I can't thank
you enough." He looked worried for a minute again then.

"Will they go to prison because of me?"

"Whoever goes to prison will go because of them and
what they did. You didn't commit the crime. They did,
or one of them did, and the others must have known
about it. And they left her unconscious. We already have
some pretty solid evidence against them, and we're
waiting for some more to come through. But there was
no eyewitness to place them there, or establish how she
was when they left. It's all been guesswork on our part.
This tells us that we're on the right track." He nodded,
and felt less responsible for their fate. "We don't arrest
people unless we have strong evidence against them. We
don't just do it on assumptions."

"It's sad really," Adrian said softly, "some of them seem
like really good guys." He had always admired Jamie
from afar, and thought he looked like a really nice guy,
and he thought Chase was handsome, like a movie star,
and Gabe Harris was really buff. Steve and Rick seemed
kind of stuck up to him, and he didn't see Tommy Yee
very often, as he was always practicing or studying. "Will
they go to prison for a long time?"

"They could. That depends on the judge and how he assesses the circumstances and what happened."

"Is the girl okay now?"

"Yeah, more or less. That's a terrible thing to have happen."

"They were really, really drunk. They could hardly stand up or walk."

"That's not smart either. I want to thank you both for coming in. This is going to help us a lot. I'll type this up anonymously. And I'll keep your contact information and Sam's separate in my safe."

"Will I have to go to court?" He looked suddenly panicked.

"No." And if he did, Gwen knew she could arrange to have him heard in chambers, given his age and his asthma. "If you both wait a few minutes, I'll type this up really fast and have you sign it. Is that okay with you?" They both nodded, and she walked them out to the waiting room and left them there. Adrian looked around at the people who came in and out. He was finding it interesting more than scary now, and whispered to Sam that he would have loved to see what kind of computers they used. Sam smiled. Their visit had gone really well, and Gwen had put Adrian totally at ease. She was back less than ten minutes later. Adrian read and signed his statement, and she handed her card to each of them, with her cellphone number on it, and thanked Adrian again for being brave enough to come in, and for being a responsible citizen. Sam told her that his cellphone number was on the card he had given her, and it was the best way to reach him. Adrian left the station feeling ten feet tall, and pranced around as they walked to Sam's car.

"She thought I was a senior!" he said proudly, and Sam laughed. He had kept her card, and promised himself to call her if he ever went to Boston, where she was based. He hadn't been as impressed with anyone in a long time.

As they drove away, Gwen walked into Dominic's office, and handed him a copy of Adrian's report. He read it and looked up at her.

"I told you, sooner or later, someone always talks." She smiled at him.

"Who was he?"

"A junior at Saint Ambrose. A wonderful, funny, geeky kid. He must have some kind of shit home situation, because he has a child advocacy attorney appointed by the New York courts to protect him from his parents. He was a really nice guy. He drove all the way up from New York to bring the boy in to us. We're almost there, Dom," she said. "When we get the preliminary DNA reports, if one of them is a match we'll have what we need to arrest them for rape, and obstruction for lying to us." He looked at her and they both knew that would only be the beginning. Depending on how they'd plead—probably not guilty—there'd more than likely be a trial, hopefully a conviction, their sentencing, and then the time they'd have to spend in prison. Ruined lives for nothing, and all the suffering of the parents, Vivienne's and their own. Some of them would never recover, especially whichever one had raped her, if that was the case.

"They told me we might have the preliminary report sometime tonight, or over the weekend," Dom said quietly.

"We'll get it when we get it. And then we'll deal with it, and we'll have the press to cope with, and the boys' parents." Neither of them was looking forward to it. There were going to be a lot of bumps in the road, but they were ready for whatever came. If the DNA wasn't a match with the boys, they'd have to start from scratch, looking for the rapist in a broader search. They were ready for that too.

*

Once back at Saint Ambrose, Adrian thanked Sam again for going to the police with him. He felt suddenly free from the burden he'd been carrying for a week, and he could breathe again. Sam hugged him, and a few minutes later he left. As he headed for the road to the freeway, he thought of Gwen, the policewoman. She was a fine-looking woman. But more than anything, for Adrian's sake, and the girl who had been raped, he was glad he had come. Meeting Gwen was just a bonus. He was thinking of everything Adrian had told them as he drove back to New York, wondering how it would turn out and whether one of them had really raped the girl, as unlikely as it seemed at a school like this. In the law, he had learned to expect surprises, and so had Gwen.

Chapter Eleven

Sundays were always quiet on campus. Students used the time to catch up on doing laundry, reading, studying, going to the library. They hung out in small clusters, and the atmosphere was finally calming down. There were only two news trucks left, and they had been relegated to the far parking lot, where they weren't a constant intrusion or an eyesore. No one had forgotten what had happened on Halloween, but it was no longer at the forefront of everyone's mind. New friendships had begun to form between male and female students, and the noise in the cafeteria was loud and jovial. Sports practices were going smoothly. Gillian was pushing the teams hard and expected a lot of them. Adrian moved back to his room in the dorm. He hadn't had an asthma attack since Thursday, the night before he and Sam went to the police. Gwen had sent Adrian and Sam a text to thank them for coming in.

Jamie and Chase were in their rooms. Chase was doing an English assignment that was overdue and having trouble concentrating. And Jamie was in his room next door, staring into space, wondering how Vivienne was doing, but there was no way for him to find out. He had a constant sense now of waiting for something bad to happen, some form of retribution, and wondered if it would be like that forever. His life had become a hell of anxiety and depression. He hadn't spent any time with the others. They were staying away from each other, and every time Jamie saw them in class, at meals or in the gym, it brought it all back to him again. He still hadn't started his essays for his college applications, and no longer felt worthy of the glowing praise he knew his teachers would write for him. He hadn't given them those forms to fill out yet either. He wondered if the others felt the same way he did. Chase didn't want to talk about it, afraid that someone would overhear them. Everything they did now was colored by what had happened on Halloween.

Tommy Yee was in a soundproof room at the music lab, practicing his violin. He was practicing more than he ever had, and playing worse. The violin the school had lent him was of poor quality compared to the one he'd had. It was a lifeless block of wood in his hands, which was how he felt too. He was tired all the time, couldn't sleep at night, and could hardly put one foot in front of the other. He woke up crying almost every morning, remembering what he'd seen, and Vivienne's lifeless form when they left her.

*

The doctors released Vivienne on Sunday morning. Her mother had brought two big suitcases up from New York, with everything she'd asked for—all her favorite sweaters and skirts, and the stuffed pink teddy bear she still slept with at home. Chris had decided that it would be easier to fly to L.A. from Boston than New York. Nancy looked around the apartment before she left New York to go back to the hospital, and realized how depressing it was going to be, knowing that Viv was in L.A. and not coming home. It had been hard enough when she left for boarding school. But if it was better for her to be in California now, Nancy didn't want to stand in her way, and had conceded. Vivienne wanted to put as much geographic distance as she could between herself and everything that had happened at Saint Ambrose. And Nancy was going to visit her in L.A. But knowing she wasn't coming home for the holidays would make it even harder for Nancy. She wondered if this was her payback for tearing her away from Chris too quickly for reasons of her own. You couldn't force things like that. They hadn't made any decisions about school yet. She'd learned her lesson, and wanted to give Vivienne time to decide what she wanted. All Nancy wanted for her now was what was best for her, and for her to be in the best place to recover from what had happened.

Nicole and Gillian had come to see Viv the night before she left. They had brought her a teddy bear, which seemed silly, but Maxine thought it might bring her some comfort. They had purposely not brought her anything with the Saint Ambrose emblem on it. It was easy to imagine that she would want to forget everything about the school and what she had lived through there.

"Girls' volleyball won't be the same without you," Gillian said, and Vivienne smiled at that. She was excited to be going back to L.A. with her dad, but didn't feel ready to see her friends yet. She had finally texted Zoe and Lana and told them she was too busy with midterms and her college applications to write or FaceTime. They had sounded miffed when they answered. Vivienne had decided not to tell them about the rape and didn't want to see them until she was fully recovered. She was too ashamed for them to know. They had asked about the rape at Saint Ambrose when they saw it on the news, and Vivienne had responded that she knew the girl and it was really too bad. They said they were just glad it wasn't her. Her name had never been released to students or the media.

She still had headaches sometimes, and nightmares. She was supposed to see a therapist in California. She just wanted to be back in L.A. and forget her time in the East. Nicole and Gillian hugged her before they left and wished her a safe trip home. In the hall, Nicole reminded Nancy to let them know if there was anything they could do for her or Vivienne, and she promised to keep Nancy abreast of all further developments in the investigation. Nancy nodded and thanked them, and they could both see how sad she was that Vivienne was leaving for L.A.

"Do you think that's the best thing for her, to go back to California with her dad?" Gillian asked Nicole on the drive back to school.

"She's almost eighteen, and it's what she wants. After something like this, it should be her decision," Nicole said quietly.

"Her mom looks so sad." But it wasn't just Vivienne leaving with Chris that made Nancy sad. Knowing the burden Vivienne would carry forever now was making them all sad for her. She had left her recommendation forms with Nicole right before Halloween, and Nicole was going to write a glowing report for her, and several other teachers had said they would too. The drinking incident was going to be overlooked, given the circumstances, and she was leaving Saint Ambrose in good standing, which was the least they could do for her since they hadn't succeeded in protecting her from her fellow students and keeping her safe at school.

*

Chris had put the bags in the car while Vivienne walked out of a side entrance to the hospital. Several security guards stood by in case someone had leaked information, but there was no one there. No information had been given to the press about the victim since the beginning. Vivienne hugged her mother, while Chris watched them. Vivienne just looked like a beautiful young girl, in jeans, a pink sweatshirt, and a denim jacket, standing there with her mother.

"I'll FaceTime you tonight when I get home, Mom." It pained Nancy that she still considered L.A. home, and not the apartment she shared with her mother in New York. But they had only lived there for five months, so it wasn't surprising. She'd lived in L.A. all her life, and now she wanted to turn the clock back and rewind the film to happier times. Nancy would have liked that too—not to be back with Chris, but for none of the bad things to have happened. It had been a hard year for her too.

"I'm going to miss you," Nancy said, with her arms around her. Chris had promised to call the therapist the next day, and set up a schedule with her for Vivienne. They were going to do things together and he wanted her to meet Kimberly and get to know her. He hoped they'd be good friends.

Nancy hugged her one last time, and kissed her, and Vivienne slipped into the car with her father, waved at her mother, and they drove away, heading for Boston. Nancy put her head down and walked to her car for the long drive back to New York. She was sobbing as she turned on the ignition and drove out of the parking lot. Her heart ached for her daughter. She was going to fly out to L.A. to see her soon, but nothing would be the same now without her. And it killed her that she wouldn't be close at hand to help her.

"I can't wait for you to meet Kimberly," Chris said, smiling at his daughter.

"Yeah, me too," Vivienne said, staring out the window as they headed toward Boston. She wondered if Kimberly knew about what had happened, but didn't want to ask him. From now on, she knew that would define everything, whether people knew that about her or not. To Vivienne, it now seemed like the most important thing about her.

*

The phone rang at Taylor's home on Sunday night, just as they were about to sit down to dinner. Charity had prepared a simple meal; neither of them was eating much lately, and Taylor had dropped ten pounds in the last week from the stress he was under. The call was from Detective Dominic Brendan.

"The preliminary report came in an hour ago," he said in a neutral tone. Taylor had been waiting for the other shoe to drop for several days, and now the moment of truth had come. "We'll have a more detailed report after this, but these results tell us what we've been waiting to find out. If it wasn't a match with any of them, we'd know it now, and the boys would be off the hook." Taylor held his breath and waited. The lives of six boys and their entire families would be impacted by the report they were waiting for. "I don't have good news," Dominic said seriously, "or maybe it is good news for Vivienne Walker. We have a match. There's no question. The match is Rick Russo. So they've all been lying to us, protecting him. And Vivienne was too. The others are accessories for being present at the scene, and have obstructed justice by lying about the rape. They all must have known it was him. We notified the circuit judge last week. He's prepared to sign a warrant tomorrow morning. We have it ready for him. I'm sorry, Mr. Houghton, but we're going to arrest all six boys tomorrow. The judge will let the other five out on bail most likely. He may keep Rick Russo in custody if he thinks he's a flight risk, or set a high bail." Taylor knew Rick's father would pay it, no matter how high it was. And no matter how obnoxious Joe Russo was, he felt sorry for Rick's parents. It would be a terrible blow for them. "It should be a relief for the victim's family that the boy who raped her has been identified and will be brought to justice." Taylor couldn't breathe for a minute, his throat felt tight and tears filled his eyes. The lives of six young men were about to change forever, as well as their parents' lives. All would be convicted felons if found guilty, and one of them would be a registered sex offender.

"Will they be tried as adults?" Taylor felt sick at the

news Detective Brendan had just delivered. He knew all the boys well.

"That's up to the judge. It could go either way. The DA will want them tried as adults. The average sentence in the state of Massachusetts, as an adult, is five to eight years. There's no sympathy for rape, even at seventeen, and it plays heavily in the press—a rich boy at a fancy school who thinks he can do whatever he wants, and rapes a girl. She played a part in it too, since she was drinking heavily with them, but no one deserves what happened to her. Juries don't like cases like this. Neither do judges. It's a hot potato and there's hell to pay if there's leniency involved. I'm afraid you've got a mess on your hands."

"I do. Thank you, Detective, and for letting me know tonight. What happens now?"

"We'll get the warrants signed tomorrow morning, and then we'll come to arrest the boys. It's best if you don't warn them. We don't want any of them flying the coop, and I imagine they all have the wherewithal to do that, with their parents' credit cards." He wasn't wrong in most cases, except for Gabe. "This is strictly confidential information, for your benefit, to give you a heads-up."

"I appreciate that. And after you arrest them?"

"They'll spend a day or two in jail, until the arraignment. They can either confess and plead guilty, or plead not guilty, which is most likely what their lawyers will recommend. They can change their pleas later if they want to confess. The judge will set bail at the arraignment, or not, depending on the gravity of the crime. He could release them on their own recognizance, which he may with the others, but not Rick Russo. And about a year from now, we go to trial. It's a long process. The hands of justice move slowly, and their lawyers will do everything they can to slow it down, but they can't put it off forever. The evidence against them is strong. They'd be fools to go to trial, and their attorneys will tell them that too. Some hotshot lawyer may think he can get Russo off. I doubt he can." Taylor could see a tough year ahead of them, for himself, and for the school, but the wheels of justice were already turning. They were in the system now, and they all had to see it through. But he couldn't imagine Rick in prison for five to eight years. It was crushing to think about, although he didn't for a moment deny the gravity of the crime.

"See you tomorrow morning," Dominic said, and they hung up. Taylor went to find Charity, who had put their dinner in the oven to keep it warm for him. He looked gray when he found her in the kitchen.

"They've got a DNA match on Rick Russo. They're going to arrest them all tomorrow. The others will be charged as accessories and with obstruction of justice for lying about it, presumably to protect Rick."

"Are you going to warn Shep?" she asked cautiously.

"I can't. I gave my word to the police. They don't want any of them to run." She nodded agreement.

They sat down together at the kitchen table, holding hands, trying to imagine the tornado that would come next. She turned off the oven and forgot all about their dinner. Neither of them could have eaten a single bite.

Chapter Twelve

Dominic Brendan called Taylor once the warrants were signed, at eleven o'clock on Monday morning. Taylor asked him if he could have the boys waiting for him in his office, rather than picking them up all over the campus, arresting them in their classrooms in plain sight of their classmates, and disrupting the entire school with drama the other students didn't need to see.

"That sounds sensible," Dominic said, wanting to cooperate with him. Taylor had done everything he could to help them, in a calm, intelligent, compassionate way. Dominic had great respect for him, and how he ran the school. It was just unfortunate that something like this had happened. It wasn't entirely unusual. "Just don't inform the boys of why they're there. We don't want anyone making a run for it, and a high speed chase." He was only half joking. Anything was possible, if they panicked when faced with arrest. They both wanted to keep drama to a minimum. What was about to happen was dramatic enough. "We won't speak to the press," he told Taylor, "but once they're in jail, it's open season.

I think the judge may put a gag order on it, because they're minors, but something is bound to leak. It can't be stopped."

"I expect that." He and Charity had talked about it all night. They would just have to batten down the hatches and weather the storm, as she put it.

Taylor called Nicole and asked her to join him in his office, but didn't tell her why.

"Is there some reason why you need me this morning?" she asked him when she got there. "I have a mountain of work on my desk." He sighed in answer.

"I can't tell you, Nicole, but I think we both need to be here. I'm going to bring the boys over in a few minutes." He had checked their schedules, and notified their teachers, and asked them to send the boys to his office. A few minutes later they arrived, in their blazers and uniforms, looking nervous to be summoned to the headmaster's office and wondering what was happening now. He invited them to sit down. He looked serious, but not ominous, and five minutes after the last of the boys walked in, Detectives Martin and Brendan arrived. There were six sheriff's deputies, and three squad cars waiting outside. They had arrived on the campus as discreetly as they could so as not to alert the press or alarm the students.

The boys' eyes opened wide when they saw the detectives walk in to Taylor's office. They wondered if some new evidence had surfaced, or if Vivienne had told them the whole story.

"We'd like to make this as easy as we can," Detective Brendan said to the group. "You're all under arrest," he said to them collectively. "Richard Russo, you're under arrest for the rape of Vivienne Walker on the night of the thirty-first of October, and obstruction of justice in the investigation." He read him his Miranda rights, and then named each of the other five boys, arresting them as accessories to Rick's crime, and also for obstruction of justice, and read them their rights as well. The boys sat silently in shock as the deputies handcuffed them. They used the plastic cuffs, which cut into their wrists. When they got to Tommy Yee, he burst into tears before they even touched him.

"You can't do this to us," Rick Russo spoke up the moment they put the handcuffs on him.

"Yes, we can," Detective Brendan said calmly. "Your DNA test was a positive match with the semen samples on the victim's body taken at the hospital."

"My father will have me out on bail in five minutes," Rick said, full of bravado, and looking angrily from both detectives to Taylor. There was pure rage in his eyes and no remorse.

"Bail won't be set until your arraignment on Wednesday," Brendan told him, unimpressed by what he said. "You'll be in jail until Wednesday," he said, as Chase and

Jamie looked at each other. They were both fighting back tears but wouldn't give in to them. Steve Babson was shaking visibly, and Gabe started to cry as soon as Tommy did. They all had so much to lose.

"I'm sorry, boys," Taylor said somberly.

"No, you're not," Rick shouted at him, with his hands attached behind his back. "You helped them do this."

"We cooperated with the police," Taylor said clearly. "A young woman on our campus, your fellow student, was raped and left unconscious with alcohol poisoning. She deserves all our efforts to find who did that to her. I'm just very sorry that the six of you are the accused. All I wish is justice for her and all of you, if you're not guilty. If you are guilty, the crime can't go unpunished. You were my responsibility while you were here, and so was she. I have known each of you for three years, and have a relationship with all of you. This is a great sadness for me as well, and for your families." He nodded at Dominic Brendan then, who signaled to the deputies to take them away. They all went peacefully, and Taylor and Nicole could see that all the boys were crying when they left. Rick's tears appeared to be of fury, not fear or sorrow, unlike the others. There was a side of him no one had guessed before, even without alcohol.

Brendan came back into the room after he had seen the boys put in the squad cars, and on their way to jail.

Gwen Martin was still with Taylor and Nicole. All three of them looked profoundly depressed.

"What an awful morning," Taylor said, and invited the detectives to sit down for a minute before they left. Nicole had Taylor's assistant bring coffee for the four of them, which no one touched.

"It's going to be a mess now when their parents and attorneys get involved," Dominic predicted, and Taylor nodded. He was going to call and tell them what had occurred in a few minutes. It wasn't a total surprise, given what had happened and the fingerprint matches, and it had included them in the excessive drinking. But this was going to be a shock to their parents, who must have been praying, as they all were, that the DNA didn't match.

"They took it better than I expected," Gwen said quietly. "They're actually nicer than their parents," she said with a sad smile.

"That's often the case," Taylor admitted, thinking of Jamie and Shepard Watts, who had been a beast to deal with since it started, and would undoubtedly be even worse now. Their friendship of three years had dissolved in the last two weeks, and Shep had shown a side of himself Taylor hated to see, which wasn't worthy of him. He was willing to do anything to save his son, no matter who he sacrificed.

"We'll try to get a statement from Vivienne now, once the dust settles a little," Gwen said. "The boys will calm down once they're out on bail, particularly if they have a year until a trial, if they plead not guilty and stick to it. This will all seem unreal to them in a few days. But they're going to have to face it eventually. There's no running away from this. Will you let them come back to school while they're out on bail?" Gwen was curious. Taylor thought about it for a minute and glanced at Nicole.

"We can't. They're innocent until proven guilty here too. But we'll have to suspend them immediately. There's the question of the tequila incident, which is grounds for immediate expulsion here. We'll either expel them or suspend them, but either way, they're not coming back, at least not until they're acquitted at a trial. They can complete the school year on home study, but we won't give them their diplomas until they're acquitted. We won't graduate them if they're convicted. The crime is too serious. And their shot at a top college next year is gone, probably forever, if they're convicted. They'll be felons, and Rick a registered sex offender."

"They can finish high school in prison," Gwen said. With juveniles, she was always somewhat torn between the victims and the perpetrators, because the perpetrators were victims in a way too, through their own fault and foolishness, and because they often didn't fully understand the consequences until too late. But in this case, with an innocent juvenile rape victim, she felt no mercy.

Dominic Brendan stood up then, and Gwen followed suit. "We've got work to do. I imagine their attorneys will be all over us by this afternoon," Dominic said quietly. They left a few minutes later, and Taylor was just about to talk to Nicole when his assistant said that Shepard Watts was on the line and it was urgent.

"Here we go," he said to Nicole, and took the call as she whispered "Good luck!" and left the room. It had been a morning she knew she would never forget. The media would be next. "Hello, Shep. I'm sorry," he said, before Shepard Watts could say anything. They both knew why he was calling. Jamie must have called him as soon as he got to jail.

"If you are, you'll do everything in your power to get Jamie out of this nightmarish mess. I don't know what happened that night and neither do you, but if Rick Russo raped the girl, Jamie was not an accessory and had nothing to do with it. He's a terrific kid, and she must be some kind of slut to have sucked them into this, probably literally, and now he's in jail. I can promise you, Taylor, I'll destroy you and the school if you don't get him out of this and have them drop the charges. The others can burn in hell for all I care." Shepard sounded on the verge of tears, and in fact had burst into tears when Jamie called and said he had been arrested and was in jail. Jamie had sounded surprisingly calm and apologized profusely to his father. Shep had already called the attorney they had hired for Jamie at the time of the fingerprints, and he was on his way there. But he had also told Shepard that he couldn't get Jamie out on bail until it was set at the arraignment, if the judge set bail. He could choose not to, given the gravity of the crime and the charges. It was entirely at the judge's discretion. Shepard had gone ballistic when he told him.

"I want the charges against Jamie dropped!" he shouted at Taylor again over the phone. "Do you hear me?"

"I'd like nothing better than to get them all out of it if they're innocent. It's not in my hands, Shep. It's up to the police. The girl didn't bring charges either. They were brought by the state. This is a serious, violent crime. She was raped. No woman deserves that. She's not a 'slut.' She's a terrific girl. They have a DNA match with Rick Russo, with solid evidence, and they all lied in the investigation. There isn't a damn thing I can do about it. I hate this as much as you do. Everything goes to hell when kids get drunk like that, but not every man or boy commits rape when they've been drinking. Your son didn't, but he covered up the crime to protect his friend, they all did, so now they're all in trouble."

"I'm just telling you, Taylor, I expect you to do something to get the charges dropped against him, or you'll rue the day you met me!" Taylor already did. Shepard's loyalty to his family and his children was admirable, but the evidence couldn't be denied, as his son's attorney had told him too. Shep had demanded that he find some loophole or technicality to get Jamie out of it, and the lawyer had told him that rape was an explosive issue and the court was not likely to be sympathetic to any of them. The public outcry would be considerable. And whatever the judge did would go viral. Jamie had to go through the normal proceedings like everyone else: waiting for the arraignment on Wednesday, pleading guilty or not, arguing to convince the judge to set bail despite the violence of the crime he was accused of being an accessory to, paying his bail, and then building the case to go to trial. Or, if Jamie admitted guilt to being an accessory and lying to the police, trying to get the best deal they could for him to plea-bargain the sentence and have the charges reduced, if the judge and district attorney were willing, which was unlikely in the current climate. There was no mystery or magic to it. Jamie Watts was in a very serious situation, as they all were, and no amount of threats or shouting at Taylor was going to change that. Jamie understood that far better than his father.

*

When the boys arrived at the jail, looking frightened, they were fingerprinted again, their mug shots were taken, and a police officer told them to take their clothes off and put them in plastic bags with their names on them. They were strip-searched, and a cavity search was performed by another officer. The boys looked horrified by the time they were taken to three cells and put two to a cell in orange jumpsuits, with rubber flip-flops. Their valuables and wallets had been inventoried and checked in. Three of them were wearing Rolex watches, and two of them Tag Heuers, which were their prize possessions. They were each allowed to call their parents, and the conversations had been brief and agonizing. There had been tears on both sides.

Chase and Jamie were assigned to the same cell. Chase had called his lawyer instead of his parents, since his mother was in the Philippines on location in the jungle somewhere finishing a movie, and Matthew was both the star and the director of the film in Spain. Chase knew there was no way he could leave. The attorney said he would be at the arraignment. Gabe had filled out a piece of paper, requesting the services of the public defender.

"Shit," Jamie said, looking at Chase. "We're fucked."

"Maybe not," Chase said quietly. "A lot could happen between now and a trial." He seemed resigned to what had happened to them, after the initial shock. And in a way, he felt they deserved it. Rick was still mouthing off that his father was going to get him out, but they had been clearly told that bail would be set at the arraignment, and they weren't going anywhere until then. They were all within talking distance of each other, but none of them felt like talking. They had two days to wait for the arraignment, in the narrow cells, each one equipped with a bunk bed with a paper-thin mattress, a set of sheets they'd been handed that were frayed, stained, and thread-bare, a towel, a filthy pillow, a military surplus blanket, an open toilet that was badly stained too, and a small sink. They were taken to shower once a day, and to the cafeteria with the other prisoners for meals. For now they were being charged as adults, not juveniles, although that could change. There were about sixty men in the jail at the time. Most of them looked like drug dealers and a few like hardened criminals. They stuck out like neon signs as the rich boys they were. Even Gabe had that look by then, with his clean-cut appearance and short hair. He bumped into one of the men on the food line, and the man turned around and barked at him to watch who he was pushing. Gabe apologized and shrank away from him. None of them were equipped to cope with the setting they were in, or the people in it.

By the time their lawyers showed up the next day, the boys looked tired and badly shaken. Each of them would be represented by his own lawyer. The public defender who came to see Gabe was in a hurry and told him that the arraignment was standard procedure, and to plead not guilty. They could always alter it later. She said she had been assigned to the arraignment, but wouldn't be handling the matter for trial, since she was pregnant and would be on maternity leave by then. The six of them looked like lost boys as they sat in their cells the night before the arraignment.

Steve Babson's mother had come up to see him that day and was staying at a motel. The other parents would all be there the next day with the attorneys, except Chase's parents and Steve's father. The lawyer had advised Matthew and Merritt by email that Chase had been arrested and was in jail. Chase could imagine how they felt and what a disappointment he was to them. Tommy skipped meals and stayed in the cell, and kept saying that his parents were going to kill him.

There was a surreal quality to the whole experience. The next morning, they were handed their own clothes, which consisted of the school uniform they would be allowed to wear to court. The cops at the jail didn't expect to see them again, since they were sure their parents would post bail and the judge would set it. Only Gabe knew that his parents wouldn't be able to, so after the arraignment he would be in jail alone, without the others, which was terrifying. Without bail he would have to stay in jail until the trial, for about a year, unless his lawyer arranged for a plea bargain, in which case, things would move more quickly.

They were brought up to the level of the courtroom in a service elevator, in metal handcuffs, which were removed just before they entered the courtroom, and four sheriff's deputies stood close to them, ready to grab them if they ran. They were much too frightened to go anywhere, and shuffled to the defense table where their attorneys waited for them, crowded together, a line of the most expensive legal help available. Gabe's pregnant public defender looked harried and didn't speak to the others. Four of the lawyers were conferring quietly, except Tommy's lawyer, who was at the end of the row and sat slightly apart. The boys each took a chair next to their attorney, and sat quietly. All of their attorneys had told them to plead not guilty, which they could always change later, unless they were prepared to make a full confession now, but they were advised against it. The lawyers had told them that the arraignment was merely a formality to bind the matter over to trial. How they pled, guilty or not, was less important and could be reversed later.

They turned and saw their parents in the front row then, which nearly reduced all of them to tears. Joe Russo looked stern in a black suit with a white shirt and black tie. He looked like he was going to a funeral and felt like it. Rick's mother was wearing a black Chanel suit and a black mink coat, and kept dabbing her eyes, and blew a kiss to Rick when he turned to see her. Shepard was wearing a serious dark gray suit and looked like the banker he was. Ellen was wearing slacks and a sweater with her hair tied back. She was pale, couldn't stop crying, and was holding Shep's hand. Shep looked angry, and glanced around the courtroom accusingly as though everyone there was to blame for the predicament his son was in. Jean Babson was alone, simply dressed and unpretentious, and she smiled encouragingly at Steve when he turned to see her, which only made him feel worse. Both Harrises had come, wearing jeans and looking devastated. Tommy's parents looked dignified in business clothes, and sat stone-faced, staring straight ahead, and made no sign of recognition to their son when he turned to see if they were there. He wished they weren't. And Chase's parents hadn't come, as he knew they wouldn't. His attorney had shown him a text meant for him from his father, saying only that he loved him and would see him on Thanksgiving, and that he knew he was in good hands with the attorney. His mother had sent a text saying only to remember that she loved him, no matter what.

Taylor and Nicole were in the row behind the parents.

There were two assistant district attorneys at the table for the state, since there were so many defendants, and both detectives from Boston sat with them.

Everyone stood up when the bailiff shouted "All Rise!" and a second later, a female judge walked in. She was in her sixties, had gray hair, and frowned as she looked at the lineup of defendants and their attorneys. She shook her head, a clerk read off the charges, and the judge told everyone to be seated. She glanced at some papers she had in front of her, which included the report from the police.

"Do we have any motions?" she asked the assembled company formally, and Jamie's impressive New York attorney stood up and addressed the judge.

"I'd like to move that the charges against my client be dismissed, Your Honor," he said respectfully. "My client has been swept up in the net of accusations against the others. He didn't see the crime occur and had no awareness of it." It was a pro forma attempt at dismissal, which Taylor was sure Jamie's father had demanded of him. The judge was clearly not impressed and denied the motion, but Shep looked satisfied that he had at least tried.

"Counselors, these are grave charges we have before us today." She addressed Jamie's attorney and the others. "A young woman, a minor, was taken advantage of and raped. The other defendants are charged as accessories, with obstruction. I am not now going to dismiss any charges against these young men, pending further investigation. Let's not waste time on futile motions to dismiss," she said clearly. "How do your clients plead to the charges?" she asked formally, and she read off their names and charges. "Will each of the defendants rise as I call your names, and tell me how you plead."

She went down the list and each of the boys stood up and said "Not guilty" in the strongest voice they could muster, except Tommy, who spoke in barely more than a whisper. Taylor shuddered slightly, thinking that it was the first time that young men wearing Saint Ambrose's uniform had been charged with felonies associated with a violent crime. It was not a proud day for the school, or for them, or for him as headmaster.

The judge looked at a calendar then, and set their next court appearance for December 18. "You can make any motions you wish to then. And that will give counsels time to study the case. Court will adjourn the day after until January 2." It was the boilerplate of the law, and all the attorneys knew that there would be many delays and continuances until they got to trial, if they didn't change their pleas before then. It all depended on the strength of the evidence, what the attorneys advised, and the deals they were able to make with the district attorney, if they were even willing to make a deal in a case like this. But it was in the best interest of all concerned to avoid a trial. Juries were unpredictable, and trials cost the taxpayers money, which the state preferred to avoid. And a rape trial would not win sympathy for the defendants. If they went forward with it, with separate counsel for each boy, it would take months to prepare, and would be a circus in the court-room and the media.

"I am going to set bail," the judge said, looking at each of the boys, "and I am quite sure, looking at the number of legal counsel I see in front of me, that money is not an object, and your families will be happy to pay whatever it takes to get you out of jail. But I want you to realize the seriousness of the charges," she said, looking sternly at the defendants. "This is not a light matter that your parents can buy you out of. If you violate the conditions of bail in any way, I will put you in jail, without bail, and keep you there until trial. I'm setting bail at two hundred thousand dollars each for five of the defendants," she read off their names, "and five hundred thousand for Richard Russo, accused of rape and obstruction of justice." She rapped her gavel then, and moved on to the next case, as the entire defense table stood up to make room for the next defendant.

"Can we go home now?" Steve asked his attorney, and he explained to him that they all had to go back to jail until someone posted their bail. He nodded and smiled at his mother. Gabe was looking longingly at his parents, since he knew there was no way they could post bail, and he would have to remain in custody for the next year. All of the attorneys were relieved because they'd been afraid that the obvious show of money would lead to a bail of a million dollars for each of them. They thought the judge had been reasonable in the circumstances. The deputies led the boys away before they could speak to their parents, and five minutes later they were in the elevator on their way back to jail. The attorneys and parents left the courtroom together and conferred outside in the hall, while the lawyers explained what they had to do next to get the boys released. The Harrises were planning to visit with Gabe at the jail before they left that afternoon, since they couldn't post bail. Joe Russo heard them talking about it, and said something to his wife.

It had all gone as they had been told it would. They were planning to pick up their sons, and then pick up their sons' belongings at Saint Ambrose, as they had been asked to do. Tommy's borrowed violin would stay at the school; his own was still with the police, as evidence for the trial.

They had all been told that the boys could not return to school until the matter was resolved, if then. It depended on individual circumstances, an acquittal from the charges, and the final decision of the school disciplinary board about the drinking incident. Their senior year was over for all of them, and it was unlikely that any of them would return to Saint Ambrose. They were not going to be allowed to say goodbye to their teachers and friends. It had come to an ignominious end. Their belongings had been packed and were waiting for them at the administration building, and could be picked up as soon as they left court. Whether or not their prorated tuition would be refunded had not been determined yet, and would be decided by the board.

All of the boys' parents went to the cashier after they left their attorneys, and posted bail. The Harrises hadn't come with them, and Joe Russo quietly posted bail for Rick, and Gabe as well. He couldn't bear the thought of the boy languishing in jail for a year, pending trial, with all the dangers that represented for him, because his parents were unable to post bail. He was sure he wouldn't run away. He had been a good kid until then, and he and Rick were friends. It was a generous gesture.

When the boys were released, Gabe said goodbye to the others, resigned to staying alone in jail.

"You too," a frowning deputy from the jail said. "All rich boys go." He was sure they'd all get off with lots of fancy footwork by their attorneys in the end, except possibly for Rick Russo.

"I'm not a rich boy," Gabe said solemnly. "There's a mistake. My parents didn't post bail."

"Well, someone did. We got the paperwork. Out. Go." He pointed to the doors, and Gabe looked confused as he followed the others out. He was sure it was a mistake and they were going to grab him by the neck and drag him back any minute, but no one said anything as he left, and their parents were all waiting for them outside the jail. Joe Russo smiled when he saw him, and he spoke to Gabe in an undervoice.

"We're not letting you rot in jail, son. Just behave yourself, and don't go anywhere. I think your parents are in the coffee shop across the street."

"You paid my bail, sir? I can't let you do that." Gabe looked shocked and grateful.

"Yes, you can. Now stay out of trouble, go find your parents, and go home. See you in court, as they say." He smiled and turned his attention to Rick, as Gabe ran across the street to find his parents. They were stunned when he walked in, and his mother burst into tears when he told them what Rick's dad had done.

"That was a really nice thing to do, Dad," Rick said with a grateful look, as his father gave him a hug. Joe brushed it off.

"Let's go home. We're meeting with your attorney tomorrow to see what he can do to get you out of this mess. And I have an idea I want to discuss with Taylor Houghton."

The group disbanded quietly, promising to call each other once they were home. None of them had made any firm plans yet, but they had to find jobs, or a way to fill their time in the coming months, and they had their homework to keep up with for Saint Ambrose so that they could eventually receive their diplomas if they were acquitted. They got into their parents' cars, headed for school to pick up their things, and after that drove to New York, infinitely grateful to be out of jail. Chase rode home with Jamie, and exceptionally was going to be allowed to stay at his parents' New York apartment, until they came back and he went to L.A. with them. They were due back in the next two weeks, and his attorney had signed responsibility for him until his parents' return.

Their departure from Saint Ambrose was brief and dry. They picked up their things, feeling like criminals and outcasts, and then left quietly. All of them were silent on the drive home. The past two days had been a harrowing experience. Tommy Yee's parents did not say a word to him on most of the drive home, just as they hadn't in court. The only thing his mother said was that he would be working full-time in the mailroom of her accounting firm and he was to practice his violin for three hours every day. They were going to rent one for him. At least they hadn't disowned him completely, which he had feared. And after that, they said not a word.

Joe Russo called Taylor Houghton the next morning, to share the idea that had come to him. It seemed like an ideal solution, and he wanted Taylor to broker the deal.

"It's very simple. We'll never really know what happened that night. And the girl should be compensated for her pain. I don't know what kind of girl she is, and you have to wonder about a girl who's willing to get drunk with six young guys. Maybe she wanted that and got more than she bargained for. She's certainly no innocent little angel either. I'd like to offer her a million dollars, in trust for her until she reaches eighteen, if she will drop the whole thing, and deny the charges against the boys." Taylor almost groaned when Joe outlined the plan, which was so typical of him. To Joe, there was no problem which could not be solved with money, no person, in his opinion, who could not be bought, including a girl who had been raped and left unconscious by six boys.

"I'm pretty sure what you're suggesting is illegal, Joe. It's bribery in some form, I can't put the school in the middle of that. I also think that she and her family would be deeply offended by it. They're not in any financial need. Her father is a successful real estate developer. But above all, you can't buy off an experience like that. How do you put a price on how this is going to affect her for the rest of her life?"

"Five million then. Or ten. I really don't care. I'm not letting my son go to prison, and ruin the rest of *his* life. Everybody has a price, Taylor. Find out what hers is. She could be set up for life, in exchange for his freedom."

"She didn't press charges, Joe. The state did. This isn't in her hands either. Even if she wanted the charges to be dropped tomorrow, I don't think the state would do it, not with fingerprints and a DNA match to back it up. The boys are all trapped in the wheels of justice now. It's not in her control. I think that if they complain to the police about your offer, you could wind up in trouble and facing charges yourself." There was silence at the other end for a minute as Taylor's words sank in.

"You won't consider it?" Joe sounded deeply displeased.

"I can't. And neither should you. You just have to do the best you can with good legal counsel, and see what happens. I'm sorry I can't help you out. I heard about what you did for Gabe Harris though, that was an incredibly kind, generous gesture." Joe Russo wasn't a bad man, he just had skewed values, and loved his son.

"I was happy to do it." He thanked Taylor for his time then, and hung up. Five minutes later, a registered letter arrived for Taylor.

It was from Shepard Watts, a scathing letter about how little Taylor had done to help his son, and announcing that he was resigning from the board. Nicole saw him reading it, with an unhappy look on his face.

"Bad news?" she asked, concerned. They'd had enough of that recently.

"Another letter from my fans. Shep Watts just resigned from the board, and withdrew his daughters' applications for next year."

"To tell you the truth," she said, "I'm relieved." He sat back in his chair and smiled at her with a sigh.

"To be honest, so am I." The Wattses were now history at Saint Ambrose, and it was a sad way to leave. But in spite of everything, he wished Jamie well. He was basically a good boy. Better than his father, who was willing to bury everyone, even destroy them, to get what he wanted. He had a feeling that Jamie was better than that. At least, he hoped so.

Chapter Thirteen

After the arraignment, while the media went crazy over Saint Ambrose and the rape case—they were calling the boys "the Saint Ambrose Six"—Dominic and Gwen cleaned up their files, tied up some loose ends, and headed back to Boston. They would come back for subsequent court appearances, but for now, the most crucial part of their job there was done, and they could go home. They were satisfied with their work, and the results. The rapist had been identified and arrested. But none of the boys, and certainly not Rick, had fully come clean about the events of Halloween night. They knew that the six boys had been there, and Vivienne with them, and that they had got drunk together. Rick had pled not guilty at the arraignment, but the DNA match with Vivienne made it clear that he had raped her, and the evidence against him would be undeniable in trial. The other boys' degree of guilt as accessories was still questionable and none of them, including Vivienne, had made a clean breast of it about that night. She didn't want to be responsible for sending the other boys to prison. Their attorneys had told them to plead not guilty. Vivienne thought that Rick deserved to go to prison, but she felt sorry for the others. Rick had put all of them in an untenable position when he raped her that night. Gwen still wanted to know what had really happened, beyond Rick forcing himself on Vivienne. The degree of the other boys' guilt as accessories to rape still hadn't been determined and none of them were talking, on advice of counsel, and Vivienne was refusing to talk too, except to admit Rick had raped her. She was clear about that. Gwen had an idea, which she shared with Dominic on the way back to Boston.

"With the DNA matches in the preliminary report, and Adrian Stone's statement, what do you think if I take a stab at it with the victim again? Now that the boys have been arraigned, she won't feel so responsible if she tells the truth. The process has been started based on the evidence we have without a solid statement from her, or even the truth. We might be able to push them into changing their not guilty pleas with a real statement from her. We still don't know what the other boys did that night, other than drink themselves blind."

"You might get something, or you might hit a stone wall again, but I agree with your reasoning. I thought she went back to California with her father?"

"She did. That's why God invented airplanes, so we can go to see victims in other cities." He glanced over at her and grinned. It had been a very full two weeks, and he was looking forward to getting back to Boston and going to a Patriots game, and a Bruins hockey game or two, in his comfortable bachelor's life.

"Are you looking for a Southern California vacation?" Dominic teased her.

"Of course." She laughed, but they both thought the time might be right to reach out to Vivienne again, and the DNA reports and the arraignment might make a difference, now that their being prosecuted didn't all rest on her.

"Why don't you check upstairs and see if they'll let you go. Do you need a sidekick? I could use a California vacation too."

"No, thank you, Detective Brendan, I'll be fine on my own." He hadn't expected to join her. Gwen could deal with it herself. He was just teasing her.

She waited a few days after they got back to ask her superiors, and they were willing to let her fly to L.A. for a quick trip if she thought it would be helpful to solidify the case against the five other boys. She booked a flight without calling Vivienne or her father. She thought the element of surprise might work better. Her instinct told her that she'd get farther with Vivienne if she kept it seemingly casual and just happened to be in town for a few days on some other pretext.

*

For the first few days after Vivienne got back, everything felt wonderful. She loved being in their house, and back in her familiar bed. Her father went to work all day, and their housekeeper, Juanita, was thrilled to see her, loved fussing over her, and was surprised that she was back before Christmas. Neither Chris nor Vivienne told her what had happened. She sensed that something had gone wrong, either with her mother or at school, but didn't ask. There were little signs around the house that told Vivienne that Kimberly was more entrenched in her father's life than he had told her. She opened one of his closets, and another one that had been her mother's, and found it full of women's dresses and sexy platform shoes. Juanita saw her checking it out, rolled her eyes, and didn't comment. She missed Vivienne and her mother, and thought Vivienne's father had gone a little crazy after they left.

A week after she'd gotten there, Vivienne was starting to get bored, as she hadn't yet seen her friends. Mary Beth had sent her a nice text from Saint Ambrose that she missed her, and Vivienne was surprised that she missed her too. There was no one else at Saint Ambrose that she wanted to stay in touch with. She wanted to leave it all behind. She thought about Jamie and Chase at times, but too much had happened and she knew they'd never be friends now. They had both gone back to New York. And after the trial, they'd be in prison if they were convicted.

She went to the therapist her father had found for her but didn't like her. She wanted to talk about the rape all the time, which made Vivienne uncomfortable and the nightmares had gotten worse. The headaches were almost gone. She was avoiding her friends because she was still ashamed and didn't know what to say, or how to explain why she wasn't in school. At best, they'd think she'd been expelled, which was a disgrace too. But admitting to getting raped was worse.

Vivienne was lying by the pool one afternoon. She didn't read because she had trouble concentrating, so she bought magazines and flipped through them. The phone rang and she answered, thinking it was her father, since no one else knew she was home in L.A. She was surprised when it was Gwen Martin. Viv thought she was in Massachusetts. She had used her Boston cellphone to make the call.

"So how does it feel to be back in L.A.?" Gwen asked her.

"Okay. I haven't seen my friends yet, but it's nice to be home." She sounded quiet and a little down, which didn't surprise Gwen. Her parents had been notified of the arraignment, so she knew that Vivienne was aware of it. "How did everything go in court?" she asked quietly.

"About the way you'd expect. They all pleaded not guilty. It's a formality. It won't go to trial for about a year. It's liable to give them a false sense of freedom, as though it's never going to happen, and then it will hit them. They all had to leave school, so I guess they're all at home now." She wondered if kids in their world would be expected to get a job of some kind since they weren't in school. "I'm in L.A. for a couple of days. I was wondering if I could come over and talk to you, since I'm already here." Vivienne hesitated for a moment while she thought about it, and then answered in a small voice.

"I guess so."

"Can I come by this afternoon?"

"Sure. I'm just hanging out. My dad's at work all day." She was lonelier than she had expected to be. She didn't feel like going downtown, and it was no fun going out without friends. She missed her mother, but not New York.

Gwen came over at three o'clock. She was wearing a denim skirt and a T-shirt and her red hair was loose, which made her look younger. Vivienne was in shorts. They walked back out to the pool. It was a big, beautiful, Spanish style house in the Hollywood Hills. They had an impressive art collection, the house was handsomely decorated, and the pool was huge. They poured two Cokes at her father's bar, and went outside to sit down. Gwen thought Vivienne looked better than she had in the hospital, but there was a sad, haunted look in the girl's eyes that worried her.

"Is everything okay with you?" she asked, and Vivienne nodded.

"It seems weird being back here and not at school," she admitted. It gave her too much time to think.

"Are you going back to your old school when you feel better?"

"Maybe. I haven't decided yet. I feel like I don't belong anywhere now. I used to FaceTime with my friends here all the time when I was at Saint Ambrose, but I haven't talked to them since . . . everything happened. I don't feel ready to see them yet. I don't want to have to explain to them why I'm not in school. And if they knew why, I'd feel like a freak. I'm still texting with one of the girls at Saint Ambrose. The school told everyone that I left because I had mono, but they know the truth. It wasn't hard to figure out when I disappeared, and then the boys got arrested. And at least I don't have to explain anything to Mary Beth." But without school now, she felt lost and rudderless, and didn't like it. "I kind of miss my mom too. My dad is pretty busy. And he has a girlfriend I haven't met yet." She didn't know why she was telling Gwen so much about her life, but she had no one else to talk to, and Gwen was a familiar face now, in a place that suddenly felt unfamiliar. Vivienne had thought it would be different. Or maybe she was different. "I'm still working on my college applications. It gives me something to do. I'm going to apply to a couple of East Coast schools too." That was a new decision for her. "What are you doing out here?"

"Working on a case, so I thought I'd call you. There's something I wanted to ask you, since everything doesn't rest on you now, Viv. The DNA report made a big difference, and a student at Saint Ambrose saw the boys leaving the scene and came forward and made a statement." Vivienne looked surprised at that. "Whatever happens, the state is going to go forward with the charges, so it's not all resting on you. I wondered if you might want to tell me now what really happened that night and get it behind you. No games, no bullshit, no covering up for them. It's going to come out sooner or later."

"Will I have to testify at the trial?" She was worried.

"You might. The state can subpoena you as a witness, even if you don't want to be one. But the judge and jury could hear you in chambers. And there may never be a trial," she said. "They may decide to plead guilty before that. It would be the smart thing to do, if the evidence is too strong against them. That's probably what their attorneys will tell them. They'd be better off pleading guilty and trying to make some kind of a deal, if the state is willing. You're not sending them to prison if you tell the truth and make a statement. You're just saying what happened. The DNA match speaks for itself, and tells the story anyway." Vivienne nodded. "The boy who made the eyewitness statement had been having asthma attacks until he came to us. I'm not telling you you'll feel great after you tell me the whole story, but it might be the beginning of healing, and putting this behind you." Vivienne nodded again. She wanted that, she just didn't know how to do it yet. She was trying to figure it out herself.

"The nightmares keep getting worse," she admitted. Gwen sat quietly, waiting, and then Vivienne started talking. It all seemed like a dream now, it seemed so unreal. She didn't know why she'd drunk the tequila with them or why she'd stayed. And she was so drunk when Rick forced himself on her, and it was so unexpected, that she didn't even know how to react. She remembered someone pulling him off her, and Jamie punching Rick in the face, and then everything went black when she passed out from the tequila. The whole night was a blur now and she was sorry she'd ever been there. She'd felt dirty ever since the rape. It made her feel sick whenever she thought about it, and Rick's face on hers.

It all sounded so banal now, and so stupid, except for the rape. One night had changed all their lives forever. Vivienne wondered if she'd ever feel the same again. She told Gwen everything she remembered. It was all very disjointed. The boys had all been nice to her, except for Rick. And when she finished, Gwen knew she had told the truth. They were just kids breaking the rules and doing something stupid. It was Rick who had changed everything, for all of them, and Vivienne most of all. She felt grown up now, but not in a good way.

"I wanted to go out with Jamie, and we probably would have," she admitted. "But Chase is so hot and so good-looking. I was flattered that he liked me. Maybe I even wanted to make Jamie a little jealous. I never even looked at Rick. I heard the others shouting at him when I passed out." Whatever had happened, the whole dynamic had been spurred on by the tequila. It was Rick who turned it into something evil and dirty. He had a violent streak none of them had ever suspected. And she had paid the highest price of all.

"I hope he goes to prison." She felt guilty saying it, but was honest with Gwen.

"I'm sure he will," Gwen said quietly. "Would you sign a statement about what you told me today?" Vivienne nodded. There was no point lying anymore. They'd all been arrested. And what happened next wasn't up to her. A judge and jury would decide.

"At first, I wondered if it was my fault, if I did something to make it happen."

"You didn't," Gwen reassured her. "Alcohol makes people do stupid things, but it doesn't turn a good guy into a rapist, and neither did you. Rick had that in him. The other boys didn't. It was just very bad luck for you that you crossed paths with him. But you can be sure of one thing: what happened wasn't your fault."

"I wasn't sure at first, but I believe that now." Vivienne looked peaceful when she said it. She wanted to put it behind her. And it was a relief to hear Gwen say it. "I'm sorry I didn't tell you the truth in the beginning. At first, I thought they'd come back and kill me if I told you. Then I started to feel sorry for them, and I didn't want to ruin their lives and send them to prison. After that, for a while I believed it was my fault."

"That's a classic female response to rape," Gwen said quietly, "and all of those reactions you had are normal. But the bottom line is that Rick did a very, very bad thing to another human being and committed a violent crime, and he has to be accountable for his actions. I'm sure his parents don't want him to go to prison, or the others, and they've got the money to hire good lawyers for them. But in the end, none of that changes what he did to you. You did the right thing telling the truth now." What she said also made the other boys' actions seem more benign. Their big mistake had been lying about it afterward, and not turning Rick in. It would have been different for them now if they had. They had tried to stop Rick; it was just too late. They were watching Chase and Jamie fight and didn't see him do it. "I have my computer in the car. If I write this up, and you look at it and agree with it, can we print it and you can sign it for me? You'll be done with it then. You don't have to keep running it through your head, wondering if you 'made' him do it. You didn't *make* him do anything," Gwen reminded her. Vivienne nodded in answer to her question.

"You can use my printer," she said softly. She didn't feel guilty about telling the truth now, or wrong. She didn't feel elated, or suddenly free, but some part of her felt relieved, as though she had gotten a jagged rock off her back that had been crushing her. She couldn't breathe whenever she thought about it, and now she could, like the boy with asthma Gwen had told her about.

Gwen was back in a few minutes, wrote it up quickly on her computer, and showed it to Vivienne.

"See if that looks right to you." Vivienne read it, and when she did, she realized how terrible what he had done to her was.

"That's what I said," Vivienne said simply.

"Did I forget anything, or did you?" Vivienne shook her head. They went to her bedroom then, and used her printer, and Vivienne signed it. "Do you want me to leave a copy with you?" Gwen asked, but Vivienne shook her head. She knew the story. She didn't need to read it again, and didn't want to. "Thank you for doing it," Gwen said. "It's the right thing to do."

"I know it is. Thank you. I'm glad I did it."

"Something tells me you'll sleep better tonight." Gwen smiled at her and they walked slowly to the front door. They both knew that they had done what they were meant to do, and then Vivienne looked at her.

"Did you really come out here to see me and not on some other case?" Vivienne asked her with eyes full of innocence. Gwen didn't like lying to the kids she worked with, especially not the victims, who had to learn to trust other humans all over again after what they'd been through. It was the ultimate abuse of trust, particularly if they were raped by someone they knew.

"Yes, I did come to see you," she said truthfully, and Vivienne looked impressed.

"I guess it really is important."

"It is. Very important, for you, for us, and for them. It's another piece of the story, like a puzzle."

Gwen hugged her before she left, and then Vivienne went to her room and lay down on the bed. She felt lighter somehow, as though a great weight had been lifted from her. She told her father about Gwen's visit when he came home, and he looked at her seriously.

"I'm glad you did that, sweetheart. I was hoping that you would." They'd been wanting a statement from her since it happened.

"I'm glad I did it too. It sounds like Rick is going to prison anyway, and he should." She could see that now, and say it without remorse. And she was glad her father thought giving a statement was the right thing too. That meant a lot to her. Then he turned to her with a smile.

"I have a surprise for you. Kimberly is coming over for dinner tonight. I'll order some Mexican food from our favorite restaurant. She's dying to meet you." Vivienne wasn't sure if she was ready to meet Kimberly or not. She felt slightly disloyal to her mother doing so, but she didn't want to disappoint her father.

He ordered their favorite meal from the Mexican restaurant nearby, and Kimberly showed up at eight o'clock wearing a skin-tight white sweater dress that was startlingly short, and high-heeled white platform shoes. She was a beautiful girl; she'd been a model briefly, and worked in a dress shop on Rodeo now. She beamed when she met Vivienne.

"Your dad has told me so much about you," she said, and went to help herself to a glass of wine, came back barefoot and snuggled up to Vivienne's father, which felt awkward watching them. She talked a lot, and Chris seemed enchanted with her. "We had some great poolside parties here this summer. You should have been here," she said to Vivienne, and when they sat outside, she went upstairs and came back with a sweater. It was obvious that Kimberly had been living there, and the clothes in her mother's old closets were hers. At one point she talked about going to Mexico with Chris last year, and he gave her a quick look and she changed the subject. But it wasn't lost on Vivienne that her parents weren't separated last year—they were still married and living together. She realized that this was the girl who had broken up their marriage, and the reason her mother had run away to New York and filed for divorce. And she had never told her about it. It gave her new respect for her mother.

When her father was out of the room, Vivienne casually asked her, "So how long have you known my father?"

"Three years," Kimberly said breezily. She wasn't very bright, but she was sexy and beautiful, and she was clearly very much in love with him. He looked crazy about her, although he was old enough to be her father, which didn't seem to bother either of them, but made Vivienne uncomfortable.

Vivienne said she was tired after dinner, so she went to her room, and left them to enjoy each other. She wasn't angry at him. It was too late for that. He seemed happy with Kimberly, which was hard for Vivienne to believe. But she felt sorry for her mother, and impressed that she had never said anything bad about him when she could have. A lot of women did bad-mouth their ex-husbands to their kids, but Nancy never had.

Vivienne looked at the time, and realized that her mother was probably still awake in New York. It was only midnight there. She called and told her that she missed her, and then she asked her the question that had been eating at her all night.

"Why didn't you ever tell me about Dad and Kimberly? Did you know about her?"

Nancy hesitated before she answered. "Yes, I did. You didn't need to know."

"I thought you were so mean when you left him. I think she's been living here with him since we left."

"I think so too," Nancy said sadly, and now Vivienne was there also.

"I want to come home after Christmas. It's nice being here with Dad, but I miss you," Vivienne said, and her mother smiled at her end of the line.

"See how you feel then," she said, trying not to feel jubilant. Viv told her about seeing Gwen then, and giving her a statement—the truth this time, all of it. She told her mother that she didn't remember everything because she was so drunk, which Nancy had suspected. But she did remember Rick on top of her, rapidly plunging into her and shuddering almost at once. She would never forget it. "How do you feel about giving her the statement?"

"Really good. I think it was the right thing to do. I kept thinking that somehow I caused it all to happen. But Gwen says I didn't, and I believe her now. It's just too bad for everyone that it did."

"Yes, it is," her mother agreed with her. They talked for a few more minutes and then they hung up. Vivienne went to bed after that. She could hear her father and Kimberly laughing at the pool. He seemed so silly with her. Then she fell sound asleep and woke up the next morning. She had slept like a baby. Gwen was right. It was her first night without nightmares since the rape. And she felt more like her old self again.

Chapter Fourteen

Gwen took the red-eye from L.A. to Boston after she saw Vivienne, and went straight to work when she landed in the morning. She saw Dominic when she walked in, and he looked up from his desk.

"So did you get what you went for?"

"I did," she said quietly, as she opened her computer case and handed him Vivienne's statement. He read it, and looked up at her, impressed. Vivienne's account of what had happened didn't surprise him, but he was stunned that Gwen had gotten it from her. Vivienne had flatly refused before, and insisted she didn't remember anything. But in fact she remembered a lot.

"How did you do it?"

"She was just ready," Gwen said modestly.

"You are masterful."

"Thank you."

"Are you going to send it to their attorneys?" he asked.

"I'm sending it to the DA. I already did. We can wait a little while before sending it to the defendants' attorneys. That's really up to the assistant DA."

"I see six guilty pleas in our future. They'd be crazy to go to trial with a victim statement like that. Everything about it rings true, and corroborates the rest."

"I think it is true. She thought something she did made him do it."

"You set her straight?"

"Of course." She headed to her office then, glad that she had gone to Los Angeles to see Vivienne. It had been so much the right thing to do. And aside from strengthening the case, she knew it would help Vivienne in the end. She was slowly finding her way back.

*

Matthew Morgan flew in to New York two days before Thanksgiving. He had post-production work to do there on the film he'd shot in Spain, and Merritt was flying in the next day. Chase had been there since the arraignment, waiting for them, and they had agreed to spend Thanksgiving in New York. Matthew was thrilled to see his son. They had a lot to talk about. He hadn't seen him since everything had spun out of control in Chase's life. Matthew was heartbroken over all that had happened, and Chase seemed somber and quiet the night Matthew arrived and they went to dinner at a neighborhood deli near their apartment.

"I don't understand how it got so out of hand, and Rick went so crazy," Matthew said to his son. Chase was a good boy, and had always been levelheaded and sensible. And Rick had always seemed like a decent kid too. Nothing he had heard from the attorney made sense. It was an ugly case. The attorney had told Matthew that if convicted, Chase would go to prison, as an accessory, and for obstruction of justice, and he admitted that it would be a hard case to win. The evidence was damning, and he said there was a recent eyewitness report from another student, tying all six of them to the scene of the crime at the right time, and testifying about how drunk they'd been.

"I don't understand it either, Dad. I don't know why it happened. We all went a little nuts, and we were drunk as skunks on tequila. I got in a fight with Jamie." His father smiled.

"You haven't done that since sixth grade. Where'd you get the tequila? Did someone buy it for you?" Matthew narrowed his eyes at his son. He was a good father and had always been as present as he could be, in his line of work. Before Chase went away to school, he and Merritt tried to alternate taking films that would require their being away on location, so one of them would always be at home with him, and they had been. They paid close attention to him. Merritt was a terrific mother.

"I took the tequila from your bar in L.A. when I went back to school," Chase said quietly in answer to his question. He had never lied to him.

"Terrific, so now I'm an accessory to the crime. You know the school's policy about drinking. That really wasn't smart. Had you done that before?" Matthew tried to sound neutral about it, but he was disappointed in Chase.

"Once last year, with a bottle of wine. And Rick Russo had a flask of his father's that night with vodka in it. They started with that." Matthew didn't look pleased but it was too late now. The worst had already happened.

"It's one thing getting drunk with a bunch of guys, it's another thing when one of the guys rapes a girl. What was that about? Is it true, or did she set you up? What kind of girl is she?" Matthew was mystified at Chase being present at a rape.

"She didn't set us up." Chase looked mournful. "She's a wonderful girl. I would have dated her, but she got to know Jamie Watts first. She wasn't dating either one of us."

"Is she a tease, or a flirt?" Matthew was trying hard to understand. But even if she was, it was no excuse for rape.

"She got drunk with us. I think she was trying to be cool. We were all stupid that night." But Rick Russo was more than stupid. He had committed a heinous crime.

"Rule number one for girls: Don't hang out with a bunch of drunken guys in an isolated place. That wasn't very smart, and definitely not cool. But she didn't deserve to get raped. And you don't deserve what's happening to you now, since Rick raped her and you didn't," Matthew said. His agent had been sending him clippings from the press and they were very bad, predictably saying that a bunch of rich boys had brutally raped a girl at a fancy boarding school. "Did someone start it?"

"I don't know, Dad. I can't remember," Chase said, staring into his plate. He could hardly eat and had lost weight. "I keep wanting to tell her how sorry I am, but I haven't had the guts." Matthew nodded, watching his son's face.

"And you all pleaded not guilty?"

"Our lawyers told us to. They said we can always change our pleas later, and the arraignment is just a formality. And we all denied it when they questioned us."

"Have *any* of you told the police the truth?" Chase shook his head. "Why not?"

"Too scared. They arrested us the day after they got the DNA match with Rick. Until then there was no evidence, just our fingerprints on the tequila bottle, but we admitted that."

"What does she say?"

"She hasn't made a statement either. She didn't bring charges, the state did after she was found unconscious with alcohol poisoning. I called the campus police after we left and they found her right away. But we left her and we shouldn't have."

"This is not a pretty story, Chase," Matthew said, looking grim and worried. Their lawyer was right. This was going to be hard to defend, and a jury would like it even less. "I'm assuming that she really was raped. It's not a trumped up story." There was a question in the way he said it.

"No, it's not. We were just drunk and stupid. Rick went crazy."

"Why hasn't she made a statement? She must feel guilty about something." It was a keen observation.

"I don't think she wanted to be responsible for our going to prison. And maybe she didn't want to admit she was drinking with us."

"Where is she now?"

"I think she went back to L.A. with her father. Her mom lives in New York. They're getting a divorce, like you and Mom." He looked grief-stricken when he said it.

"What do you want to do now? According to the attorney, this will take a year to get to trial. You can't sit around and do nothing. I have to do some work in New York. You can stay here with me, and work with me on post-production. Or you can go home to L.A. with your mother on Friday. We're spending Thanksgiving together here, but after that she's got to go to L.A. and wrap up her own film. And I'll come back to L.A. in a few weeks so we can all spend Christmas together there." Chase didn't ask if he was still seeing the same actress he'd had the affair with. His parents had been staying on opposite coasts since they'd separated, or they were on location. "You can work for your mother too. But you can't sit at home watching TV for a year." Rick's father had told Rick the same thing, and had him working in his office, carrying boxes and doing menial work. No one would have hired him with rape charges pending. Gabe was working at the gym with his father, cleaning up. Steve was looking for a job delivering pizzas, and Jamie hadn't found anything yet but he was looking. They had a lot of time to kill, and they couldn't go to any school with the rape hanging over their heads. No school would have had them. None of them were going to graduate this year, and their hopes for college, for the kind of colleges they wanted to apply to, had gone right down the tubes. Chase had wanted to go to Tisch Drama at NYU, or major in film at USC or UCLA.

"You'll need to be available for court appearances. We should talk to your mother about her plans when she gets here tomorrow." It was going to be a hard Thanksgiving this year. Matthew hadn't talked to her since it happened, nor had Chase. She was flying in from the Philippines, and had been in a remote area where they couldn't reach her.

Matthew paid the check and they walked outside into the cold night air, and he looked at his son. He still looked like such a kid, but he wasn't. He was a man who might go to prison.

"I just want to say one thing. Someone started the drinking and it got out of hand, and a terrible thing happened. A girl was raped. You all did a bad thing by being there and were part of it, and lied about it afterward. Now you have to clean it up and do what's right, whatever it costs you and no matter how hard it is. You all have to clean it up. You owe it to the girl who got hurt, to your friends, and yourself. You have to do it as a man, Chase. No false loyalty to your friends if they're doing the wrong thing. You all did the wrong thing. Now do the right thing, whatever that is." After that, they walked back to their apartment building with Matthew's arm around Chase's shoulders. He was glad his father was home. Things were always better when he was. Nothing had been the same since he and his mom had split up, even if they were on good terms.

Merritt came home the next night, and they talked about it again. She agreed with Matthew, and she said that no matter what his friends did, Chase had to do the right thing. After telling him what they thought, they let him figure it out for himself.

They had a quiet Thanksgiving at their apartment, catered by a restaurant. They didn't want to have to deal with people asking for autographs in a public place. They got besieged by fans when he went out with both his parents. It had already been in the news that Chase was one of the six boys being accused of rape and other charges at Saint Ambrose. It was a good time to lie low.

Chase decided to stay in New York with his father for the time being. They were going back to L.A. for Christmas with his mother. But in the meantime, he could help his father with odd jobs. Merritt left for L.A. on Friday and told him, as she always did, how much she loved him. He noticed that his parents still seemed to be on decent terms, which he knew didn't mean anything. They were always civil to each other in front of him, and never argued, but they were still getting a divorce, so he assumed that his father's affair with the actress Kristin Harte was still on. His mother had slept in the guest room in New York. He saw the sad look in her eyes. Now he didn't know if it was because of his father, or because of him, which was a terrible feeling. He hated to hurt her.

Chase was lying awake every night, thinking of everything his father had said. On Sunday morning, he walked into his father's bedroom with tears in his eyes and a tortured expression.

Matthew was reading the Sunday *New York Times* in bed and looked up at his son.

"What happened?" How much worse could it get?

"I want to give the police a statement now and tell them what happened that night. Everyone's lying. I can't

271

do it anymore. I want to change my plea to guilty. I didn't know Rick had raped her until after he did. But I've been lying to protect him and everyone else. The others will hate me for it, but I don't want to lie about it anymore. I want to do what you said and finish it right." He felt better when he said it.

"I'll call the lawyer in the morning. You can think about it tonight." Matthew was calm when he spoke to Chase, but relieved that he'd come to the right conclusion on his own.

The next morning, Chase said he hadn't changed his mind, and Matthew called the lawyer to tell him, and he said he'd contact the police in charge of the case.

"I'll see if I can get a deal for him, a lesser charge, or a lighter sentence, or both." He called back half an hour later. They had an appointment the next morning at the police station near school for Chase to make a statement and change his plea. They had refused to make a deal. They were taking a hard line on it, and charging them as adults. "They're afraid of the media if they make a deal with you. You and Merritt are too well known. It would cause an explosion in the press and go viral."

*

Chase and Matthew drove to Massachusetts the next day, and their attorney met them there. Gwen and Dominic had been advised and drove in from Boston to take the statement.

Chase looked quiet and serious as he did it. He told them everything he remembered, although a lot of his memories of it were confused because of the tequila. Gwen spoke to him softly when he finished.

"I know you told the truth, Chase. The victim made a statement recently. Your story corroborates hers on every point. She didn't want to do it until now either. She didn't want to be responsible for any of you going to prison."

"How is she?"

"She's doing better," was all Gwen was willing to say. Their attorney told Matthew and Chase afterward that Chase had done the right thing by confessing. Vivienne's statement would have buried him, if he continued to lie to them about it. The attorney said he might be able to get Chase sent to a lighter security prison, but that was probably the best he could do. The attorney thought he might get a year or two as an accessory, and another year for the obstruction. It sounded like a life sentence to Chase, especially for a first offense. Matthew had to fight to keep his composure.

They had Chase sign his statement, and they went to court to enter the guilty plea. They spoke to the judge in chambers. She gave him a sentencing date of January 8, and agreed to let him remain out on bail, as long as he was staying with either of his parents. Matthew said he was. Then they left and stood outside in the cold winter air.

They drove back to New York, and neither Matthew nor Chase said a word. When they got back to the city, Matthew turned to his son. "You did the right thing, Chase. I'm proud of you," and then he hugged him as tight as he could, and they went back to the apartment. Chase looked around and realized that five weeks from now, he might be in prison, or shortly thereafter. Merritt knew what they were doing that day, and Matthew had called her after they saw the judge. They were both going to be at the sentencing with him. They agreed that whatever happened, they would stand by him.

Chase texted Jamie that night. "I told them the truth, and changed my plea to guilty. I'm sorry. I had to." Then he sat down to write Vivienne a letter. He'd wanted to do that ever since it happened. He regretted everything about that night, especially what had happened to her. And now he was trying to do all he could to make it right, and do the right thing.

Chapter Fifteen

Five days later, after many agonizing nights, Jamie called his lawyer. He admired what Chase had done and told his attorney he wanted to do the same. He hadn't told his father, but the lawyer called Shepard and felt he should inform him, before Jamie changed his plea to guilty. They weren't pleading guilty to rape, and he wasn't accused of it, but rather to having been there, drinking to excess, having become aware of the rape after Rick had done it, and abandoning Vivienne while unconscious from the alcohol, and lying about all of it later to protect Rick and the others. The only thing Chase had done right was call campus police to report her whereabouts when they left her. Jamie had punched Rick as soon as he became aware of what he'd done. And Steve had pulled Rick off her.

Shepard told their attorney not to do anything yet when he called him, and he had a major confrontation with Jamie, with Ellen present. The lawyer had told Shepard that he thought Jamie was right to step forward and change his plea. He couldn't win the case, and Jamie being honest would only help the outcome and possibly lighten his sentence. And morally it was the right thing to do, not to shield Rick, who didn't deserve it. The truth was the only way to go. It didn't change the fact of the rape for Vivienne, but it proved Jamie to be an honest person, no matter how foolish they'd been to get so drunk. It was a powerful and costly lesson to all of them. But his father was violently opposed to his entering a plea of guilty, and forbade him to do it.

"Are you insane? Do you want to go to prison for years? We have one of the best criminal lawyers in New York for you. He can get you off," Shepard insisted.

"He says I can't win the case, Dad," Jamie interrupted him, "the evidence is too solid against us. They know we've been lying. And Vivienne has made a statement, the lawyer said so. We've all been lying, Dad, and the cops must know it. Our stories weren't even the same. Chase confessed five days ago, and entered a plea of guilty. I want to do that too." Jamie couldn't stand it anymore. He wanted to tell the truth. "And even if I could win the case, I don't want to do it by lying."

"Do you know what you could do to that girl in court? Drinking tequila with a bunch of guys behind the bushes at midnight? You could make her look like the slut of the century, and she probably is. If Rick raped her, she probably would have screwed all of you. And I don't care if she's the Virgin Mary or Mother Teresa, when the defense lawyers get her on the stand, they can make her look like a prostitute." It was his fondest wish and what he had told the attorney he wanted to happen. It was what he had implied to Taylor too.

"She's already been through enough, Dad," Jamie shouted at him. "How much more do you want us to do to her? Wasn't getting raped enough? I *like* her, Dad. She's a good person. I wanted to go out with her, and she liked me. I kissed her and Chase was jealous of me. He wanted her too, and he went crazy, and I went just as crazy. We got in a fight over her."

"You didn't rape her," Shepard shouted back at him, as Ellen watched in horror, listening to what her husband wanted to do to an innocent girl, and all to allegedly protect their son. And everything Jamie had said was right, about being honest.

"I won't lie about her on the stand, and let you pay the lawyer to destroy her, so I don't have to go to jail. It's wrong. She's an innocent girl and she got raped. We ruined her life. Or Rick did, and we were there, even if we didn't know he was doing it."

"You were drunk." Shepard dismissed it, while his wife listened. "And Rick raped her, you didn't."

"How can you think it's all right and want to make her look like a slut?"

"Because I'm sure she is. Nice girls don't hide in the bushes, drinking tequila with a bunch of boys at midnight," he shouted in his son's face. "You didn't rape her, Rick did. So you lied about it, so what? Who wouldn't? I'm not going to have a jailbird for a son because of some piece of garbage like her."

"What if Rick had killed her? Would that be okay too? What's wrong with you, Dad? I'm going to do the right thing, whether you like it or not. My life wouldn't be worth shit out of prison if I listened to you. I'm not going to lie anymore, or have your lawyer destroy her on the stand. We owe her something for being there, getting drunk with her, and not protecting her from Rick. I had no idea he'd do something like that. I won't lie to protect him."

"You owe her nothing. Why won't you let us help you, however we can?"

"Because it's not honest, or fair. I'm going up there tomorrow to tell them the truth. If you don't like it, I'm sorry. But it's time to do the right thing here. I'm not like you," he said with all the disgust he felt for his father, and Shepard hauled off and punched him in the face as hard as he could. Blood spurted from Jamie's nose immediately. He fell backward onto the floor, and was dazed for a minute, and then his father kicked him in the stomach and walked out of the room. Jamie was doubled over, bleeding all over the rug, as his mother rushed forward to comfort him. She led him to the kitchen to clean him up. The other children had heard them but didn't know what it was about. Shepard slammed out of the apartment a moment later. Jamie was sitting on a kitchen stool, still bleeding, with an ice pack on his eye and his nose, his gut still aching from where his father had kicked him. He looked at his mother with all the regret he felt.

"I'm sorry, Mom. I'm sorry I was there at all, and lied about it." If he hadn't, he wouldn't have been charged with obstruction of justice.

"We'll get through it," she said gently. "Are you going up there tomorrow?" He nodded.

"I have to. I should have done it in the beginning."

"I'll come with you," she said, and he hugged her. They both wished none of this had happened, but it had, and now they had to deal with it. Jamie knew he would never feel the same way about his father again, and nor would his mother.

She called the attorney that night, and he agreed to meet them at the police station near the school, and assured her that Jamie was doing the right thing. He had urged him to tell them everything he knew earlier. But he'd been determined to protect Rick at first, and his friends, out of loyalty to their friendship.

The next day at noon, they met with Gwen Martin and Dominic Brendan. Ellen was with Jamie and his attorney, and he told the same story as Chase and Vivienne, adding in some details Chase had forgotten. His remorse for not coming forward sooner and all that had happened was obvious, and he signed his statement. He had a terrible shiner and his nose was bruised and swollen but not broken. Gwen asked him about it with some concern, and he was honest about that too.

"My father didn't want me to come up here, or change my plea. I had to. I'm sorry I didn't tell the truth in the beginning." She nodded, satisfied with his honesty now, and sorry about what his father had done to him, and the kind of man he was. Money and success didn't make him a good person and he was a terrible father. Jamie was a better person, despite the charges against him. And he would be a good man one day.

"I'm sure your father doesn't want you to go to prison." Gwen tried to make Jamie feel better.

"Neither do I," he said sadly. "But we did a terrible thing getting drunk, being there, protecting Rick, leaving her there."

"Have you told Vivienne that?" she asked gently, remembering what she had said about him. He shook his head. "Maybe you should." He had thought about it, but didn't know what to say. Maybe now he would.

Gwen took Jamie and his mother to see the judge in chambers, as she had with Chase, and they changed his plea without his having to appear in court. They left a few minutes later, and Ellen drove him back to New York. His father hadn't come home the night before. The judge had given Jamie a sentencing date of January 15, and told Gwen to extend Chase's as well. She would sentence them both on the same day.

When Gwen went back to the office, she looked at Dominic. "I think we need to take a trip to New York to see the others. They need to come to Jesus on this. They'd be even crazier to go to trial now, with signed statements from two of them, and a statement from the victim that corroborates everything they said. Jamie's memory of that night is almost identical to Chase's, and he said they haven't spoken since the arraignment, and I believe him. I'll call their attorneys tomorrow. NYPD can give us an office to meet them in or we can go to their homes." Dominic agreed with her.

"Let's get down there before Christmas." They were getting close. Chase had requested permission to go to L.A. for Christmas to see his mother. His father was taking him, and the DA had agreed. "You know what this is about," Dom said to her. "It's not just about rape, right and wrong, and the obvious. It's about which of these kids has a moral compass, even if their parents don't, like the Watts boy. The boys who do have a moral compass, and a conscience, will turn out to be decent people and good men one day. They've learned a hell of a lesson here, but in the end, they're finding their way to do the right thing."

Gwen smiled at him. "You're a philosopher."

"No, just a cop." She agreed with him, and it was a good point.

All four attorneys thanked her for the call the next

day, and agreed that in the circumstances, changing their pleas made the most sense. She told them that the DA's office was not making any deals to plea-bargain or for leniency, but it would go better with the judge if they all came clean and made statements, if they were willing. The attorneys said they would advise their clients accordingly. Some already had.

She and Dominic drove to New York the next day. They had new cases on their desks, but this was still their priority right now, to wrap up the Saint Ambrose case. NYPD had agreed to give them an office to work from. They had taken rooms in a small seedy hotel near the station.

"First-class all the way," Dominic said when he saw it, and Gwen laughed. The hotel was awful, but it was still New York.

They met with Gabe and his parents first. His parents were heartbroken at what had happened. His scholarship at Saint Ambrose had been his big opportunity for the future and he'd blown it. Gabe reiterated that he hadn't seen Rick raping her. He'd been trying to break up the fight between Jamie and Chase. But he had left her like the others and lied about all of it to protect himself and his friends. He knew he had let his parents down in a major way, and felt terrible about it. They blamed the rich kids at the school and the poor values some of them had, and their parents. They said they were sorry they had ever sent him there. And now he'd be going to prison.

Tommy Yee came in next and his statement was similar to the others, although he remembered less than them since he'd been throwing up from the tequila most of the time. He said he hadn't told the truth afterward because he didn't want to get them all in more trouble than they were in and he was scared.

Steve Babson came in with his mother, and his statement was almost identical to Gabe's. He had no insight about why it had happened but said he regretted it deeply. He said his father had disowned him, and his parents were getting a divorce, but Jean Babson was staunchly standing by her son.

And the Russos came in last. Rick started out by being cocky and ended up in tears within minutes. Joe had still wanted to buy Vivienne off, but his attorney had strongly advised against it, and said it would make it all worse. Both of Rick's parents looked crushed, and Rick blamed the alcohol for his raping Vivienne. His situation was more complicated, since he would be tried as an adult for rape. Gwen didn't find him as remorseful as the others, although his crime was far worse, and he was less concerned about Vivienne than himself, which spoke volumes to her. He confessed to taking her by force, but showed far less compassion for her than the others had.

After they left, Gwen thumbed through the statements. "Full house," she commented. All had entered a plea of guilty, which the judge said she would accept without seeing them in person, and they all had the same sentencing date, January 15. "Now we can get some other work done," Gwen said with a sigh, but she was still sad over the case. So many lives had been affected, and bright futures wasted—six young men who had been on such a shining path, and would have a hard road now, and Vivienne impacted most of all, especially if she didn't fully recover and remained too deeply scarred. It was too soon to tell. The six boys would have to navigate the shark-filled waters of the prison system. The judge was probably going to sentence them as adults, because the crime was too serious not to, and the punishment had to be equally so. The parents she had seen had had their lives rocked as well. Two of the fathers hadn't even come in, Steve's and Jamie's, and had abandoned their sons. No one came out a winner in a case like this.

"When are we going back?" she said to Dom, looking tired.

"I'm staying here tonight," Dominic said sheepishly.

"Hot date?" She smiled at him.

"Sort of. The Bruins are playing the Rangers at Madison Square Garden. I bought tickets online last night. Wild horses couldn't drag me away from that. I'll go back tomorrow. You can take the car, if you want. I can take the train."

"Maybe I'll stay too," she said, thinking about it. "I still have Christmas shopping to do for my nieces and nephews. I haven't had much time lately. Do you want to go back around lunchtime tomorrow?" He nodded.

"Sounds good to me." They went back to the hotel, so he could get ready for the game, and she could put on flat shoes to shop in. Gwen had listened to so much misery all day, she was looking forward to some shopping to relax her. She was looking for something in her purse, when she came across Sam Friedman's card, from the time he had brought Adrian Stone in to see her. In a crazy minute, she decided to call him. He had put his cell number on the card, but she called his office. If he wasn't around, she could leave him a message or try his cell. She had liked him, and she never met anyone except cops and teenage sex offenders and victims and their parents. It would be nice to talk to a normal person, and he seemed like one.

She was surprised when he answered. It was a little late for him to be at the office.

"Sam Friedman," he said brusquely.

"Hi, it's Gwen Martin, Boston PD. I met you when you brought Adrian Stone in to see me." He laughed.

"You must think I meet beautiful red-headed detectives every day, or movie stars, so I wouldn't remember you. Hello. To what do I owe the honor of your call?

Everything okay with my client?" He sounded worried for a second.

"As far as I know. I hope his asthma is better. I'm in town. We've been taking statements all day from the boys. We're wrapping up the case. They've all switched their pleas to guilty, and are being sentenced in January."

"You must be pleased."

"Yes, and sad too," she said, sounding more tired than she wanted to admit. "It's such a damn waste. Most of them are probably good kids, and they just threw it all out the window with a bottle of tequila. It breaks your heart sometimes. The boy who raped her is another story. The whole thing is tragic."

"I know. I see some pretty nasty stuff sometimes too. Parents who treat their kids like shit and should never have had them and don't deserve them, like Adrian. His parents should be in an insane asylum, and he pays the price for it. So how long are you in town for?"

"Till tomorrow. I just finished work and thought I'd do some Christmas shopping, and I found your card so I called you. I think that should be your line, but you get confused about traditional roles when you're a cop."

"Just don't shoot me. Tell you what. I've got about two hours' more work, maybe three. Why don't you go shopping, and I'll take you to dinner at a little Italian restaurant afterward. Does that sound feasible?"

"It sounds fantastic. Shopping *and* dinner? Couldn't

be better." She wouldn't have told him, but she hadn't had a date in six months, and she had really liked him when they'd met. She didn't know when they'd see each other again, if ever, and now here they were.

"It's not very gallant, but I'll meet you there. It's near my office." He gave her the address. "Nine o'clock? Does that give you enough time? I've got a report to finish for a hearing tomorrow."

"I'll be there. And, Sam, thank you! You really perked up my day."

"Mine too. See you later."

Gwen arrived at the restaurant on time, lugging four shopping bags with her.

"Successful mission?" he asked, visibly pleased to see her. She realized that he was even more handsome than she remembered. She had changed into heels in the cab, brushed her hair, and put on lipstick. She was faintly embarrassed when he noticed her shoulder holster in her jacket, but she didn't want to leave it at the hotel once she knew she was seeing him. "I think you're the first woman I've taken to dinner who came armed." She laughed and they ordered dinner.

The food was delicious, and they talked constantly throughout the meal. He was from a Jewish family of lawyers; she was from a Catholic family of cops. He was impressed that she had a master's in criminology. They liked the same movies and books, and loved to travel.

Venice was her favorite place on earth. His was Paris. And they both loved kids. He was three years older and hadn't been in a serious relationship in four years, and neither had she. They both explained it as having no time. They ended up talking about their work, and found that it had much in common. They talked until the restaurant closed at midnight and they were the last people there.

"Do you come to New York a lot?" he asked her.

"Never. We just came this time because we had four statements to get here. Do you ever come to Boston?"

"I haven't been there in ten years," he admitted, "although I went to school there."

"Let me guess. Harvard?" He nodded. She had suspected it during dinner.

"I was supposed to be making millions by now as a Wall Street lawyer. It hasn't worked out that way, but I love what I do. Half the time, I don't even get paid. I do a lot of pro bono work for the courts, for people like Adrian, who needed a neutral mentor to oversee his case." He took her back to her hotel in a cab. "What are you doing for New Year's Eve, by the way?"

"Nothing yet." She smiled at him. She'd had a wonderful time, and loved how smart and caring he was. She had seen the evidence of it with Adrian. And he had loved how she talked to him. Her looks didn't hurt. He was a good-looking man too—he went to the gym and she could see he was fit and in good shape. He played squash twice a week.

"Would you like to come down here and watch the ball drop in Times Square on New Year's Eve? It's corny but it's fun. Or we could do something more dignified, if you prefer."

"Times Square sounds great." They were at her hotel by then, and he handed her her shopping bags. "Thank you, Sam, I had a great time."

"So did I. So do we have a date?" Gwen nodded, and he kissed her lightly on the cheek. "Wear something warm. There's a cute hotel around the corner from where I live in the West Village. I'll book you a room there." She liked that he didn't assume she was going to sleep with him the next time she saw him, just because he'd bought her dinner. She waved as she walked into the hotel with her shopping bags, and he hailed a cab to go back downtown. Gwen smiled all the way to her room, and was still in a good mood when she met Dominic to go home the next morning.

"How was the game?" she asked him when she got in the car with all her shopping loot.

"It sucked. The Rangers won. They played a great game, though. It looks like you cleaned out the stores."

"And I had a date," she said, smiling broadly.

"How did you manage that? Are you picking up guys in department stores now? Talk about desperate."

"Oh shut up. I called the lawyer who brought the kid in for the eyewitness statement. I found his card in my purse. We had dinner."

"You've probably been planning it all along. Did you wear your gun?" She nodded. "How did he like that?"

"He loved it. We held up a liquor store after dinner, and split the money."

"Smartass. So are you seeing him again?"

"New Year's Eve," Gwen said, looking victorious. She hadn't had a date on New Year's Eve in three years. Their line of work wasn't conducive to a heavy dating life.

"Well, I'll be damned. Good for you. I may get rid of you yet, and finally get a partner who eats."

"Oh, just shut up and drive," she said, staring out the window with a smile. She'd had a text from Sam that morning, telling her what a good time he'd had. She could hardly wait for New Year's Eve. As she stared out the window as they left New York, Dominic glanced over at her and smiled. She was a great cop and a good woman, and he was happy for her.

Chapter Sixteen

Christmas was difficult for all the families involved in the Saint Ambrose case. They each felt as though their days were numbered and time was running out. Gabe's parents had to explain to his younger siblings that he might be going to jail for a long time. They all cried when they told them. Tommy's parents were still not speaking to him, and he felt lost in a solitary world.

Steve Babson had Christmas alone with his mother. She was sober and went to an AA meeting every day, sometimes more than one. His father had moved out, but it was more peaceful that way. After years of abusing both of them, he was gone, and his mother had filed for divorce. It was actually the nicest Christmas they'd ever had, which surprised them both. But now he had prison time to face.

The Russos had their Christmas dinner catered by one of the best restaurants in New York, but none of them could eat, thinking of what lay ahead. They tried to put a good face on it, but Rick kept coming across them crying, and he stayed in his room most of the time, so he didn't have to see it or talk to them. None of the other boys were in contact with him. And he got drunk alone in his room on Christmas Eve.

Jamie shared Christmas with his mother, twin sisters, and his younger brother. Their father was staying at the Racquet Club, and Ellen had to tell them that Jamie might be going away too.

Chase was in L.A. with his parents. Matthew was staying at a friend's, whom Chase assumed was Kristin Harte. Chase was staying at their house with his mother. His father came to dinner with them on Christmas Eve. They all exchanged gifts and had a nice time, acting as though nothing was wrong, but the divorce was still happening, no matter how civil they were to each other. And he was being sentenced in three weeks, and likely to go to prison. It was hard to forget any of it, and thoughts of Vivienne still haunted him. His mother was making him see a shrink. Jamie's was too.

Vivienne had received Chase's letter, and answered him, telling him how much it meant to her, and how sorry she was that everything had gone so wrong for all of them. She said she hoped that things turned out for the best for him. He felt relieved when he heard from her. Jamie had written to her too, and got an equally nice response, nicer than he felt he deserved. It made him even sadder that he had blown it with her. He would never know now what could have happened between them. He was going to prison instead. And he would remain a bad memory for her now, they all would.

They were all worried about the sentencing. The boys and their parents were feeling all the effects of the stress they were under, and trying to deal with it as best they could. But the days were ticking by and going too quickly. January 15 was only three weeks away.

Vivienne had Christmas Eve dinner with her father, sent over by a restaurant. Kimberly "dropped by" afterward. She was always lurking nearby, and Chris included her in their plans whenever he could. It was obvious that he wanted to be with her, but he wanted to spend time with his daughter too, and he tried to combine them whenever possible. Kimberly kept casually asking her when she was going back to New York, and clearly couldn't wait, so she could move back in. Vivienne still hadn't decided what to do about school in January. She was doing the assignments Saint Ambrose sent her, turning them in on time and getting good grades, so she could get her diploma in June.

Vivienne called her mother in Vermont on Christmas Day. Nancy sounded like she was having a good time at the house she had rented with friends. Viv closed her bedroom door so she could talk to her and didn't upset anyone.

"Mom, when can I come home?"

"Are you kidding? Whenever you want. I'm going back

to New York the morning of New Year's Eve, and I don't have any plans. Do you want to spend New Year's Eve with me? You can be my date."

"I'd love it. Can I stay? I know I said I wanted to live with Dad this year. But Kimberly gets on my nerves, and he wants to be with her. I love Dad, but I really want to be home with you. And, Mom, I've been thinking about school. Would you let me go to a day school in New York? Do you think any of them would take me mid-year? I want to stay home with you till I leave for college. I could stay with Dad next summer in L.A. I've finished all my applications, and added a few more. I'm applying to Columbia and NYU and Boston University."

"Wow, that *is* news." She sounded thrilled. "I'll call some schools after Christmas vacation and see what they say. We can visit them together." Nancy thought they should tell them about what had happened at Saint Ambrose, and they might take her mid-year, on special circumstances. Vivienne said she wanted a fresh start at a new school, which sounded sensible to Nancy too. She promised she'd book her a ticket to New York on the thirty-first. They could both hardly wait.

"I'll tell Dad," Vivienne volunteered. "He'll want to be with Kimberly anyway. She wants me out of here so badly, she'll help me pack." Vivienne sounded sad when she said it, but matter-of-fact.

Nancy was beaming when they hung up. Her daughter

was coming home. It was the best Christmas gift she could have. And Vivienne sounded better than she had in two months, and wanted to go back to school, which was a good sign. The nightmares had almost stopped. She just had them from time to time now, not every night.

They had talked about her father and Kimberly before they hung up. "I don't want to hurt his feelings. He really tried hard to make me feel at home and spend time with me. He just has a different life now, and Kimberly is a big part of it," she told her mother. It wasn't news to her. She had been for a long time, but Nancy didn't remind her daughter of that. "Do you think he'll marry her?"

"He might."

"That's ridiculous. He's old enough to be her father."

"Men are ridiculous sometimes," she said, but she wasn't as upset about it as she had been. She had just met a nice man on the slopes in Vermont. A doctor from New York, divorced, with three daughters. She had skied with them a few times. The girls were a little older than Vivienne, and he was forty-nine. She was having dinner with them that night, and they were planning to get together again in New York. Two of his daughters were in college, and one had just graduated in June and was moving to the West Coast to attend graduate school at USC.

At dinner that night, Vivienne told her father that she was going to New York to stay with her mother, and leaving on the morning of New Year's Eve, and that she thought she'd spend the rest of the school year there. She said she wanted to go to school in the city and her mother was going to start working on it. He looked a little disappointed that she wanted to go back to New York, but he didn't object. And he thought a new school was a good plan. It would have felt weird to her in L.A., and New York was a clean slate. She needed that now. Kimberly was having dinner with them that night, as she did most of the time, and she was so excited to hear it, she nearly jumped up and down in her seat, and looked at him adoringly.

"You mean you'll be gone on New Year's Eve?" Kimberly said excitedly to Vivienne, and even Chris had to laugh. "Let's go to Las Vegas and stay at the Wynn," she said, looking thrilled, and he agreed. Las Vegas for New Year's sounded corny to Vivienne, but it was the height of glamour to Kimberly and she said she loved playing blackjack and the slot machines, and going shopping there. Vivienne didn't care as long as they didn't top it off with getting married at the Elvis Chapel on New Year's Day. Her parents weren't divorced yet anyway, so he was safe for a while, although Vivienne could see it happening one day and dreaded it, if it did.

They spent the rest of the evening talking about Las Vegas and all the things Kimberly loved to do there, like the magic shows, and Cirque du Soleil. Vivienne was

thinking about going back to New York while she listened, and going back to school. They all had their lives
to pursue, and she had figured out that hers was in the
East with her mother, for now anyway. And this time she
was going because she wanted to, not because she'd been
forced.

"I can come back for spring vacation, Dad, if you want
me to, and next summer before I start college."

"Of course I want you to. This is your home too. You've
got a home on each coast." Kimberly looked a little glum
over that, and Vivienne heard her ask him later if she'd
have to move out every time Vivienne came to L.A. He
said they'd talk about it later, but he thought she should
keep the apartment for a while, so they had "flexibility."
Vivienne smiled at that. She wondered if Kimberly got
on his nerves too. She hoped so.

Vivienne started packing that night. She had been in
L.A. for almost two months, and she was ready to go home.

*

Sam and Gwen stood watching the ball drop in Times
Square on New Year's Eve. It was a freezing cold night,
but they had dressed for it, and Gwen was jumping up
and down to keep warm.

"Every time you do that, I keep worrying your gun
will go off," he whispered to her, and she laughed.

"I'm not wearing it tonight."

297

"Now I'm scared. I thought you could defend us if we get attacked."

"Don't worry. I'm a black belt in karate."

"You're a dangerous woman, Gwen Martin," he teased her.

"Not if you're nice to me." He was extremely nice to her. They'd had dinner at a lovely restaurant and he had a whole weekend planned around her. The next day they were going ice-skating in Central Park.

The ball dropped at midnight and then he turned and smiled at her. "Happy New Year, Gwen, I hope it's a great one," and then he kissed her, which took her by surprise, and she kissed him back. They stood together for a long time, and then he hailed a cab and took her to the Sherry-Netherland for a drink, and after that a hansom cab ride in the park, where he kissed her again. The horse and buggy ride through Central Park was the most romantic thing anyone had ever done for her. Gwen had always dated cops, who weren't known for their spirit of romance. It was the best New Year's Eve of her life. She went back to his apartment with him that night, rather than going back to the hotel. They let the room go the next day and she stayed with him. When they went to Central Park, they discovered that they were both good skaters, and had a good time skating hand in hand. Then they went back downtown to his apartment and made love.

They ordered food brought in that night and watched old movies on TV.

"I have such a good time when I'm with you," she said dreamily as she lay in his arms.

"Me too. I had just decided I'd be a bachelor forever and preferred it that way, and then you came along."

"I figured that too. Will you come to Boston and visit me?"

"Of course," he said happily. "This is the best New Year's weekend I've ever had. You don't think I'm going to give that up, do you?"

"I hope not," she said, smiling. Everything had happened so quickly between them, but it all fit together perfectly, almost as though they'd been waiting for each other.

"We'll have to send Adrian a thank-you note one of these days," Sam said, and she smiled and nodded, and he kissed her again. Something good had come of the Saint Ambrose case after all, for them anyway.

Chapter Seventeen

The sentencing came all too quickly, on January 15. The countdown started in earnest for all of them right after the holidays. All six boys went to the courtroom in Massachusetts with their parents. Judge Hannabel Applegarth, who had recorded their guilty pleas and presided over the arraignment, had demanded a closed courtroom, and barred the press. But as each car arrived, the media was there in force, rushing toward anyone and everyone, shouting questions and pushing microphones in people's faces. There were a dozen camera vans parked in the street from different stations in various cities. Getting through the crowd was a nearly athletic event.

Taylor and Charity Houghton, Nicole Smith, Gillian Marks, and Simon Edwards had decided to attend, and Gillian forged a path for them through the mass of reporters. They were breathless and disheveled when they got through.

"I thought they were going to rip my clothes off," Gillian complained, and she was taller and stronger than the others. When the boys arrived with their families it was a feeding frenzy as police and sheriff's deputies helped them through. The media was not being allowed in the building, and one by one the boys filed into the courtroom wearing suits. Their parents were as nervous as they were, and their attorneys met them outside the courtroom. They had all had endless meetings to discuss what was likely to happen. At the appointed hour, they took their places at the defense table, each one next to his lawyer. At the table for the state, the same two assistant district attorneys were seated, and Dominic and Gwen walked in. She was wearing a new navy blue suit and heels.

They waited another twenty minutes for the judge, and then the bailiff told them to rise, and Judge Applegarth walked in and took her seat on the bench. She looked particularly somber as she observed who was in attendance in the courtroom. The boys' parents were seated right behind them. In the row behind that, the representatives from the school. The entire country was eager to hear her decision, and to see if she would be lenient because it was an elitist school. She had gone over all the evidence and statements again and again, and spent countless hours weighing the decision, its impact on the defendants, what was due Vivienne given what she'd suffered, and the potential fallout of her decision for all concerned. It was one of the more difficult decisions she'd had to make, and she'd been meticulous about legal procedure in case of appeals, which was likely in Rick Russo's case. Their parents' bank accounts were of no interest to her, or the stature of the school. What mattered was that there were six lives at stake, and six futures, and they in turn had a debt they owed to society, particularly Rick.

Gwen Martin had delivered a handwritten letter to the judge the day before, from Vivienne Walker, which held sway with her too. It was her legal right as the victim to weigh in about the sentencing, but the final decision was the judge's. The boys could learn from this experience and become better people, or they could come away from it ruined. And it all rested on her. It was an awesome responsibility and she felt satisfied with the decisions she'd made. She hadn't come to them easily or lightly. She had no prejudice either for or against the boys. They were seventeen-year-olds, and not habitual criminals. But the rape Rick had committed could not be taken lightly.

Vivienne had very generously sent texts to both Jamie and Chase that morning and wished them luck. She was back in New York with her mother, and anxious to hear the news. Justice had to be served, but where that line fell, and the judge's interpretation of it, remained to be seen.

There was dead silence in the courtroom when the bailiff named the first five defendants and told them to stand up. The judge began speaking directly to them. She dealt with the charges of accessory and obstruction of justice first, and left Rick for last.

"I have given this matter great consideration, for your benefit, the victim's, and that of the community and the state. The interests of society must be served here. You're being tried as adults and will be given adult sentences with the scope of your crimes. Justice will not best be served by turning you into hardened criminals, nor will justice be served if this matter is treated lightly. You're not children, you're men, and you were present when a serious crime was committed and a young woman's life was put in jeopardy, and impacted forever by being raped. Whatever I decide here today, she will live with that forever. You were present when she was raped, and that makes you accessories, even if you didn't see it happening because you were drunk. The appalling amount of liquor you consumed could have been life-threatening to all of you. And you left Miss Walker unconscious, although one of you called the campus police to get help for her. Miss Walker herself has a voice in the sentencing. By state law she has the right to request that you not be imprisoned, despite convictions or guilty pleas. I received a request from her yesterday, asking for your five prison sentences to be suspended, which I have taken into consideration too, along with the facts of the case and your individual histories, for a first, albeit very grave, offense. For the charges of accessory to rape, I sentence you to two years in state prison." She paused for a long moment. Several of the boys closed their eyes at the almost physical blow, and then she went on. "Your sentences are to be suspended. However, if you are arrested for any reason during those two years, you will go directly to state prison for two years.

"For the charges of obstruction of justice, lying repeatedly during a felony investigation involving injury to a young woman is also a serious crime. I sentence all of you to ninety days in county jail, and two years' probation.

"I hope you use the opportunity I will be giving you to better yourself, to grow, to learn from it, and to redeem yourselves. When this is over, I expect you to be better people. You have a debt to society now, which you must fulfill, however unpleasant you find that prospect. I want you to *think* about this now, and in the future, and to keep this lesson with you, always. The world needs good, honest men with a strong moral compass, not weak, dishonest ones without integrity. You have a choice as to which you want to be. You may sit down," she said sternly, which they did with shaking knees. Their parents were crying with relief.

The bailiff then instructed Richard Russo to rise, and the judge looked at him sternly, and began speaking. "For the charge of rape of a minor female, I sentence you to six years in state prison, including an additional year added to your sentence because of the age of the victim. For the charge of obstruction of justice, I sentence you to an additional year, to be served concurrently with your six-year sentence. You will begin serving your sentence immediately, and will be taken into custody from this courtroom.

"The five other defendants will also be taken into custody and taken to county jail today to begin their sentences." The judge rapped her gavel, stood up and left the courtroom, and all hell broke loose.

Rick looked like he was in shock as a deputy put handcuffs on him and led him away. His father looked as though he wanted to murder someone as he talked to their attorney, and his mother was sobbing. The other parents crowded around the five boys to hug them before deputies took them away to county jail. Ninety days was nothing compared to what it could have been, but they hadn't raped her or even seen it happen in their drunken state. The boys looked nervous and smiled meekly and it wasn't lost on any of them that Vivienne had asked the judge for clemency. Gwen had informed her of that legal right and she had made her own decision.

Neither of the district attorneys had objected to their sentences. They put their papers back in their briefcases and left the courtroom, pushing their way through the crowd. Dominic leaned over to Gwen, and spoke in a low voice.

"Did you know?" She didn't seem surprised by the sentences.

"She called me into her chambers two weeks ago when she was deliberating and asked me what I thought. I suggested leniency within reason for the five accessories. I think she did a very good job of it and I think Vivienne's letter weighed more with her," she answered, and Dominic nodded and agreed. And Rick's sentence was hard but fair. He had raped her, and had received an adult punishment for it. Six years was a long time, but Vivienne's sentence as a rape victim was for life.

Deputies arrived to help the parents leave the courthouse. Apparently, the mob outside had grown. The media had been notified of their sentences, and they were going to have to press through them as best they could.

They were taken out a side entrance and rushed to their cars as quickly as possible. The Morgans had their own security, and Joe Russo looked angry to the point of dangerous. The representatives from Saint Ambrose made their way out, into their van, and headed back to the school. They felt drained but the sentences seemed fair to them too, even Rick's. Nicole thought so too.

"I was terrified they'd give them all ten years," Gillian said. "She was right. There was no point turning them into hardened criminals with a sentence that wouldn't teach them anything, just destroy them. And Rick got an appropriate sentence for the crime."

"How soon can we see him in county jail?" Matthew asked Merritt in the car on the way home. It would have been easier to fly back to New York, but the press would have besieged them at the airport. They had privacy in the car.

"I'll find out. It could have been so much worse. Three months won't kill him. It was generous of Vivienne to write to the judge." Matthew nodded, relieved it hadn't been worse, and held Merritt's hand as he had in court. She didn't seem to mind. Being terrified for their son had been a bond between them.

They were all back in New York by that afternoon. Ellen Watts went home, exhausted, and Shepard was there, going through some papers at his desk.

"Do you want to know what the sentence was?" she asked him.

"Five years? Ten? Where is he now? In jail. He'd be a free man if you had listened to me and done what I said. We could have destroyed that girl in court, if he'd gone to trial instead of pleading guilty." He was still furious that Jamie wouldn't follow his advice. Jamie had been afraid of his father ever since he'd hit him.

"They suspended sentence for the accessory charges and he got ninety days in county jail and two years' probation for obstruction of justice. The victim asked the judge for leniency," she told him.

"Congratulations," Shep said bitterly. "I could have

gotten him off if you and he had let me. So now he sits in jail and is on probation and has a criminal record?"

"He was there, Shep. It's a serious crime. There was no other choice." He looked sour and angry, and not even pleased that their son had fared so well. "I'm divorcing you, Shep," she said quietly. "You've turned into someone I don't know. You wanted to teach Jamie to fight dirty, by your rules. Shortcuts, and threats, and blackmail, and destroying an innocent girl who had already been hurt. I never knew before that that's who you are, or who you've become."

"And you're so lily pure, now he's in county jail like a petty criminal. He didn't rape her. My way, he would have been out, free and acquitted. This way, he'll always have a criminal record. What kind of job do you think he'll get with that?"

"He deserves it, Shep. They were party to a terrible thing, a serious crime, and they lied about it. They left her unconscious and she could have died. What if someone treats your daughters that way one day? You'd be out to destroy them. I'm grateful he's not going to prison and will only be in jail for three months. Rick Russo got six years."

"His father will appeal it," Shep said. "You're not serious about a divorce, are you?" He looked at her with a smirk on his face. In his opinion, he was much too successful for her to leave him. She had nothing of her own. She hadn't had a job since she'd married him. But she wondered now about how he had gotten so successful. It was by threatening and destroying people, as he would have with an innocent girl who was a true victim, not a whore.

"Yes, I am serious." She had lost all respect for him in the past two months, and knew their marriage could never be repaired.

"I'm not going to give you a generous alimony after you crossed me on this, Ellen. Our son is a convicted felon now, thanks to your advice," he said coldly. His eyes were vicious. She wondered why she hadn't seen that before.

"I'll get a job," she said quietly. "And don't plan to move back in after you left us and didn't even come to court to support Jamie today. You don't live here anymore."

"He didn't deserve my being there, and neither do you," Shep said. He picked up his briefcase and walked out of the apartment and slammed the door. His ego wouldn't allow him to feel anything over losing her, except contempt for her and their son. They didn't matter to him anymore, and he didn't consider it a loss.

*

Sam called Gwen on her cellphone after she left the courtroom, and she was happy to hear from him. "Congratulations! Well done!" he praised her. "I thought the sentence for the boy charged with rape was strong, but lenient in the right way for the others. She taught them a lesson but didn't destroy them. And the media think so too. They're calling it 'reasonable and fair.' Can I come up and celebrate with you this weekend?" he asked her, and she smiled happily.

"That sounds terrific."

"It does to me too. I'll call you later. I have to go to court. Thank God Adrian called me, or I'd never have met you."

"Thank God you listened to him and came up."

"I always listen to my clients," he said. It was why he was good at what he did. And she listened to the juveniles in her cases too. She had listened to Vivienne, and Adrian, and all of them. No one had been permanently damaged by the decision, not even Vivienne, hopefully, in the long run. Vivienne had watched it on the news and was relieved for the five boys, and thought six years was right for Rick. She felt rightfully avenged, which was healing too.

Chapter Eighteen

A week after the sentencing, Vivienne started her new school in New York, at Dalton. It was co-ed, a great school, and they had accepted her with special circumstances. She had been in New York for three weeks and was loving it this time, and enjoyed being with her mother. She was happy to get away from Kimberly and her father.

She had finally FaceTimed with Lana and Zoe when she got back to New York. She told them that boarding school wasn't for her and she had transferred to a day school in New York and was excited about it. She promised to see them in the summer, and never told them she'd been in L.A. for two months. She hadn't been ready to see them, but she would be by summer. They knew her so well, they would have sensed something was wrong, and she didn't want to talk about it.

Vivienne loved her classes at Dalton. She had some work to catch up on, but she did so quickly, and she had sent her college applications out on time. They would hear back from them in March. And she'd had letters from the five Saint Ambrose boys, thanking her for her letter to the judge. She had grown up a lot in the last three months, they all had. It was a hard way to get there.

When the college acceptances came in, Vivienne got into UCLA and USC, her two top choices before everything had happened. She got into NYU and Boston University too. She picked NYU in the end because she liked the idea of being in New York, and close to her mother so they could see each other whenever they wanted to. They were closer than they'd ever been, and she liked the man her mother was dating, the doctor she had met in Vermont. His daughters were fun when she saw them.

Her father had broken up with Kimberly, and she felt sorry for him, but she was glad too. He said he was playing the field for now, and had come to New York to visit her, and was impressed by her new school when she gave him a tour. The students were bright and lively and enthusiastic. She had made new friends and loved it. She wasn't dating. It was still too soon, but she was happy.

Chris and her mother came to graduation in June and sat together. Her mother was still tense around him, but they were proud of their daughter.

Vivienne had heard that the boys were out of county jail by then; they'd got out in April. She didn't hear from them and didn't want to, but Gwen Martin had told her. She had a boyfriend in New York now and called from time to time to see how Vivienne was.

Vivienne had heard from Nicole Smith too. She said

that everything had gotten back to normal at Saint Ambrose. The graduation ceremony had gone smoothly, and Nicole told her that everyone still missed her.

Nicole didn't tell Vivienne that the school's enrollment had suffered slightly from all the media attention, which a lot of parents didn't want for their children, and the rape had been national news. But they weren't the first school that had survived a scandal and gone on to continued success. It had been profoundly upsetting but they had come through it. Taylor Houghton was still staunchly in place. Larry Gray had retired after graduation and Nicole still loved her job, her colleagues, and the school. They were all desperately sorry about what had happened to Vivienne.

It was quiet when everyone left the campus after graduation. It took another week to wrap things up, and slow down for the summer. The Houghtons were going to their house in Maine, and the students would be with their families until September. The third female dorm would be ready by August, since they were adding another eighty girls to their enrollment, according to plan. In the end, Saint Ambrose had survived the storm and was better and stronger for it. They had all learned valuable lessons. It had shaken them to their foundations, but they were back on course now.

*

Merritt Jones arrived in New York to see Chase. He was living with his father at the apartment, and had been accepted at the New School on probation for September. It was a respectable college, and he had a job at Starbucks for the summer. County jail in Boston, where they were sent for a change of venue, had been awful but had gone quickly. He never complained about it and was grateful not to be in prison. Merritt had visited him once a month in jail, and Matthew had gone up weekly. Some of the other parents had too, but not all. She was about to start post-production on a film in L.A., so she had come to see Chase before she got too busy. She was considering another new script at the moment, but hadn't decided about it yet.

Matthew had invited her to lunch when she got to New York, and she had agreed to see him. She was staying at their apartment and kept to herself. These days, it was rare that she and Matthew were in the same city at the same time. She was spending more time in L.A. and he in New York. She tried to visit Chase when she knew Matthew wouldn't be around. They were on decent terms, but their divorce would be final soon.

He suggested they meet at a diner they both liked, where people didn't bother them even if they recognized them. Going there brought back memories, which she forced from her mind. He was sitting in a back booth, waiting, when she got there, and smiled as she slid onto the banquette across from him. "How're you doing?" she asked him. It was nice to see him. He looked well and was as handsome as always. She'd never gotten used to his looks—they struck her every time, even now, when it was over between them.

"Pretty good." He smiled at her. "Not as well as our son. He's lifting weights, looking healthy, he has a great tan, he likes working at Starbucks and he's excited about starting the New School in September. Considering what we were facing six months ago, I think he's in good shape now. County jail was an eye-opener. I don't think he's had a drink in eight months."

"He seems happy to me too." She smiled at Matthew. "What about you? New projects?"

"Some. I'm enjoying hanging around with Chase for the moment. I want to slow down on the location shoots," he shared with her. She smiled at the man she'd been married to for twenty years and who was about to become her ex-husband. At least they were still friends. He was staying at a friend's while she was at the apartment with Chase while she was in town, as a courtesy to her.

"How'd the movie wind up?" Matthew asked her.

"We're going into post-production." It had always been nice sharing the same business. There was something he wanted to say to her, but he didn't know how. "Something on your mind?" She knew him well.

"Chase isn't the only one who had some serious

cleaning up to do, after the mess he got himself into. I've been an ass, Merrie. I know it. We both know it. I don't know what happened. You were away a lot, with three pictures back-to-back. I got lonely. I told myself you didn't love me anymore, or some equally stupid bullshit to justify my screwing up. And I got involved with Kristin. I'm sorry. I'm desperately sorry. I still love you, I always will. I'd give my right arm and leg to put us back together again. I don't suppose there's any chance you'll ever forgive me?" He was abjectly contrite as he looked at her and she smiled at him.

"Oh I don't know, maybe a year in county jail would do it for you too. Or hard labor splitting rocks in Siberia somewhere." She laughed. She'd been thinking about it too, but she didn't think he was interested and was afraid to ask him and get rejected. "What about your little friend? What are you going to do about her?" She was referring to his affair with Kristin Harte, a very beautiful twenty-four-year-old actress who had torpedoed their marriage with his help.

"I told her two months ago that I'm still in love with you. She moved out that night, which was my intention when I told her. And if the tabloids are to be trusted, she just got engaged to a billionaire Texan."

"I'll have to remember to send her an engagement gift," Merritt said as he came around the table and slid into the booth next to her and kissed her. "Will you take me back, Merrie?" he asked humbly. She nodded, and kissed him.

"It's not every day I get proposed to by a famous movie star," she said, and he laughed.

"Oh shut up. I've never won an Oscar, you have two."

"I'd trade them both to be back with you," she said softly. "I've missed you. What woke you up?" She had thought he never would and had given up on him, and had accepted that it was over for good.

"Chase. I told him how much I missed you, and didn't know what to do about it. He said to tell you. I guess he was right. He told me to 'clean it up and do it right,' which is what I told him when he got into his mess. We all make mistakes, terrible ones sometimes, like Chase, but good men correct them."

"You're a good man, Matthew Morgan. I always knew that about you." She smiled at him.

"I love you," he said softly.

"Yeah, me too. I'll have to thank Chase when I see him tonight." She was smiling broadly and Matthew kissed her again. They had gotten lucky. Terrible things had happened, his affair, their separation, Chase's conviction and time in jail, and through it all they still loved each other.

They walked out of the diner together after lunch holding hands. A fan ran up and took their picture. The sun was shining, Matthew was back, Chase was okay. It was a beautiful day.

Danielle Steel

Have you liked Danielle Steel on Facebook?

Be the first to know about Danielle's latest books, access exclusive competitions and stay in touch with news about Danielle.

www.facebook.com/DanielleSteelOfficial

THE DARK SIDE

Zoe Morgan has met the man of her dreams and is about to start her own perfect family. But when she gives birth to her longed-for daughter, she discovers the true impact of a tragedy from her past, with powerful consequences.

Paperback published April 2020

LOST AND FOUND

Sifting through old photos, Madison Allen, a renowned photographer, reflects on what might have been. She'd had three important men in her life – but her job always won out in the end. So she embarks on an adventure to reunite with the men she had loved and let go.

Paperback published June 2020

CHILD'S PLAY

After losing her beloved husband, Kate Morgan successfully raised their three children single-handedly. However, as adults they are determined to deviate from the paths she planned for them. But Kate will discover that sometimes the choices our children make are the right ones. Because happiness is living the life you choose.

Paperback published August 2020

SPY

Britain, 1939. At eighteen, Alexandra Wickham seems destined for a privileged life. But a world war and her own quietly rebellious nature lead her down a different path. While her country pays the terrible price of war, Alex learns the art of espionage, leading to life-and-death missions and extraordinary adventures.

Paperback published October 2020

NEIGHBOURS

After the death of her teenage son, legendary movie star Meredith White has spent the last fifteen years living as a recluse within her magnificent mansion in San Francisco's Pacific Heights. Lonely and alienated from her daughter and granddaughter, Meredith knew nothing about her neighbours who lived on the same block.

That is until a major earthquake stuns the city. When Meredith opens the gates of her home to help the residents, she also unlocks what was missing in her life. Each of her neighbours need help beyond shelter. Tyla, the wife of a famous surgeon, was the subject of domestic abuse. Arthur is a blind concert pianist, cared for by Peter, his young lodger. And Ava, a model, is made to feel worthless by her rich, self-centred boyfriend. In the weeks that follow, as they shelter together in Meredith's home, each of them experience the rewards and the true spirit of community.

Coming soon

PURE STEEL. PURE HEART.